Praise for *W*

'A startling read that unfurls fi   ...p... ....
a dark tale of righteous vengeance'
Val McDermid

'Fascinating, complex and sometimes controversial – timely,
relevant and filled with compassion'
Ian Rankin

'This insightful and absorbing novel explores the human
condition through a therapist's lens. Both a compelling
psychological study and a moving reflection on the power of
words and actions, it's a truly captivating read'
Angela Jackson, author of *The Emergence of Judy Taylor*

'Gripping, beautifully written, and full of priceless insight,
Words Fail Me is the rare novel that will enlighten you even
as it entertains you. An incredible debut'
Simon Stephenson, author of *Sometimes People Die*

FRANCES McKENDRICK is a psychotherapist and writer living in Edinburgh with her husband and two children. She won the Isobel Lodge Award for her short fiction, which has also been shortlisted for the Bath Short Story Award and the Alpine Fellowship Writing Prize. *Words Fail Me* is her first novel.

WORDS FAIL ME

FRANCES McKENDRICK

Published in 2025
by Lightning
Imprint of Eye Books Ltd
29A Barrow Street
Much Wenlock
Shropshire
TF13 6EN

www.eye-books.com

ISBN: 9781785634178

Cover design by Nell Wood and Craig Murray

Typeset in Charter and Chalkboard

British Library Cataloguing in Publication Data
A catalogue record for this book is available from the British
Library.

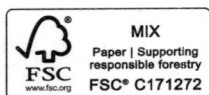

FSC
www.fsc.org

MIX
Paper | Supporting
responsible forestry
FSC® C171272

Words Fail Me is entirely a work of fiction.
The characters and their situations are
not based on any real people, living or dead.

*

*We must not try to cure adolescents as if they were
suffering from a psychiatric disorder…
There is only one cure for adolescence,
and this is the passage of time*

Donald Winnicott

For Ben

Tomorrow, on what, according to the Met Office, is shaping up to be a gloriously warm September day, I will die so that you can live. There's something almost elegant about that, don't you think?

Oh, I know, if we were having this conversation for real, you would argue that you live just fine thank you very much, you cheeky bitch; but that's not really true, is it? Yes, you exist, as you have done since you were five, when he started hurting you. But existing is not the same as living. You'd say that no therapist in their right mind would give up their life for the sake of a client – it's not even a thing! And I'd reply that no, I don't suppose it is, but don't worry, nobody will make the connection between us, and my death won't, I imagine, make the papers.

You'd cast up the maxim that I trotted out in your (and every client's) first-ever session – therapists don't save people; they help people to save themselves – asserting that what I'm about to do makes me a bad one, and I'd say yeah, fair enough, but that's hardly relevant given that tomorrow I'm meeting my maker.

Then, incredulous, but still curious despite yourself, you'd regard me with those pale blue eyes and chew on your lip a little before breaking out in a wavering smile and asking: you're not serious, are you?

And I'd say, of course I am, because you, Kass, have to live.

Spring Term 2022
Early January – late February

High School Counselling Service (i.e., me, Jane, 41, in a very small, out-of-the-way third-floor room with a window looking out onto sky, in a big Scottish state school whose catchment covers several affluent areas and council housing estates)

Hazel (S4)
Age 14
Initial appointment
Teacher referral – Hazel disclosed eating disorder
No other pastoral involvement that I know of

Hazel Session 1
'Hi Hazel, lovely to meet you. Come on in…'

Hazel looks around the room, shrugs off her schoolbag and sits down on the armchair. I fuss about, rifling through papers on the bookcase. I'm not actually doing anything; just giving her a moment to take in her surroundings.

In a room that's only fractionally bigger than the stationery cupboard directly beneath it – I know because I've measured both – any scents carried in by teenage bodies, from the choke of celebrity perfumes to the vinegary hum of menstrual blood and the heady glandular funk of pits and groins awash with new and enthusiastic pubescent hormones, tend to find a captive audience in me. Hazel's delivered a chemical kick of lemon fabric softener designed to evoke a sparkling morning on the Amalfi Coast or some such, which has immediately connected with the spore of a headache I hadn't realised was there.

Hazel's face is flushed. She's late and probably ran across the quad to get to my room. If memory serves me, she's come from Mandarin, which is in a shabby prefabricated outbuilding with a corrugated roof at the far end of the school.

As long as the window stays open, we are not required to wear masks for counselling. I'd worried she would feel cold, but clad in only her shirtsleeves she doesn't seem to have registered how glacial it is in here. In my woollen wrist warmers and knee-length faux-fur coat, I'm still chilly.

'Okay,' I say, settling into my chair. You've come out of Mandarin, is that right?'

'Yes,' says Hazel and smiles, revealing attractive protruding canines in a set of otherwise perfectly straight white teeth. No doubt she hates them.

'Is that a good thing then?'

'I'm not very good at languages,' she explains and nibbles at the edge of her finger – a hangnail perhaps.

'Me neither. What's your favourite subject?'

Hazel stops nibbling and considers the question, then says, 'Probably DT.'

'Ah, okay. What is it about Design and Technology that you like?'

'I dunno. I like making things, I suppose. And I like the way the room smells, and that there's always music on but it's still really calm. Everyone just gets on with their own work – it's pretty chill.'

She doesn't mention the teacher, but this sense of calm, of industrious autonomy, where no one mucks about, is surely their doing. I imagine a room warm even in winter, swept-up drifts of sweet-smelling sawdust and a neat wall of numbered tools, each one accounted for at the end of every lesson.

'It sounds lovely. I've never been in the department – I didn't know it was like that.'

Note to self: don't pull Hazel from DT classes.

'Have you ever been to any sort of therapy before?'

Hazel looks down, fiddles with the rubber band on her wrist. On another young person I'd immediately suspect the band was there as an alternative to cutting, but in the few minutes since she entered the room, she's used it to tie up her froth of reddish blonde hair and then taken it down again at least twice. I don't know why it doesn't snag, like it would in my hair. I don't know why her mother doesn't give her proper hairbands – maybe she does, and Hazel loses them. Maybe the rubber band signifies a deeper neglect. Maybe I'm an arse for thinking that. Freud said sometimes a cigar is just a cigar. Sometimes a rubber band is just a rubber band.

'No, I don't think so,' she replies, a dismal note in the delivery, and my attention snaps back. The colour has gone from her cheeks.

'Okay. So, sessions are fifty minutes long, same as lessons. See the clock there? I'll let you go a minute or so early, so you have time to get to your next class. Does that sound okay?

'Yes Miss.'

'My name is Jane, and it's okay to just call me Jane.'

'Jane,' she repeats.

I nod. 'So, Hazel, in this room you can say what you like, and I won't tell anyone. There are only two exceptions to my confidentiality. Firstly, if you were to tell me anything that makes me think you are at risk of *serious* harm, or that someone else is, then I will have to tell Mrs Morrison, our Child Protection Officer, but in almost all circumstances I'd discuss it with you first. And by serious, I mean really *serious*.'

She looks unconvinced, so I rattle off what, in the context of breaking confidentiality, does *not* constitute serious harm: smoking, vaping, drinking, smoking weed, most self-harm, sex with other young people, bitching about parents, gender issues, sexuality worries, evil thoughts, stealing…etc etc. These being the issues which, in the past, young people have assumed I would have to report. Then I add that the only other exception to my confidentiality is supervision. I have a supervisor with whom I talk about my clients. But she's a therapist like me, works across town, is ancient, and doesn't know anyone here. I'm also a member of a supervision group which meets infrequently online, but again, the people in the group are nothing to do with the school and are all bound by a code of ethics not to repeat what they hear.

'Yeah, that's fine, except you didn't mention, like, eating disorders… But I kind of think maybe that's why I'm…because I need help talking to my parents…'

Usually this is the point in a first session where the kid, having been very wary that I might contact their parents, looks to be appraising me, and it feels like a big moment. Will they or won't they open the door to whatever mess they are in and let me walk through to them. But Hazel has just said very clearly why she is here.

'I see… So, you think you might have an eating disorder…'

She squirms slightly in her seat.

'Take your time. It can be hard to open up to someone you've just met.'

'It's not that. I just, I sort of tried to say it to my dad once in the car and he said I didn't, like, fit the criteria of someone with an eating disorder and put the radio on.'

Nice one, Dad.

'What do you think he meant by that?'

'He meant I'm too fat.'

'He doesn't understand that eating disorders aren't really about weight.'

Though I'm making sure that my eyes don't drop to her body, I've already clocked the well-developed breasts in the pristine school shirt, then the straight sweep from her waist to her thighs encased in the ubiquitous black tube skirt (though she doesn't hitch hers up), opaque bobbly black tights, black Converse... Neither slender nor particularly curvy, she has the ten-a-penny, utterly lovely, almost-adult physique of a hundred other girls who will rush across the quad to get to lessons today.

'Can you remember when you started thinking about your body? Did someone say something?'

I don't add that body shaming almost always plays a part in the development of eating disorders; that they are opportunistic, searching for a chink, a tear – a way in.

Hazel shifts forward a little in the armchair, then swallows and launches into the story she needs to tell.

'I was eleven, I was still at Primary. It was the Christmas holiday and I'd had really bad flu for, like, almost two weeks. Then, on the day school started back, I got norovirus. I was puking for, like, three days. When I finally went to school my mum came with me. She wanted the school nurse to check me over. The nurse put me on the scales. My parents have scales at home, but I'd never really taken any notice of them. The ones at school were much larger, with a big round face like a clock. The nurse read out my weight and she was frowning. She pointed to the numbers and explained where I was, compared to where she thought I should be. I felt silly for not knowing there was a way my body *should* be. She said I'd probably lost a bit of weight because of the illnesses. Then she said it was a great excuse to eat cream cakes.'

Hazel has been staring into the middle distance somewhere west of my knees. Now she steps out of the memory for a moment and looks at me to check I'm understanding. When she sees that I am, she goes back in.

'My mum thought it was so funny – getting told to eat cake. She said, 'That's my kind of prescription!' She picked me up after school and we went to a café and ate éclairs. I had three – it was great. Then Auntie Gina turned up – she's a big deal in the police force. When mum went to the loo, Auntie Gina looked at me stuffing my face and said, 'Steady on Hazel, you don't want to ruin your lovely new slimline figure now, do you? You look just like your mum did when she was your age.'

Hazel pauses here, for the rush of shame necessary for her eating disorder to thrive. She's focused on me now, desperation in her wide eyes, the first shimmer of tears.

'I...I was so confused. Mum and the nurse wanted me to eat loads, but now I could see that they were just being kind. I had to stay thin. I remembered the numbers on the scale. I wrote them down, and I promised myself that I'd try not to eat very much.'

Fucking Auntie Gina. What a bastard.

'I don't think they were just being kind Hazel. And I think your auntie should not have said that to you.'

'I couldn't stop thinking it. My mum is beautiful and really slim – I wanted to stay like she was when she was eleven. So, I cut right down on food and started weighing myself on my parents' scales.'

'But you were still growing. You *are* still growing...'

'That doesn't matter. I had to stop the numbers going

up.'

She pauses; I wait.

'I was so hungry and sad all the time…'

'You must have felt dreadful…'

'I did. But I failed, I couldn't keep it up. I started eating again and sort of forgot all about the scales and what my auntie said. I felt much better.'

'But at some point, it started up again…'

Hazel nods. 'It was near the end of S1, in the summer. We had to wear shorts. This boy in my class said I had meaty thighs…'

Again, on her face the shame, and over it the tears that now flow freely.

'What does that even mean?' I say, and immediately regret it because I know fine well what meaty thighs means.

The slightest of frowns and a narrowing of her brown eyes as Hazel assesses whether I'm as dull-witted as my last comment suggests.

'It means fat. And I wasn't fat back then. I was just sort of straight up and down. But I looked at my thighs and I could kind of see what he meant…'

Here we go. Teenage girls rarely extend compassion to themselves.

'And then all the girls started talking about thigh gaps. Do you know what they are?'

'Unfortunately, I do.'

I do. And there's a part of me that doesn't want to be thinking about them yet again. I just…it's a lot. So many of these kids…

In case I'm bullshitting her, Hazel unnecessarily explains, 'So, you know there is meant to be a gap at the top of your thighs when you stand up. And if you haven't got one then you're fat…'

So simple. So stupid.

'Ridiculous. It's not healthy…'

Fuck's sake, Jane, that's twice now you've used the word healthy. All she'll hear is *fat*.

Hazel neither agrees nor disagrees. 'People started instagramming their thigh gaps; soon everyone was doing it.'

In S1. Eleven- and twelve-year-olds.

She's stopped crying, and through still-wet lashes, she stares hard at me with huge glassy eyes, but her mind is reaching back to her past.

Women in ancient Greece applied an extract of Atropa belladonna to their eyeballs for its pupil-dilating properties, which gave an eye-widening effect. A risky business considering that all parts of the plant are poisonous, especially the berries which, when ingested, can affect the nervous system, causing severe symptoms including sweating, vomiting, coma and death.

I haul my thoughts back to Hazel, who's now fixing her ponytail in place with the rubber band for the umpteenth time.

'So, I stopped eating again. But I was really serious this time. I'd fuss about making toast and jam in the mornings so my parents would see me walking out the door with it. Then I'd stick it in a hedge on the way to school.

I imagine a hedge full of sparrows eating toast, their beaks sticky with strawberry jam.

'...I'd go to the library at lunchtime instead of the canteen. And just eat at teatime.'

'You must have been starving...'

'I was. But I got thin. My thighs were thin, I had a gap at the top. You could see my ribs. I used to gaze at myself in the mirror. My clothes sort of hung off me, and it looked good. I felt light, and the empty feeling was...well, it felt like success.'

'Weren't your parents concerned?'

Hazel raises her hands to pull her ponytail tighter and considers the question.

'They were so busy with work, and I think when I started to lose the weight, they probably thought it looked good too. They are both kind of into being ripped – my dad's a GP and really into training. He's always going on about fitness and exercise and burning up calories. And my mum works at a spa in a big hotel. She's obsessed with juicing. She has a goldfish bowl of wine on a Friday night – her 'wee treat', but that's about the only unhealthy thing she does. She liked that I'd ask for a green juice at night. She didn't realise...'

The reference to the goldfish bowl of wine has opened the filing cabinet of my unconscious and unearthed my parents arguing over the glass orb which my father had found for homing the little tetras I'd set my heart on. My mother had heard on the radio that such old-fashioned vessels were inhumane, and was snorting with laughter at my father's dismay when she insisted it be returned to whatever skip he'd found it in. 'But they're about as far from human as you can get!' he'd protested. She'd given a derisive snort which meant *no dice*. I remember how he rolled his eyes and told me to get my coat; that we were going to a proper pet shop, and he was going to spend proper money. A memory with no edges, this one is as perfectly round as the whole scene had been, watched through the warp of the offending bowl.

I sigh, Hazel sighs.

I say, '...It acted like a laxative.'

Somewhere, not too far from here, someone is using a pneumatic drill, and the noise reverberates off the surrounding buildings in a brittle shudder.

'Yeah. If I'd slipped up during the day and eaten, like, a bag of crisps or something, I'd have a green juice and then it'd be okay.' She pauses, caught for a moment by the memory.

She didn't vomit like so many of them do, because she had the green juice; what the hell was in it?

She continues, 'I looked good, but I felt awful. I couldn't focus in classes and I had no energy. I just felt so sad all the time.'

'No wonder you felt sad, it's a lonely place to be, and you were starving. Diarrhoea's not much fun either.'

'No, but I kept that to night-time, so it wouldn't happen at school. Anyway, Mum started noticing. She bought loads of really nice snack food. I've got a total sweet tooth. I kept not eating during the day, but I started pigging out after tea. Mars bars and biscuits and stuff. I put the weight back on... And then I started having periods. My body really changed. Not in a good way.'

'You're becoming a woman.'

'A fat one,' Hazel snaps, bristling with contempt for herself.

'No, not a fat one. You're becoming an adult, with an adult's body. You need it to move, and to do all the things you want to do, maybe even to have a baby one day...'

Why did I say that? Hazel looks more than a little revolted by the idea and I have the creeping sensation that I'm starting to lose her.

'Where are you now in all this?' I ask.

Hazel sighs. 'I think about it all the time. I know it wasn't good, what I did to get thin. But I'm always thinking about doing it again. I forget all the bad stuff and focus on how really great it was to be thin and light. And about how much willpower I had. How disciplined I was.'

She glances at the clock, starts speaking faster. Eager to fit in as much as she can.

'But I can't seem to do it any more. It's gone the other way – now I'll come home from school and be so hungry that I'll have a huge bowl of rice with loads of sweet chilli sauce, and I'll eat, like, a whole pack of cookies after tea. I just never feel full. It's disgusting. I've gone from being so disciplined and thin, to stuffing myself.'

All said in the one breath, and now she flops back in her chair.

I give it a beat.

'You've forgotten what it's like to eat normally. Your body is busy doing all the things it needs to do to turn you into an adult. It needs you to eat healthily.'

Fuck. Why can't I come up with another word for healthy?

'I don't want to eat normally. I want to be a size six.'

Irritation rises in me like it always does when these girls start revealing the extent of their faulty thinking. The sensation never lasts long, gets quickly replaced by dread and the overwhelming pity that my supervisor Estelle likes to drill down into. Estelle sees pity as othering the client, as a condescending emotion that therapists should be wary of. I get that – I really do. But I wonder how she would feel, day after day, watching lovely kid after lovely kid being consumed by eating disorders they are powerless to resist. And Hazel's story, though pretty grim, isn't half as bad as some.

I hold Hazel's eyes with mine, hoping she's listening. 'I know you do, but very few women are size six naturally. You have to be tiny for that. Normal girls and women just aren't that small. To stay size six, you'd have to exercise all the time and never eat. It's just not possible without getting really ill…'

I pause for effect. Is she hearing me?

'…But you asked to come here, and I'm guessing that means that part of you wants help to eat normally again.'

As I say this, I can see the gloss of denial slip over her eyes. I'm dealing with two entities: Hazel, and the eating disorder, represented in my imagination by a smirking demon sitting by her side, its scaly arm draped around her, its clawed hand squeezing her shoulder. (Must remember to tell Estelle, who'll appreciate the imagery.) The more I say about the futility of trying to make herself perfect by starving herself, the tighter the demon grips. I can see it now, laughing at me, at *my* futile attempts to make her see sense. Right now it is relaxed in repose, but experience tells me that this creature could not be more ferocious.

'Are you looking at anything specific online?'

'What do you mean?' Hazel says, the twist of discomfort on her lips telling me my instincts are right.

'You know what I mean.'

'I try not to… I dunno. It's just…those girls want what I want, and they can be really encouraging. But some of them are so harsh when they see someone mess up…'

I want to shake her – shake all this crap out of her. I'm angry at her for feeling like this, which is ridiculous. I've seen the pro-ana and thinspo sites, have sat slack-jawed at the horror I saw there, yet still a tiny part of my middle-aged, should-know-better self *gets* the attraction, understands the draw, feels the pull…the seduction. What hope is there for these not-yet-grown children sitting alone imbibing this stuff via their phones?

'Really encouraging? The girls on these sites look emaciated, skeletal. They look like they're starving, which they are… Do you understand this?'

Hazel shrugs.

'I do… I mean, of course I do. It's like half of me does,

but the other half... I'd *like* someone to describe me as emaciated, as tiny. That's like my dream... I know I had bulimia, but now I think I've probably got binge-eating disorder.' She declares this in the callow manner of the teens of her generation who are both the beneficiaries and the victims of growing up in a society which talks more openly about mental health.

I'm slouching: how does Estelle achieve consistent good posture? I straighten my back and uncross my legs.

'I'm not a huge fan of self-diagnosis, Hazel, but given what you've told me, it sounds like you might be right. And eating disorders need to be named. Denial is the biggest gun in an eating disorder's arsenal. It enables it to thrive. Do you understand what I mean by that?'

Hazel nods, yes, she understands.

'...Which is why it's so great that you've told me. This is the first step to getting better...'

'People think binge-eaters are just greedy,' she snaps.

'Yes, but they're wrong. You've been struggling with this for years now. I wonder if we could think a bit about the root of it all.'

'The root of it all is that I'm fat,' Hazel says, gripping the flesh of her thighs.

Part of me wants to lean over and grab her hands, pull them on to my thighs. See what she thinks of them.

'But I can see that you are not fat. You have decided your body is unacceptable. Why?'

'I told you; it was what my aunt said, and that boy...'

'Do you like your aunt?'

Hazel curls a lock of hair escaped from her ponytail round her ear.

'No, not really. But I try to because she and Mum are so close.'

'So, you don't like her, don't respect her.'

'No.'

'What about that boy in your class?'

'Ugh, no.'

'Why didn't you like him? I mean before he said what he said.'

Hazel screws up her face and says, 'He's one of those boys that got into porn too young, and now he just sees girls as, as…well, we all just try to avoid him.'

She says this wearily; just one of those things one must learn to live with, like income tax and endless housework. But she's only fourteen.

'One of those boys that got into porn too young. You say this like they are a category of boy…'

'They are! They get obsessed with porn sites, and they think that girls are just there for, you know, like sex and stuff. They say horrible things to us.'

What have we done to our kids? How lonely this boy's life is going to be. I want to seek him out, tell him what I think of his behaviour, then get him into some sort of reparative justice re-education programme. Auntie Gina too.

'Okay so you don't like him or Auntie Gina, yet you have decided your body is unacceptable on the back of some mean stuff they said to you. Your mum and the nurse, on the other hand – you like them?

'Yeah, course I do.'

'But it wasn't *them* you listened to.'

Hazel frowns. 'The nurse put me on the scales and my mum told me to eat as many cream cakes as I wanted.'

'I know, and maybe in hindsight both were unwise, but they were well intentioned… What I'm trying to get you to see is that you were influenced not by the people you liked and respected, but by the people you *didn't* like, and there's got to be a reason for this.'

'It's because what they said made sense. I hadn't noticed my body was fat before. They showed me it was, by saying those things.'

Bullshit.

The room feels to have got warmer – the heating must have come on, but underneath my fur coat I'm wearing a sleeveless blouse, and right now I'd rather not reveal my fleshy white upper arms to Hazel, so I keep it on.

'Hazel, that's the eating disorder talking. I can see that your body is the body of a perfectly normal teenage girl – it's a great body. I don't think the problem is you. The problem is external. It's not just these nasty people who've got inside your head, it's the world you're growing up in.'

Hazel, glancing at the clock, looks utterly frustrated. 'I don't understand…'

'How can I put this… Hazel, you, like almost every girl I've worked with who has an eating disorder, believe that the problem – having been triggered by some nasty person like Auntie Gina, or that little shit in your class –

comes *from you*. You think it's your body that's at fault, and that your lack of "willpower" is a character flaw. This belief is reinforced by the cruel language used by the people on the thinspo and pro-ana accounts that you look at. What I want to do is to offer you the idea that your eating disorder doesn't originate with you. And that there are external forces at work here, forces sending you messages.'

Hazel looks at me like I'm completely nuts.

'I'm talking about the messages we get from all the clothing websites, all the make-up ads, all these Instagram accounts promoting clean eating. TikTok girls with their fashion hauls. Messages telling us we must be slim, we have to have perfect skin, perfect hair. Hazel, there is a multi-billion-pound juggernaut which relies on women and girls feeling terrible about themselves. There are many, many people making huge amounts of money from the gym gear, the fake tan, the hair removal stuff, the low-cal drinks, the digital scales…. If we, as girls and women spend more and more time obsessing over how we look, we buy into the idea that our bodies define us on a scale of worth – worth in the eyes of others. Constantly asking ourselves who will desire us, who will approve of us, envy us. We become inward-looking, incapable of thriving, of challenging…changing the world.'

As the words tumble from me, and the adrenaline surges, I feel omniscient. I am Truth-Sayer. My wisdom will transform how she feels about herself. Grown-up Hazel might even go on to be a mental health campaigner – a leading advocate for people with eating disorders. Off she'll go to fancy parties, winning awards, and effusing about her high-school therapist in her acceptance speeches – ha!

Hazel stares at me, still as a statue, even her ponytail is motionless.

I suddenly feel embarrassed. I am a ranter and a fantasist. A ranter in a cupboard at the top of a stair.

'I'm sorry, that was a bit jumbled, and maybe a bit much...'

We sit in this for fifteen, twenty seconds – I notice that my *Hoya carnosa*, in a small terracotta pot, cascading down from the one shelf in my cupboard-room, is looking more grey than green. The cold, maybe? Hazel smiles, perfectly snaggletoothed, and it's like the sun coming out from behind a cloud.

Then she says, 'It's okay, there were just quite a lot of new...but I think you're saying that there are all of these people selling stuff, who get fat off of me trying to get thin, or something like that.'

The relief. 'Hazel I couldn't have put it better myself.'

'Could you say it all again, but slower?'

Slower and more articulately.

I take off my coat.

Later, as I walk home, I imagine walking into the local cop shop where Auntie Gina, in full uniform, is deferentially ushering out a group of council high heid yins and some visiting foreign law-enforcement delegates, who will provide an audience for my tirade.

Then it's to the posh squash court for a wee chat with dad…

The problems Hazel left my room with were unchanged from those she brought, but some of the pressure has been released and I think that, together, we've laid the groundwork for what could prove to be a strong therapeutic alliance. Job done.

So, why then, am I left feeling useless? Like what I have to offer is somehow…meagre?

Vaishali

Age 17

Self-referral

Started puberty early, has been harassed by men ever since

Mum has chronic endometriosis, spends weeks of the month in bed

Both parents work in tech

Some responsibility for looking after younger siblings

Pronouns they/them

Hates their curves

Solid friendship group since primary school

Straight-A student but struggling to concentrate

Terrible periods – could they also have endo?

Presenting issue: anger, distress, hates body

Vaishali Session 5

They sit there with the type of body which would make Sophia Loren envious. I'm very uncomfortable about the fact that each and every time they come in, the first thing I notice is their incredible figure. Not so incredible for Vaishali who refers to it as 'my curse' which they bring as the subject for therapy every week. Vaishali requested that they be called 'they' at school, which the school agreed to do, as is our policy, and also agreed not to tell Vaishali's parents, as is their right. Vaishali explained that it is not that their parents would not understand if they told them; they just aren't ready to tell them yet. Also, with their mum's health problems, and their little brother and sister to look after, Vaishali doesn't want to give their parents anything else to stress about.

'I'm wondering where you would like to start today?'

Vaishali starts where they always start. 'I want rid of this body.'

'I know you do.'

'This morning on the bus…I'm sick of having to move because of some bloke old enough to be my dad…'

I feel the pull of automatic recoil, ignore it. Covid rules are loosening but buses with their vaporous air and handrails coated in human grease, still feel risky. I'm lucky enough to live close enough to the school that I can walk to work, as do most of the kids, but some of them still have to travel by bus.

The lockdowns are like a dream I had, stretches of time that somehow don't count. A blip. Endless Zoom calls for work and play, my household of one subsumed at Jessie's insistence into her ever-expanding menage, making our bubble. When I finally succumbed to the virus, it hit me like a bad cold, nothing more. At the start of the pandemic, when Covid appeared to be killing people at random and fear spread across the globe more efficiently than any virus ever could, I worried for others but felt unaccountably Zen about contracting it myself. When this came up in conversation with my supervisor Estelle, she, not being one to mince her words, pointed out that I already had a deep-seated belief that I knew what was going to kill me – and it wasn't Covid. Though this was the first time I'd really considered it consciously, I knew instantly that she was right. Covid will not be the thing that gets me in the end. Still, I don't like to be ill.

'It happened again?' I ask them.

'It happens all the time,' Vaishali replies. 'Today I got asked if I'm a St Trinian. I wanted to say, no mate, I'm a real schoolgirl, which makes you a fucking paedo.'

Ha!

'But you didn't. You froze.'

'Yeah, as always.'

I can't tell whether anger or shame is the prevailing emotion.

Vaishali sits forward and strokes the leaves of the variegated ivy which spills out of its small pot onto the table that sits between us. According to NASA, *Hedera helix* is a top performer in air purification.

'My mum's got this in the garden.'

'You know it's not our choice what we do. Most people freeze.'

'Yes, I know...' they say, tolerating me repeating the same old line to them. '... I just don't want this body any more.'

'But isn't it these men who are wrong, not your body? Perhaps if we lived in a better society where sexism and misogyny didn't exist, you would like your body, or at least accept it? Actually quite like being female...'

They shake their head, their long hair rippling as smooth and reflective as treacle. If I ask them what conditioner they use they'll say some cheap and nasty stuff from Superdrug, and I'll be forced to recognise that it is being seventeen which imparts that shimmer, and then feel a bit downcast. So I don't.

'No offence Jane, but you're dreaming. What you're describing is utopia, and utopias don't exist. My reality is getting leered at, yelled at, commented on, every single day. Nothing I can do will change that, except changing myself. I don't feel like this bombshell people keep telling me I am. I want to be able to run without worrying about people staring at my tits.'

Vaishali slumps back in the chair, defeated.

If I had a pound for every girl who came to me with this problem... It is the younger ones that really break my heart – the eleven, twelve, thirteen-year-olds, who still call break 'playtime', who take teddies to sleepovers, who have little yet in the way of sexuality, but whose bodies have exploded into puberty. Children with women's bodies, and now, suddenly, all the shit that brings with it.

As if to hammer home the point, my womb twangs in a painful proclamation that my period has just started. As the cramping subsides, I feel smug at the foresight which saw me put a pad on this morning. It's taken thirty years, but I've just about mastered the art of not spending a whole day each month with toilet tissue stuffed down my pants: a sign of adulthood if ever there was one, surely.

I don't really know what to say, so I say, 'Hmm.'

Was that a flash of anger at my sub-standard response?

The shoulders of Vaishali's blazer are up around their ears making them look like a *Beano* character and I have to suppress what would be a completely inappropriate smile.

'What? Do you think I should just put up with it?'

Vaishali is more combative than usual – or they aren't, and it's just me imagining they are, because I'm worried that I'm coming across as old and out of touch, or because they suddenly remind me of Minnie the Minx.

'I don't think you should have to put up with any of it,' I say uselessly.

Vaishali sighs, crosses her legs. They are having trouble sitting still today – all that angry energy. 'You're a good person, Jane. Don't worry about it.'

Relieved I say, 'Vaishali, you are a kind person.'

They smile, 'Touché.'

I smile back.

'Okay. I get it. The point is that it doesn't matter what I think you should or shouldn't have to put up with, you still have to put up with it.'

'I do.'

'You do... I'm just so sorry you have to...'

Vaishali sits forward again and chucks their hair over their shoulder, 'Oh, for god's sake, Jane, it's not you, it's men! And those stupid bitches in Sarah's clique. But mostly men...'

I can't seem to shake off the feeling that I should somehow be doing better with Vaishali, that I'm failing them. Just need to get back to core conditions – respect, congruence, empathy. Stop feeling so bloody guilty.

'Today, in Drama, we were doing our warm-up exercises – you know, rolling our shoulders and stuff

– and Mr Kimble walks in and says, "That's right, push those chests out ladies…" He was looking directly at me.'

I say, 'What a creep!' Very congruent.

'I know!'

'Then at lunch, Mr Huntley comes up and tells Sarah K her skirt is so short she may as well get herself to the strip club up the road to earn some extra pocket money. I mean, she'd rolled it right up, but still, is that really okay?'

Yet another story about Mr Huntley: I can't work out whether this guy is just a prick or actually dangerous.

James Huntley is a broad-shouldered, good-looking and well-dressed (slightly tweedy with some discreet Ralph Lauren) sleazeball in his late thirties who slimes over the young female newly qualified teachers (NQT's) whenever he gets half a chance. Rumours of inappropriate behaviour circulate. The kids tell me the just-tipping-into-awful things he says to them but forbid me from passing them on. My male friends among the teaching staff sigh and shake their heads at his mention.

But it's a big school, and he's well-liked by many. The first and only time we spoke was the day when, having forgotten my packed lunch, I braved the lunch hall, and he sat himself down in the free chair next to mine. Though I've been at the school much longer than he has, I'm rarely roaming free within it, and he must have thought I was an NQT, because he saw my polite smile as an invitation to introduce himself with a kind of lofty benevolent confidence, edging into flirtation, that hinted at a status superior to mine.

When, after talking about himself for a good ten minutes, he eventually asked my subject, I told him I was the school counsellor and that I'd been in the job for twelve years. The affable generosity of moments before disintegrated before my eyes. I was not as he thought I was, and whether or not he knew it, he was angry at me for having misled him, though I had said nothing much other than my first name. His once expansive body language bordered on hostile, as he trotted out the old cliché that he'd have to be careful around me or I'd try to psychoanalyse him. I just wanted him to get up and leave me alone.

At the best of times I find the lunch hall a nerve-wracking place to be – social anxiety more than true shyness – but generally when I get chatting to someone the fear passes. Some teachers, far from seeing my occupation as a threat, find it interesting, ask me questions about the problems people bring, how I got into counselling in the first place. Occasionally I've made a new friend, someone whose face I can search for in the lunch crowd as I uneasily make my way towards them, tray in hands.

Not so with James Huntley. Despite his obvious discomfort and mine, he stayed put, forced me to be the one to leave, but not before complimenting him on his beautiful wedding ring.

Focus, Jane.

'No. It's very much not okay. She is a pupil in this school and no teacher should be referring to her in that way. Do you want me to report it?'

I feel my own anger (or maybe it's Vaishali's?) rising inside me. Must resist the urge to try to 'fix', but then again, I have a bit of clout, I could at least mention it at the next Pupil Support meeting…

Vaishali shakes their head. 'Sarah already did report it, but nothing will happen. Nothing ever happens. At least it wasn't me, for once. Usually it's me who gets told off for having my skirt too short, when I don't even roll mine up. It just looks short cause my legs are so long.'

I look at their endless Pretty-Polly-model's legs, which is bad because I always resist the urge to look at clients' bodies in case they think I'm making judgements about them. Which I almost certainly will be. I say judgements – more like information gathering – bodies tell me stuff.

Even if I lost a stone, I doubt my legs would look like that.

'You feel like you get picked on by some teachers…'

'Yeah, some of them…'

'Are you able to say why you think that might be?'

'I think it's because of how I look, but maybe also because I'm brown.'

'So, the reasons you get picked on are not only sexist but also racist.'

'Yes. Maybe. I don't know…'

'I'm wondering, does being they, rather than she, help with any of this?'

Vaishali frowns, and I feel like I've asked a stupid question.

'No. Yes... I don't know. It dilutes it a bit. If I'm not always this kind of mega-female, if other people are accepting me as not that, by using my pronouns, I feel like for once they are seeing beyond my "curves".'

They make speech marks in the air, I guess mimicking all the people – mum and aunties and school nurse, me probably – who have scratched about trying to find the best way to refer to their voluptuous body.

'Pronouns are important to you.'

'Yes. Very.'

'Can I just ask though; would you want rid of your "curves" if you weren't getting sexualised all the time? Could you, do you think, be happy with the fact you have a young woman's body?'

'What, and accept I'm going to get harassed for the rest of my life?' she says, arching a beautiful eyebrow.

'I mean hypothetically, if no one was going to harass you...'

'Jane, you're dreaming again. You don't get one without the other.'

'I know. But you are stuck with this body, and unless you learn one day to accept it you will always be unhappy with it – because of other people's awful behaviour. I mean, that's just terrible. To forever want rid of the perfectly good body you've got.'

'I don't see that I have any other options, Jane.'

'But there's got to be something here about embracing the body you have, standing up for it, not letting the bastards get you down, not letting the patriarchy win...'

I started this session sitting back in my chair, I'm now

on the edge of my seat, gesticulating into the space between us.

Vaishali laughs and says, 'Give it up, Jane! You should go on a march or something, get all this anger out.'

Go on a march or something.

I feel anachronistic, irrelevant. Like my kind of feminism is dead in the water. Am I just not getting it?

I fail Vaishali time and time again – the not-quite-good-enough therapist. If they had other options, I'm pretty sure they wouldn't come back. In my head I can hear my supervisor Estelle telling me that I'm doing my best but given the circumstances no one's best would be good enough. I know this, yet, still, after Vaishali leaves, I sit and squirm in my own inadequacy for a bit, water my plants from my own flask, then go and boil the kettle.

Kass (staff)

Age 31

Member of support staff

Self-referral

No mention of family

Struggling to make ends meet

Very late for session

Presenting issue: thinks she might have anxiety, finding it hard to make friendships at work

Seemed indifferent to my explanations about biological manifestations of anxiety and ways to expel stress hormones from the body

Very boring first session – something she's not yet ready to say, maybe?

Kass Session 2

Counselling courses teach that when you get bored and sleepy in the room with a client, it could mean there is something they are *not* talking about. Something they are avoiding talking about. This is probably, mostly, true. One exception is those younger girls, S1 or S2, doyennes of the fifty-minute filibuster, who whine endlessly about their bitchy friends. I find it almost impossible to follow or care why Megan said whatever to Naomi, about Susie behind Heidi's back, because the kid is totally fine and wasting my time. I know this says more about me than my client; that the child in front of me deserves my full attention and forbearance as much as the next person, so I try extra hard to concentrate on the most undramatic of dramas rehashed for me, often in semi-American twang.

Kass, however, is thirty-one. I'm not entirely sure what she does here – some sort of administrative role. Her very pretty face is free of make-up, and she has straight mouse-coloured hair and striking pale blue eyes. She looks older than thirty-one.

Last week she came in quickly, sat herself down in my chair, the back of which is visible only to birds. No one but clients ever visits my room at the end of the hall at the top of the stairs, but there is a small window in my door, a portion of which is not covered by the poster I stuck over it, and it is true that were someone to come along, they would be able to see the legs of whoever was sitting in the client's chair.

Some of my clients – adolescents and adults – don't mind other people knowing they are attending counselling sessions; for others, like Kass, privacy is central to maintaining the 'therapeutic frame'. At the start of the work, rules and limits, such as the time and setting, are agreed to establish a safe and effective environment; these boundaries provide the edges of the frame, the importance of which is drummed into rookie therapists almost from day one of training. The therapist who fails to keep the frame intact, holding the client safe within it, invites questions regarding their practice.

Our first session was so mind-numbingly boring that, this week, I've come prepared. Right now, Kass is sucking the life out of me with banal office-politics chatter which doesn't match the stricken expression on her face and the general tense vibe which hangs about her. She describes herself as having anxiety, but I see the wary unease and tension that signals underlying trauma, somehow different in quality to the stress and worry other anxious clients present with.

I interrupt her, 'Kass, you came here saying you thought you were suffering from anxiety. I don't doubt that, but I wonder if we might think about areas of your life other than work...'

Kass screws up her forehead and immediately I have the feeling that if she were the bank teller in an American heist movie, this would be the moment where she pulls down the security grille.

'But it's work that causes the anxiety...' she says.

'Yeah, but does it though? Or maybe it does, but there might be other causes. Anxiety tends to attach itself to any situation available to it, though its true roots may lie elsewhere.'

Looking unconvinced, Kass says, 'I don't know what you mean...'

'Well, if you were an astronaut, then it's possible you would be anxious about doing all your technical tasks correctly, getting your calculations right, even though you know you are more than capable...'

'No wonder – that would be incredibly stressful, and if I did something wrong, I could endanger my own life *and* the lives of the other astronauts.'

'Okay, bad example. Let's try another. Say you were a librarian, putting all the returned books back on the right shelves – a task that you do every day as part of your role. It's possible that you might start getting anxious about doing this correctly, or within the time you've set aside for it, because the anxiety is not actually about the task, which you know you can do well and have evidence of doing well in the past. The anxiety exists outwith the job but attaches itself *to* the job, and kind of feeds off it, if you get what I mean.'

'I think I *do* get you,' says Kass, 'but I don't see what those examples have to do with me. Neither the astronaut nor the librarian is having issues with their work colleagues like I am. I'm anxious because they make me anxious!'

Either she's deep in denial, or I'm barking up the wrong tree.

'I know you say that Kass, and honestly, I will hold my hands up and apologise if I'm wrong, but I just don't get a sense that that's what's going on here. They do sound annoying with some of the things they say and do... that one you say taps on her teeth with her shellacs... But I don't get a sense that you are unhappy at work *as such*. I mean they are annoying, sure, but they also sound like they're your friends – not just colleagues. Friends who you find annoying, probably because you are working at such close quarters with them. But that very real anxiety you experience, that I can see in you – that feels separate. And I realise I don't know anything about you other than your work life, which is fair enough as this is only our second session...'

'There's not much to tell,' she says and looks to the side, dropping eye contact.

Yeah right.

'Have you got a family?'

Or are you on your own like me?

Am I being too directive, bullying, even? I've got my hunch, but is that enough to lead her towards a path she's clearly reluctant to go down? Is this really therapeutic? She's so new to our therapy, which means the power dynamic is leaning heavier on my side. But am I misusing that power?

She could always refuse to answer. But then she trusts me to be professional, to know the right way *to do* therapy. Refusing might feel confrontational, a bit rude.

'I have a son,' she says bluntly, as if giving me a present that she wanted to keep for herself.

Lucky you.

'How old?'

'Six.'

'Does he have a name?'

'His name is Lewis.'

Christ, she's cold. Most parents bubble over with information when you ask them about their kids, but not Kass. I don't think she likes me any more, and I feel like I've lost her. She probably won't come back next week.

'That's a nice name.'

Nothing.

I could reel this back in, make it better, ingratiate myself and just let her waste her allocation of sessions. She'd come out of therapy singing my praises and feeling lighter for having a good old moan about her co-workers. But I'm not sure I could live with that. I know it can take time for an alliance to develop, for trust to grow, but this is school counselling, eight sessions is usually as many as I can push for – we don't have the luxury of many months of therapy, and she needs help now because it's obvious there's something not right here.

In for a penny, in for a pound.

'You seem reluctant to tell me about your son, and I'm wondering why that might be.'

She frowns, 'I'm not sure that's true...'

'Okay, I might have got that wrong. I'm a bit like a detective sometimes, asking questions to try to get an idea of what life is like for you. And I frequently get things wrong, so bear with me, and please don't be scared to put me right, okay?'

'Huh... Okay.'

'So, is it just you and Lewis at home?'

'Yeah.'

'Can I ask does his father play a part in his life?'

'I'm really not sure this is relevant to me having anxiety...'

Yes, but you are strongly resistant to talking about this stuff, which makes me think I'm on to something.

'Okay Kass. How about this? I can stop asking questions about your family and your life outside school. We can go back to where we were, and I won't intrude into these areas again unless it really does seem relevant...'

Kass, plucking a stray thread from the pale blue

jumper she's wearing, looks faintly interested in what I'm about to say next.

'… So, we can totally do that if that's what you want. Or – and bear with me yet again for a moment here – you can choose to go to places where there is pain. It might be incredibly hard-going. I don't know what *it* is, so I can't say what it might be like, but I'm guessing it won't be easy. We only have about fifteen minutes left of our session today, but we can pick up again next week… I have this idea in my head that your anxiety stems from somewhere deeper than your issues at work. I have nothing to base this on other than the fact you look…so wary all the time. So ready to run.'

Kass laughs – a hard sound that slaps the walls. Why?

'Something I said made you laugh; can you tell me what it was?'

'No,' she replies, but she is staring intensely at me, deliberating, '…but I *will* answer your questions, since you've been honest about why you're asking them.'

'Okay, great. And of course, you can choose to stop at any time. And I should have asked last week, have you ever done any type of therapy before?'

She hesitates before saying, 'Yes. Years ago now.'

'And would you feel able to tell me what that was for?'

'No, I would not,' she snaps.

'Alright. Let's go back to Lewis. What's he like?'

At my mention of her son's name, she gifts me a small smile.

'He's… he's not like other kids. He's an angel. I mean not all the time – he can be naughty sometimes, but he's good… He's a really good little person.'

I return the smile.

'And what about other family. Your parents – are they still alive?'

She nods. 'Yes.'

'And do you get on with them?'

Kass uses one thumbnail to scratch back and forth over the other. Eventually she says, 'I don't really see them.'

'Because you don't get on?'

She shakes her head slowly, 'No, I mean…it's hard to explain. They're not bad people.'

'But you don't see them…'

'I can't.'

'Why not? Do they live far away?'

'No.'

'Then why don't you see them?'

'I just can't.'

'Okay. Any siblings?'

'No.'

'You are an only child? And you don't see your parents. That sounds hard.'

'No.'

'No what?'

'No, I'm not an only child. I just don't have siblings. *Lewis* is an only child.'

'Do you mean you had a sibling who died?'

Kass mutters, 'Something like that.'

No siblings, but not an only child. Doesn't see her parents who live close by even though they are *not bad people.* And Lewis is *a good person.*

'What about other family members, extended family...?'

She shrugs, 'There are people, but I'm not close to any of them.'

'It must be hard not having people who can take Lewis off when you need a bit of time to yourself...'

I've said the wrong thing because Kass is suddenly angry. She says nothing, keeps her features neutral, but it's there in the twitch of a tendon in her neck, in the hardening of the line of her jaw. And then a serrated intake of breath by a body sensing threat. The last thing I meant to do was corner her.

'I've said something to upset you, but I don't know what it is...'

'You're fine, don't worry about it,' she says, unconvincingly.

'I don't think that's true. What did I say to upset you?'

Not gentle enough Jane; tread more softly.

'You've not got kids, do you?'

Is it that obvious?

'No, that's correct,' I say slowly, '...but I'm an auntie, in the way that your mum's best friend is your auntie, to all my friends' kids. My pals are always saying how much they're looking forward to relatives taking their kids off their hands so they can have a break. That's all I meant by it...'

She softens a little and says, 'I just didn't like the way you said it. *Taking Lewis off,* like he might not be safe.'

'You worry about your son's safety?'

'What mother wouldn't?'

But I'm not a mother so I wouldn't know about that... Is that what you're implying Kass? Or maybe I'm projecting my own stuff, and you didn't mean that at all.

'But I was talking about *family* taking him, not some stranger...'

Kass is very agitated, scratching at her nail and fiddling with her rings.

'It's just us... Me and Lewis,' she says.

I'm starting to wish we hadn't started talking about her family. Soon she's got to go back to the harpies in the office – her word not mine. And she was late for this session, so we don't have that long to go. If clients are talking about particularly difficult stuff, like I've done with Kass, I always warn them ten or fifteen minutes from the end, and again when time is nearly up, so they can have a chance to come back from wherever they went during the session, ground themselves, fix smeary mascara, before going back into the world.

We sit in silence. Something seems to settle in Kass. She folds her arms over her middle but it's not defensive. I think she's calming herself. She's okay with the silence, but I'm clearly not because I interrupt it and say, 'I'm sorry if that made you feel even more anxious...'

Looking for Kass to make me feel better. Not therapeutic, and now I feel a bit pathetic.

She doesn't respond. It looks like she's consciously deep-breathing into her diaphragm. I don't know what's happening, so instead of clumsily cutting into her silence again, I attempt to tolerate it while she uses it well.

Five minutes left. I doubt she will say much more. She may not even return next week. In my stomach a knuckle of hunger uncurls and I'm glad next period is lunch.

Then she says, 'Lewis doesn't know who his father is, and to be honest, I don't think I do either.'

Clients will do this sometimes. Just when you think you've lost them, or if nothing much has been said during a session, right at the end they drop a bomb. Something about escape being imminent. We learn in training that clients will only give us what we can handle. I don't really know if I believe this, but it makes sense that they might want to test the water by telling us the big thing right at the end of the session, just in case we don't react in the way they hope we will.

'Okay... Could you tell me a bit about why that is?'

She's regarding me intently again, as if trying to judge whether letting me in is a good shout or a big mistake.

She sighs, or takes a deep breath – I'm not sure which – before saying, 'When Lewis was conceived, I wasn't doing too well...'

She's looking off to the side, but glancing at me, I guess to see if she can read my expression, which I keep neutral while I nod in acknowledgement of what she's just said.

She takes the nod as her cue to continue. 'I, I went on dating sites... Have you heard of Tinder?'

I get this a lot – kids asking me if I've heard of

Snapchat or TikTok or Reddit. And that's okay because to them our age differences are unfathomable and I was born in 'the olden days', but Kass is only ten years younger than me. I thought of us as peers but now I see she doesn't share this view, which is useful information.

'I have, yes.'

I cross my legs and adjust my skirt, now feeling old and matronly compared to Kass, who, as has just been established, is of a different generation, *and* much slimmer than me. There is a synthetic shine on my tights that isn't supposed to be there because it said *opaque* on the packet. That's what you get when you buy Asda instead of John Lewis.

'I was going on Tinder *a lot…*'

'You wanted to meet someone; that's only natural…'

She looks embarrassed, but there's no shame in going on Tinder. Did she just wince?

She says, 'No, I didn't want to *meet someone*, at least not in the way I think you mean it.'

'Ah, okay, you wanted a hook-up.' See Kass, I'm not old, I know the lingo.

'Sort of… I wanted to find men to have sex with…'

'Okay… Like you said, you weren't doing too well, and you wanted to find men to have sex with… Do you think you were looking for validation maybe? For intimacy, affection?'

A tiny shake of her head. 'It wasn't that kind of sex.'

'What kind of sex was it?'

'The opposite of what you said…' She looks up at me through brown eyelashes. She wants me to guess because she's finding it hard to say.

'Okay, so maybe you were looking for sex that feels wrong? Feels bad? Maybe even quite aggressive?'

'Yes, and the rest...'

'So that's what you like? Your thing. You like to be dominated by a man...hurt, even?'

'No... I don't like it... I'm not even straight...'

'Then why...?'

'Because I wasn't doing too well.'

'So, this was some kind of punishment? Some part of you felt you deserved to be hurt in this way, treated badly...'

'Sort of...'

'So maybe I'm half right...but there's more to it...'

'Yes.'

'You actively sought men to have this certain kind of sexual experience with... Why?'

That intense stare again, that weighing up. Should she or shouldn't she?

Hard, sleety rain hits the window outside.

She closes her eyes and says, 'Because it felt like coming home.'

1996

Jessie's red hair is like a net for catching the sunlight which shakes in her curls every time she sneezes.

'Jessie, stop fucking sneezing, will you?' says Neil.

Jess gives Neil the death stare.

'And just how the fuck do you propose I do that? I've got fucking hay fever and we are sitting in a field.'

Neil just turned seventeen – the first of us. He passed his driving test and bought a banger. Six of us squashed inside it today and drove away from the city to… I don't actually know where we are, so I ask.

'Somewhere nobody thought to mow the grass,' replies Jessie.

'Jessie, have you never been to the countryside before?' asks Neil. 'This is not a field, it's a meadow. That thing over there with all the leaves is called a tree.

An oak if I'm not mistaken. And the watery thing down there is a river – R-I-V-E-R.'

'Thanks Neil. I can't actually see anything because my eyes are so itchy, so that's really helpful of you.'

Neil reaches out and pulls a lock of her hair.

Jessie, squealing, jumps onto Neil, who, delighted, attempts to fend her off. She grabs the cap from his head and is up and away, running through the long grass, crowning glory bouncing as she goes. He is straight after her.

'Arseholes,' says Leila, getting up and handing her half-smoked cigarette to Ross, who's reading a graphic novel and takes it without looking up.

I smell Timotei shampoo as Leila lies down behind me, Benson and Hedges breath in my ear. She fits her knees into mine and pushes with her hand so I'll lift my head to let her slip her arm under my neck. I can feel her breasts against my back through our T-shirts as she holds me as close as can be and says, 'I love you Janey, and one day you are going to be okay.'

I close my eyes as a tear from one leaks out across my nose and into the other. They are all like this, my friends, since what happened happened. It's like they had a meeting to discuss strategy, decided how they would deal with me. How do you deal with someone who flits from mute, to numb, to tearful, to fizzing with bad energy, sometimes all in the space of one day? With doggedly optimistic and loving supervision, apparently.

Leila and the sun are warming my skin. I am level with the grasses and the wildflowers whose names I don't know. I plan to teach myself one day, my parents never having been much good at flower identification. Or helping with homework. Or cooking and cleaning. Our house was always just at the point of tipping over into hazardous-to-health. Every so often they would reluctantly step up and blitz it together, yelling at each other whenever one of them had finished a task, like they were a team in *The Crystal Maze*. What they were good at was adventures and trips and dressing for the occasion. They were good at spending all the food-shop money in one go in a restaurant. They saw weekends as the time for exploring. We'd come to places just like this meadow, but no one ever remembered to bring the flower identification book that my mother picked up in a charity shop. They were only slightly better at birds.

Bees drone somewhere nearby, and a beetle runs up a blade of grass not far from my face. The odd little breeze shivers over us and is gone. Jessie's wrong about mowing grass; surely that makes hay fever worse.

It's getting hotter.

In the distance I can see Jessie and Neil walking back towards us. Both tall and strong-looking. She's wearing bootleg jeans and a cropped crochet halter-neck which shows off the flat plains of her stomach, and he's in a Public Enemy T-shirt and ridiculously baggy cargos. For a couple of seconds, the shimmer of a heat haze makes them wobble, indistinct, like subjects in a watercolour painting.

I did John Everett Millais for my Higher Art exam. The painting was *Mariana*, the woman in the blue velvet dress, gazing out the window and pausing in her embroidery to stand and stretch. Her fiancé should have returned long ago. With the passing of time, represented by the autumn leaves scattered on the ground at her feet, she's come to realise he never will. Now she hopes death will release her from her yearning, and presumably from the twin points of pain she's attempting to rub away with her pale little hands from either side of her coccyx. I've seen my mum in this pose many times; back pain's not for sissies, was her line, always reaching beyond pain to the joke, but still wincing. I can't remember why Mariana's fiancé has fucked off. Is he away with another woman? Someone who doesn't spend her days yearning at windows maybe. I don't know, or much care – I just like the dress. Millais has turned paint into velvet and it's incredible. The richness of the pile, the glow and shadow of the blue.

That blue.

Angie's come back from checking out the river, mud on the knees of her dungarees and slightly out of breath, excited to tell us what she's discovered. She takes a band out her pocket and ties her hair into a messy knot on the top of her head. 'There's a pool upstream – perfect for swimming...'

Ross looks up from his book, squints at Angie.

'We didn't bring anything to swim in.'

'Oh, for fuck's sake, Ross. It's boiling! Come on ladies...' she says, mimicking our old PE teacher.

She undoes the clips at the top of her dungarees and

steps out of them before pulling off her stripy T-shirt and dropping it on the grass.

'I'm just not doing that,' says Ross, embarrassed by Angie in her bra and pants.

Naturally athletic, unlike me, Angie is a tiny, slim, fair-haired person, and also unlike me, up for anything that involves liveliness.

'But I'll come and sit by the river,' Ross concedes.

Neil is already stripped to his boxers, with Jessie almost down to her underwear too.

The four set off towards the river, Neil and Angie running ahead.

Both my knees crack as Leila hauls me onto my feet. In the far distance a car windscreen glints and flashes as it wends along the motorway between fields of tall emerald-green crops – corn? Leila and I walk together after the others with the sun beating down on our heads.

The bright wings of a butterfly flitting between the grass and the flowers catch my eye and there is movement and birdsong coming from the trees down by the river. We follow a little stony path along the curve of the riverbank until we reach Angie's pool. On either side, the trees, hung with clusters of white blossom, dapple the sunlit water with shade. Hawthorns, Neil says, and I'm inclined to believe him because Neil is clever. Their tiny browning starflowers spread across the shining surface of the pool where little insects dart and hover. It will be colder than it looks.

Ross, who's found himself a rock to sit on, removes

his Docs and dips his big feet into the water. Jessie and Angie hold hands, picking their way barefoot over the slimy green rocks at the side of the pool, but Neil, in boxers and trainers, runs headlong into the water, plunging down through the floating blossom with all the grace of a Labrador.

Leila gets out of her clothes and motions to me to do likewise. She looks funny standing there in her green Converse Hi-Tops and nothing but her underwear. Leila's body is like mine – just sort of normal, at least compared to Angie's compact, petite frame, or Jessie's perfect willowy model proportions.

'Keep your sandals on,' she orders.

It's a relief to be out of my clothes, but standing in my underwear I feel exposed and fold my arms across my breasts, words of protest catching in my throat.

Noting this, Leila says, 'None of that Janey. It'll do you so much good.'

She takes my hand and leads me towards the water where Jessie, Neil and Angie are splashing about, squealing and laughing, wet skin and hair flashing in the sunlight.

My body won't go any further. It's too much. I can't go in.

Ross has noticed. He puts his Docs back on, hops off the rock and comes over to us.

'I can't...'

'Yes, you can...' he says gently, and pulls off his T-shirt revealing angry red acne in a landscape of inflamed ridges and peaks all across the exposed white skin of his back and chest. An unexpected kindness intended to draw me out of myself just long enough to get me into the water.

But I still can't do it.

Jessie, who has stopped leaping about, stands statuesque at the dead centre of the pool like some Olympian goddess, hair plastered to the side of her face. Our eyes lock. She extends a slender arm and beckons to me.

I nod.

'Okay then...'

Ross and Leila put their arms around me and the three of us run across the rocks and into the water. Jessie shrieks with delight.

Spring Term
Late February – early April

Fraser (S6)

Age 17

Referred by Pupil Support Administrator – 'He seems really down...'

Presenting issue: intrusive spiralling negative thoughts about himself / trouble sleeping

Young carer for mum who has arthritis

Met bio dad only twice

Good friendship group who all get on well with mum

Lots of sci-fi metaphors

Girlfriend of 2 months, also in S6

Movement from parental attachment onto peers

Frustrated by caring duties

Adores mum, worries about her

Much of sessions taken up with these worries

Fraser Session 5

'I need to tell you something, but I don't know how to say it.'

'Okay. Is that because it's maybe a bit embarrassing? Or upsetting?'

'Yeah, sort of both. But worse.'

Fraser stares at the floor. He's been doing so well these last few weeks, but something looks to have set him back. His hair, whipped into stiff meringue-like peaks, glistens with wax; presumably a homage to some footballer of whose style I'm unaware. He's wearing a bright PE kit which makes the alabaster skin on his lean arms and legs seem even paler than usual. When he glances up at me to see how I'm dealing with the idea of something worse than embarrassing and upsetting, his face is flushed scarlet.

Fraser makes my heart hurt; if I'd had a boy, I would've liked him to be like Fraser. It's his particular mix of integrity and gentleness that gets me. He's also an only child like me, though not an orphan. I see other only children of course but feel a kinship with Fraser regarding our sibling-less status that isn't roused in me by anyone else. He could go far in life, should he ever get the opportunity. His mother is determined he go to university, but Fraser anticipates an ever-attenuating future as her arthritis gets worse and the council's care package ever sketchier.

'Fraser, look at me. Whatever it is you have to say to me, it will not change how I feel about you. Do you hear me? Nothing you could say will do that.'

Fraser sits back in his chair and bites his lip hard. For a second, I think he's going to cry, but he doesn't.

'My girlfriend says I'm abusing her.'

There is a brief fluttering noise outside that tells me a pigeon has landed on the windowsill, as they sometimes do. Fraser, who has a view of the window behind me, hasn't noticed.

'Okay. Well done for saying that out loud, Fraser. Not an easy thing to do at all, but very good that you have. Now, can you say a bit more about why she thinks you are abusing her?'

Fraser looks utterly exposed, Bambi-like.

'We were…last night we were having sex, and I did it to her the other way…'

'I'm sorry Fraser, you're going to have to be a bit more specific. But please know I really have heard it all before in here, so you needn't be embarrassed.'

Fraser looking wretched, almost whispers, 'Anal.'

'Ah okay. So, you had anal sex with her.'

'Yes, but she screamed out… Said I'd hurt her. Like *really* hurt her.'

'Then what happened?'

'Then she jumped up and got dressed. I didn't understand why she was upset, didn't know how I could've hurt her, I thought… Anyway, she was crying and getting her stuff, then she went home. I've tried phoning and texting, but she just sent me a text saying that she felt like I've abused her, and she needs time to think.'

Behind me the pigeon taps its beak against the window. The same thing happened yesterday. Is this the same bird? It's interested in the glass bell jar I'm using as a small terrarium, or perhaps more what it contains. I'm growing two different tropical varieties from seed – *Psychotria viridis*, and *Psychotria emetica* – just to see if I can. Emeticas produce the most intensely blue berries, which is why I'm having a go. I tried it on the windowsill in my living room at home, but nothing happened, so I brought them here and *voilà* – saplings!

'Okay. What a tricky situation. Let's see if we can try

to make sense of it. Can you tell me, did the two of you talk about doing anal beforehand? Did you have lube? Try with a finger first?'

Bewildered, Fraser shakes his head and says, 'No, I just, uh, put it in… I didn't realise… Is that really bad?'

Tap tap tap.

Fraser's oblivious, but the noise of the pigeon's determined little beak against glass, irregular like water droplets on linoleum – my mother's silk blouses drip drying on the pulley – is very distracting.

You don't want what's in there, little birdy. Once grown, one variety would make you hallucinate and the other very sick indeed. Last week, after asking about the bell jars, Kass pointed out that I could get in trouble for having poisonous plants in a school, which, stupidly, I hadn't actually considered; but then again, they are just babies which I will take home as soon as they are established, and anyway *most* plants will make you ill if you eat them.

'I mean, it's not great, but you obviously thought that's what you were supposed to do. Fraser, other than what happened last night, do you and your girlfriend usually get on? Are you the type of couple who argue a lot?'

Fraser frowns. 'I don't think so. I mean she once got upset at me because of what I said when we were… well, when we were doing it. Apart from that, we get on great.'

'Can you maybe tell me what you said that time?'

The high colour returns to Fraser's face, and I feel

like I'm torturing him.

'I called her a wee slut…and some other stuff.'

'Why did you do that Fraser?'

'I just thought that's what you were supposed to do… That's why I tried to, you know, her bum…'

I say as gently as I can, 'So, let me get this right… You thought you were supposed to call her certain names like slut, and have anal sex with her. You thought that was a normal part of sex. Can you tell me *why* you thought you were supposed to?'

Fraser shakes his head, the shame of having to talk so candidly to a middle-aged woman just too much.

I wonder what he sees when he looks at me, and, not for the first time, what his mother looks like. My sense of my physical appearance hovers somewhere around my mid-thirties, but my reflection in the mirror tells a different story. I mean I'm not bad for my age, but neither am I used to it. By the time I've grown into my early forties I will be way beyond them.

'Can I take a wild guess and say you got this stuff from watching porn on the net?'

If facial expressions were audible Fraser's wince would crack the windowpanes. As will that pigeon if it doesn't quit.

'Yes. But not just that. Other boys at school all ask each other if they've done this or that or boast about having done stuff.'

Getting up to sort out the mad bird I say, 'Sorry Fraser, I just have to sort out this mad bird…'

I carefully pick up the bell jar and place it on the

floor. The pigeon swivel-eyes me and flies away.

I return to my seat.

'...But I'm guessing *they* – the boys at school, I mean – are also basing what they think you should do in bed, or wherever, on what they see in porn?'

'I suppose so, yeah.'

'I think I know what's going on here.'

Fraser looks up. Is that a flicker of hope I see shining through the shame?

'Porn is like a sex manual for your generation – it's where you get your ideas about what you are supposed to do in bed – but it's a crap one. I take it you see anal sex quite a lot on Pornhub, or whatever site you are on? I'm guessing you also hear men calling women "little sluts".'

Fraser nods. Eyes to the floor again. Counsellors' carpets must be among the most stared at in the world. Mine looks like it hasn't been hoovered in a month; clarty cleaners.

'Okay. If you can bear it, I'm going to have to give you a bit of sex education now. Can you bear it?'

An almost imperceptible nod of his shiny head. Two large tears like beads of weighted glass are swallowed by the carpet.

Oh Fraser, if only you'd just been flicking through *Big and Bouncy* like Adrian Mole – I doubt you'd be in this mess.

'So...sex in pornography generally bears no relation to sex in real life. It usually shows a woman having stuff done *to* her, rather than a couple doing stuff *together*.

It's often quite aggressive, or even violent, which is not what real sex is, or should be. Sex needs to be about respect and enjoyment for both people – it's supposed to be fun, pleasurable! – but in porn the men often don't give a crap about the women.'

Fraser's focus is all on me now, rapt. So, I take this as my cue to continue.

'Real sex is about two people who are really into each other. And, especially for teenagers just starting out, it should be about exploring what each other like, asking what feels good. And it can be a bit messy, a bit noisy, but it's exciting. And of course, both of you need to consent. You definitely should have asked if she wanted to try anal.'

'I didn't think I had to because they don't in the videos...'

'Have you not had Sex Ed in Social Education?'

Fraser, scratching at his wrist, says, 'I remember the teacher saying something about real sex not being like porn. Something about *The Fast and The Furious* not being like real driving...To be honest they have talked about it quite a lot in school, but I just sort of forgot...'

'The thing about anal sex is that you don't just have to get consent, you need to both be aware of what it involves. It can really hurt, and can actually be really damaging, if you don't do it really gently, especially at first, and if you don't use lots of lube.'

And don't do it until you're at least thirty-five and sensible.

'I didn't know any of that!' Fraser says, shaking tears

from his eyes. 'I don't even want to do it any more. I just did it because I thought it was what I was supposed to do.'

It's uncommon for a straight boy to talk about this stuff with me, though I had one skinny little thing whose girlfriend unexpectedly implored him to 'treat me like a whore', after the most preliminary of snogs, completely throwing him off his game.

'Oh Fraser, some people do enjoy that kind of sex, and that's up to them, but as I said, it's not something you'd just do spontaneously – you work up to it. But no wonder you thought it was normal.'

Looking sheepish, he says, 'The girls in the videos all seem to love it.'

Christ.

'I'm not sure they do, Fraser. Those girls are acting. They are *pretending* to love it. And sometimes they are pretending to love it because they are trafficked and to do otherwise would be extremely dangerous for them.'

'Oh!'

'Yup.'

Fraser stares at me, horror slowly pulling at his features as the reality of what I've just said sinks in.

'Really? I mean about the trafficking.'

'Yeah, really.'

'Fuck.'

'Indeed.'

Fraser, attempting to rake his hands through his hair, is thwarted by the wax. He resorts to leaning forward and steepling his fingers over his do, in an *oh fuck, what have I done?* kind of a gesture.

'Is she right then? I mean does what I did make me an abuser?'

'Listen, technically your behaviour in bed was abusive, yes, but not intentionally, and you aren't going to do these things again are you?'

'No!'

'Well then, you are just going to have to have an honest conversation with her about it all, however awkward and horrible it is for you, to make things right. Do you think you can do that?'

I'm confident he *can* do this, but 'feeling awkward' is the new enemy of intimacy. Being trapped in their houses through two lockdowns divested so many kids of their ability to talk to each other face to face about even the most mundane of subjects without excruciating awkwardness. I won't be surprised if he chickens out...

'I can try. I could send her a long message explaining...' he says, reaching into the top of his schoolbag for his phone.

'If I were you, I'd do it face to face. Less room for misinterpretation, don't you think?'

'I suppose so,' he agrees reluctantly. 'Jane, do you have any books I can borrow?'

'Books?'

'I mean about, you know, all this stuff...'

'Sure. I think that's a great idea.'

So far so good, but we have further to travel to reach the heart of the session. He's clawed his way through embarrassment and shame, learned necessary lessons, but we are not done yet.

He closes his eyes against tears that still come. For a kid who learned years ago the language of suppression and sublimation that teenage boys use to survive, the tears he's shed today speak of a pain which feels almost unendurable.

The heart of it, I see now, is fear. They've not been together long, and he's frightened he will lose her, *has* lost her. He cannot fathom why she noticed him in the first place, let alone what made her arrive in his DMs like some advanced humanoid alien erroneously landing on Earth. He's previously described how they will often stream past each other in the melee of the busy school corridor: she a bright polestar flanked by her glossy pack, the aloof and exalted 'Geminis', he with his ragtag ensemble of gamers, drama nerds and ballers. That slide of her eyes to meet his, heads thrown back over shoulders for the briefest of moments, slivers of smiles catching. Hooked, both. But maybe not any more.

I'm acting the good therapist, containing his anxiety. I sound reassuring and calm. But I'm not calm inside. I want to kill whoever's done this to Fraser, but it's not any one person. What kind of world have we made for these kids, that makes abusers out of sweethearts like Fraser?

After he leaves, I check my saplings, which appear to have survived, and return them to their place on the little window shelf which I'm extremely proud of having installed precisely for the purpose of nurturing baby plants. Being with my plants helps calm me down. I have larger shelves full of them at home, which I also erected myself – I even constructed a unit out of bamboo, from scratch, which sits neatly in front of the bay window, and on a good day basks in light and warmth. Who knew that a passion for botany would result in a proficiency in DIY? My parents, both useless in this department, would be very proud, I'm sure. What would they make of the conversation I just had? What must it be like to have a job that doesn't involve bearing witness to other people's sorrow?

Kass Session 3

I think I understand now. Why Kass laughed that brittle laugh last week when I said she always looks ready to run. Running wasn't an option.

I know she told me more than she intended to in our last session, and I wasn't sure she'd come back, yet here she is, bundled up in a green puffer coat, tight black jeans and boots with a small heel. I put the radiator on when I came in this morning, but something must be wrong with the boiler because we may as well be sitting in a refrigerator. Kass says it's the same in the room she works in, and we talk a bit about whether or not the Head may decide to close the school.

'Kass, these sessions are for you to use in any way you like, but I am wondering how you felt after telling me such difficult stuff last week, and if you might be okay to kind of pick up where we left off – or if you think that might be too much…?'

She sits contemplating the question, as comfortable in the silence as a person could be, considering the context. Just as it's tipping into uncomfortable for me, she says, 'I didn't feel as bad as I thought I would – at least it didn't make my anxiety worse. I went back to the office and didn't even notice the others… I didn't like how you pushed me to talk about things I didn't want to talk about, but I'm kind of glad you did, because… well, I suppose you were right about this being about more than just work.'

'I'm sorry you felt I pushed you…'

Stop being so defensive Jane – you took a risk, and it paid off. Drop it.

Kass inclines her head slightly, says, 'That's okay, I mean I'm kind of glad you did... And to answer your question, I think I would like to pick up where we left off...but I don't know where...'

She doesn't know how to start, so I say as gently as I possibly can, 'You managed to tell me about finding men to have sex with – violent sex. You said it felt like "coming home", and I took from that that you meant someone had hurt you in your past, when you were younger. Because we tend to seek out the things and situations which feel familiar to us, even if they harm us.'

I sit and watch her think. Why is she so good at silence?

Eventually she says, very quietly, 'I was so out of my body all the time – I was so numb. It made me feel real, even if it was really...really bad for me.'

Who was it? Her father? An uncle, sibling, cousin? A family friend? Surely not her mother...No, she wouldn't be looking for men if that were the case.

'Do you want to tell me who it was?'

A whisper. 'Not yet.'

'Okay. Thank you for trusting me with this. Telling me can't have been easy...'

Someone – or some people – hurt Kass, I'm guessing, when she was much younger than she is now. Lewis is six, so Kass must have been twenty-four or thereabouts when he was conceived. So, in her early twenties she was looking for the kind of familiar violent experience that would make her feel something.

Kass is deep in her thoughts and seems very far away. Is she hearing the rain battering the glass, the wind shaking the windowpanes? I hope it has stopped by home-time.

We sit.

And sit.

Then she says, 'So, yeah, it was one of them who got me pregnant.'

'Yes.'

'I don't know which one, and I don't want to know. Lewis doesn't need a dad, especially not someone like that.'

'No. How did you feel when you found out you were pregnant?'

'Surprised! I didn't think I could... I mean I'd never got pregnant before... I didn't think I could...'

'You hadn't used protection with these men that you met through Tinder?'

Again, the checking glance: will I shame her?

'No.'

She could have got any number of STDs. No sense of self-preservation or self-worth. When she said she 'wasn't doing well' in her early twenties, she really meant she was in self-destruct mode. Which often happens as a result of a history of trauma. And not only was getting pregnant with Lewis the first time she fell pregnant from a Tinder hook-up – she also never got pregnant during the original abuse either, whatever it was.

'So, you were surprised, and it sounds like that might have been in a good way…?' I say, hopefully.

'I mean I was a mess…' she counters, 'but yeah, strangely, when I saw those two lines on the test, confirming what I'd begun to suspect, I felt weirdly happy.'

'You already suspected…'

'Yeah. Like I said before, I wasn't usually in my body if you know what I mean. I mostly tried to ignore it, cover it up, pretend it wasn't there. I didn't track my periods like some women do. My periods had always been all over the place anyway. Sometimes I wouldn't bleed for months and months. I only started to suspect because the signs became impossible to ignore. My boobs – they've never been big, but they had got huge and sore. And I was so hungry all the time.'

Kass's description of early pregnancy could not be further from that of the smug newly up-the-duffs on American reality TV shows, yet still I suffer that familiar jolt of jealousy.

'So, you did a test.'

'I did so many! Do you know you can get a pack of five out the pound shop for a quid? They are cheap as chips – just wee skinny paper things – but they work. I used all five in the first pack, then went out and bought another two. The week before, I'd finally been given a council flat after years on the waiting list, and now I was sitting on the floor in my new bedroom looking at fifteen positive pregnancy tests. Couldn't believe it…'

'So, no more Tinder…'

Why am I making the presumption?

'No more Tinder, no more cutting – I don't think I told you about that, but I used to do it a lot, anyway… No more alcohol, no more fags. It just all sort of stopped, and something else kicked in. I knew I couldn't do any of that stuff without it affecting my baby, and I actually didn't want to. All I wanted to do was make sure my baby was okay. Better than okay…'

I got away with the presumption – the relief is balmy. Move on now.

'Were you working at the time?'

'No. I was on housing benefit and job seeker's allowance. I'd get sent for interviews and mess them up – I'd just freeze. After I did the test, I went to the doctor, who said she thought I was already further on than twelve weeks. She was really kind. I think she thought I should've known sooner but she guessed it wasn't because I'm stupid, it was because I was, well, you know…'

'Because you were traumatised.'

'Yes. She was the first person to tell me that. I used to go to her because I couldn't sleep, or when I did fall asleep, I'd wake up again a few hours later. I had flashbacks – I didn't tell her what they were of, just that I couldn't cope with them. She wanted to put me on the waiting list for counselling, but I just couldn't. At the dole office I think they all just thought I was mental, 'cause one week I'd burst into tears and then the next I'd be shouting at them for something they'd said that wasn't really that bad. Dunno why it was always the dole office where I lost it, but in those days – the days before Lewis – I either felt everything so strong I couldn't bear it, or I felt nothing at all – I'd be totally blank.

'My first scan showed I was sixteen weeks. I had to tell the dole. The guy said, so, a Saturday night up the town, was it? I think he thought he was being kind, saying an explanation out loud so I didn't have to, but it made me feel like shit. He couldn't conceive of me having got pregnant in a good relationship… But I suppose he was right in a way, only the reality was much worse than he could have imagined… Anyway, the pressure they'd been putting on me to find work kind of went away. They said I should still be looking, but no one hassled me any more, they were just ticking boxes after that.'

'Did you have any family around to help you?'

'No. I, uh, I'd pretty much cut off from them a few years before. I couldn't do it any more…pretend. As long as I was still seeing them, I'd still be hearing about him; there would still be the risk of seeing him…'

Him, she said him.

'You never told anyone in the family what happened?'

'No.'

'Can I ask why not?'

The limpid blue eyes, searching my face for some clue that I deserve her trust. Do I look trustworthy to Kass? Do I remind her of anyone? Where did she place me that first day we met, in those crucial milliseconds of snap-judgement making?

'They would never have believed me.'

'Why do you think that is?'

She is shifting in her seat, getting agitated – a creature suddenly caged.

'Jane, this is getting too much – I don't want to…I can't…'

I raise the flat of my hand to show her she needn't. My rings need a rub with silver polish, which I've run out of, which I'll forget until the next time it occurs to me, then forget again…

'…And you don't have to. That's fine, Kass. You are doing just brilliant. Shall we get back to you having had your scan?'

'Yes please…'

'Have a drink of water.'

She picks up her water bottle and takes a sip, puts it down again. More quickly than I'd anticipated she might be, she's back in a safer place – an open space with room for her mind to roam.

'I had a friend for a while who sort of knew. She knew I couldn't talk about it, and she was good, she didn't try to make me, she was just there for me when she could be. But she moved away.'

'Did she come to the scan?'

'No. I did that by myself. I do everything by myself.'

'What was it like?'

'It was in this nice new building. You know the clinic next to the swimming pool? Very clean and bright. I hated when the nurse put the gel on my belly. Didn't like how hard she pressed with the scanner thing, but they have to, I suppose, to try to get a good picture of the baby.'

'What was it like when you saw your baby on the screen for the first time?'

A smile broadens across Kass's face. 'It was...it was pretty amazing. I've got this thing about the sea. I like bioluminescent sea creatures. You know, the ones that light up in the dark? I don't mean the scary-looking ones with all the teeth in the Mariana Trench, although they are also very cool. I mean other ones, like jellyfish and squid. In the dark they are transparent, but parts of them glitter and glow. Do you know what I mean? Have you seen the jellyfish where the light ripples up through their tentacles?'

'Yes, I know exactly what you mean – they are extraordinary.'

She nods. 'Well, that was what the bones in his little spine looked like – almost glowing. And the curve of his skull, it shone, and it looked strong. His ribs were like stripes of neon paint done with a tiny-tipped brush. And his fingertips – he looked like he was waving at me.'

Spine, skull, ribs, fingertips. Her own bright fish in the dark depths of her womb. Right there, yet so far away. If I glowed in the dark, I would be the greenest of greens.

'...And his nose! A little upturned nub of a nose...'

She sits inside the memory. Smiling. Then all at once something shakes her out of it. She reaches for her bag on the floor down the side of the chair and rummages about inside it. She takes out a tatty-looking purse and from one of its compartments produces a scan photo, which she offers to me to take.

It looks like any other scan photo.

'Lovely,' I say.

'And this…' she says, taking the picture from me and replacing it with a normal photo, '…is Lewis now. Well, a couple of months ago.'

Lewis, wearing red wellies and a brown T-shirt over bony shoulders, is crouched next to a bucket; inside is what looks like a crab. He beams up at the camera with Kass's sky-blue eyes – a little paler perhaps. He has a very round head, like little boys at that age tend to, light brown, mouse-coloured hair like Kass, and a pointy snaggletooth to the left of his front teeth which reminds me of Hazel. His skin, despite a mucky smear on his chin, is creamy pale gold, the camera capturing the fair fuzz that begins just below his temples and runs down the side of each cheek, sunlit.

He is unspeakably beautiful and I'm glad when she puts the photo back in her purse.

'Isn't he cute?' says Kass.

'He's extremely cute… It can't have been easy…'

'What can't?'

'Being pregnant on your own. Then raising a child on benefits, without any emotional support or financial help from your family.'

'It was almost impossible, financially I mean. I couldn't afford to buy new. I got most of the baby stuff from charity shops and Gumtree, but it still added up. I got the cheapest reconditioned pram, and it was still a hundred quid. All his babygros and bedding were second-hand, apart from a couple of bits from Morrisons, and the bloody mattress. Did you know that it's not safe to have a second-hand cot mattress? If I bought new, like the baby bath, because I couldn't find what I needed second-hand, I had to buy the cheapest, and cheap things are flimsy – they break, so it costs you more in the end. Thinking about it, he hardly slept on that mattress because he was always in with me – still is. Naps, I suppose, but he always had them in his bouncer...'

I didn't know about the mattress. I do know that when a baby comes their mother is subsumed.

Kass continues, '...So much stuff you have to have for a baby. Someone told me you just need a drawer and a blanket for a bed, but it's not true, you need piles and piles of... And I was constantly washing – used so much detergent. He used to puke on me all the time... So much detergent and having to have the radiators on all the time to dry everything. And I was permanently knackered. He didn't sleep through for such a long time...'

'It all sounds extremely expensive and exhausting, and you did it on your own.'

Kass hesitates for a moment before saying, 'It was. But Jane, I was in love, and for the first time. First and only time. I don't know if you've ever been in love...?'

A searching question that wants an answer – deserves an answer. Is not getting an answer, because this is hard enough without me bringing in my stuff.

'I'd like to hear about your experience of love…'

She lets the deflection go, a small smile playing on her lips.

Outside, wind batters the building, rips through the horse chestnuts and howls along the open stone corridor to the PE department, but Kass is oblivious, swaddled in her son's first weeks.

'When you're in love, it doesn't matter how knackered you are. How many sleepless nights… I was worried about money; worried about everything being spotless and not too hot or too cold – I was worried about keeping him alive! When he'd finally fall asleep, which is what I'd so desperately want, I'd often be tempted to wake him up just to make sure he was okay. Always putting my finger under his nose to make sure he was still breathing…'

She puts two fingers under her nose, blissfully unaware she looks like she'd doing a Hitler impersonation. Am I a freak for seeing that? Would another, better therapist have?

Focus.

'…Anyway, apart from the sleeping, he was a really good baby – he hardly ever cried. And he fed well, after a bit of trouble at the start in the hospital when he would try to latch on but just kind of fall off again. The doctor didn't know why he was doing it – said he was fussing. But then one of the older mums on the ward, who already had two other kids, came over while I was trying to feed him and put her finger in his mouth while he was trying to suck. It was alarming, I didn't know what she was doing, and I didn't like it. It felt intrusive, and there I was with my boob out. But she felt about in his mouth and said she knew what the problem was. The silly wee thing was sticking his tongue to the roof of his mouth. She showed me how to pull his tongue down and then try again, and what do you know, he latched on and started sucking away like he was born to it, which I suppose he was.'

'And the love?'

'The love… Having a baby was like going from no job to being employed seven days a week, including the evenings and all night long. But I found I could do it because right from the start, when they put him in my arms, after the horrendous labour, which I'll tell you about another day, I was mad about him. With him I suddenly felt like I was right where I was meant to be, you know? I'd never felt like that before, when there's nowhere else you'd rather be, and no one else you'd rather be with… I wasn't lonely any more.'

I know that feeling, Kass. I know what it is to be mad about someone, though not a child – never a child.

Kass, now sitting straight-backed in her seat, legs folded at a balletic angle despite the bulk of the puffer, and gesticulating animatedly, is on a roll. '…He was born in January, and he brought the light in,' she says. 'That year there was the worst snow… I'd prepared for him coming, researching what I needed and trawling the charity shops during my pregnancy. Even if he'd come a month before my due date, I would've been all set up. The health visitor was amazing, she made sure I had enough food those first few weeks. So, we stayed in, all cosy, he slept loads, and when he was awake his eyes were huge, the colour of pebbles in a stream, greenish-black and shining. I'd cuddle him and we'd just stare into each other's eyes. After a few weeks, when he was awake more, and then when he found his smile, we'd spend most of the time just grinning at each other or making silly faces.'

'And that was all you wanted to do… The only place you wanted to be.'

Kass's usually guarded demeanour becomes even more expansive.

'…My love for him felt bigger than the world. It was bigger than my tiny flat, bigger than the block we lived in, I felt like it reached out across the globe, that I was part of the earth and suddenly I had a place in things. Having him rooted me, to all the good stuff I'd forgotten existed, had never really understood before – it was all in me now, and I was part of it. Probably sounds really daft to you…'

Not daft, no. Kass, you have no idea how I'm feeling right now, and that's the way it should stay.

Oxytocin is a star. Right from when Kass found out she was pregnant, raised levels of oxytocin got to work and began to trump the adrenaline and cortisol her body was so used to producing. It could have easily gone the other way. Pregnancy and birth can be extremely challenging for women who have a history of childhood sexual abuse. I don't know for sure, but I'm guessing when Kass said she wasn't doing too well, seeking men on Tinder to enact violent sex so that she could feel something other than numb, she was probably suffering from complex post-traumatic stress disorder which had been going on for years. The numbness will have been a defence against having to feel her emotions day in day out – she shut down, in order to cope, but shutting down brings its own problems. Poor Kass.

'It doesn't sound daft at all. It sounds amazing… One of the models of therapy I was trained in is called psychodynamic, and there is a guy called Donald Winnicott, whom I love – which isn't relevant, but anyway – Winnicott has a name for what you just described. He called it the primary maternal preoccupation. Which is where new mothers become completely attuned to the needs of their babies, who are utterly helpless and dependent on them. If mum is there, working out what each cry is trying to communicate – is she hungry? Does she need her nappy changed? Did she get a fright and needs a cuddle? – and attending to those needs, then the baby never experiences anxiety for very long.'

Kass mulls this over. Then asks, 'Why did you say she?'

'What?'

'You said she when you were talking about what babies need.'

Ah yes, I did, didn't I?

Because the baby who lives in my mind's eye, who plays in the place between consciousness and dreams is always a girl. But you don't need to know this.

'So I did! Probably because a couple of my friends

have little girls. Anyway, Winnicott called it the mother/baby dyad. I always imagine it as this protective bubble which surrounds mother and baby, not letting the world in. No past, no future – the focus is just on what they need right now.

He said this thing that always gives me shivers when I think of it – that there is no such thing as a baby, because he believed that at the beginning of a baby's life, the baby doesn't differentiate between herself and her mother, they are one and the same thing. See, look, I've got goosebumps…'

'I like that,' says Kass. 'And it does sound like how we were, but doesn't it put a pretty high expectation on mums to get everything right? That's bit much for first-time mums who have never done it before… I felt so out of my depth sometimes, didn't have a clue what I was doing half the time…'

She's come down from wherever she soared when she described her colossal, boundary-less, elemental love, and landed roughly on the wearisome and challenging terrain of being tasked with keeping a human alive on practically no sleep. Did I make her do that?

I nod. 'I agree totally. And how I've described the maternal preoccupation to you – pretty badly, probably – also assumes mums can somehow stop the world from getting in the bubble, when of course they can't. But Winnicott understood that there is never the perfect environment, so he talked about good-enough mothers, and by that he meant mums who, overall, manage to be there for their babies. Another name he had for it was the ordinary devoted mother.'

'Well, that sounds like me,' says Kass.

'I reckon you are more like the extraordinary devoted mother.'

Because what I'm not telling you Kass, is that Winnicott believed the care of the mother was just as important as the care of the baby. And you didn't have that care, and you managed anyway. Not just managed, you triumphed. Just look at that happy, healthy little boy with his bucket.

'Yeah right,' says Kass, but she says it kindly; she's pleased.

'And all this good-enough mothering you are doing, it means Lewis is growing up feeling secure and safe and loved. And getting all that stuff he needs to grow up happy and resilient.'

Kass nods, but she looks troubled, like something I've said has worried her.

'What's on your mind?'

'I just, I'm so glad I've given him a good start. I think my mother was probably a good enough mother too... but then all her hard work got ruined... I need to make sure Lewis stays safe, that no one ever hurts him.'

'Even if they did, like you said, you have given him such a good start that he'll be able to overcome hurtful stuff.'

A flash of anger and she snaps, 'I'm not talking about small hurts, Jane. I thought you understood...'

Idiot that I am.

'I do, I'm sorry – of course you meant that...'

She must have forgiven me because she interrupts me to ask, 'You know Donald Thingamajig…'

'Winnicott.'

'Yes, him. Did he say anything about how long the maternal preoccupation lasts?'

I reach back into my mind to my training.

'I think, if I remember rightly, he said it started in the last few weeks of pregnancy and went on for a couple more weeks after the birth. It must be an individual thing – I've known some women who felt it went on for much longer – but it's just a theory, a way of understanding a process… Why do you ask?'

'Because I think mine has lasted six years and now it's starting to wear off.'

'Okay, can you tell me a bit more about what you mean?'

'I just…it was like right from when I found out I was pregnant, it changed everything. I went from being completely alone, and just…just a mess, to having someone and being sort of stronger. Don't get me wrong, I had my moments, but I got out of them. When Lewis was three, I got the free nursery place and started working here part-time. I felt like Mama Tiger. We were a little family and for a while I was living a normal life, for the first time ever…

'But recently the bad stuff has been creeping back in…and I can feel it happening, like a darkness coming towards me, but I just don't know what to do about it… It's in my dreams again – the nightmares have come back.'

Supervision with Estelle
Session 74

During my training I drew the short straw when it came to supervisors. Other students on my course would rave about how wonderful their supervision had been, how eye-opening and epiphany-producing, and I would feel very jealous. I got a group supervisor whose psychoanalytic contributions were so wordy and jargon-filled that I would have to wait for other students' responses if I was to have any hope of working out what he was talking about. Another was, like Estelle, an individual supervisor. Unlike Estelle, she was so totally person-centred and non-directive in her approach that much of the time in our sessions I felt lost and unsupported. Estelle is very firmly rooted in her model of therapy, and hard to take at times, but I know she's good for me.

I'm sitting in the counselling agency wondering if it is a prerequisite that rooms used for supervision and therapy be dusty. It's not even actual dust – these rooms will no doubt get cleaned regularly. It's the illusion of dust that makes everything – the walls, the chairs, the carpet, the rangy *Tradescantia* with its gaudy purple leaves – just dull, dull, dull. Even Estelle. with her shiny, silvery white hair, in her bright scarf of blues and greens, looks dusty in here. And why always a bowl of pebbles on a mantelpiece or side-table? Has anyone in the history of therapy ever actually used them for grounding, or *overcoming intellectual defences*? I know the answer to this is yes, and often, but I feel closer to my father when I release my inner cynic.

And the windows are mucky! On the other side of the glass, fat snowflakes fall like feathers.

'So, you don't know who it was that abused Kass?' Estelle says, and then clears her throat.

'No, but when she talked about having cut off from her parents completely, she said that, as long as she was still seeing them, she'd still be hearing about *him*, still see *him* sometimes. Cutting off completely seems to have put a stop to any contact. So, I know he's a he, and I don't think it's her dad because she said her parents were good people.'

'I see. You seem overwrought today...'

'Do I? I suppose I'm worried.'

'What are you worried about?'

'About Kass.' Obviously.

Why does it sometimes feel like Estelle is trying to catch me out? I don't think she attempts to be non-judgemental, as I do with my clients, and I usually get the impression she is judging me big-time. If I said so, which I won't because she'd enjoy it too much, and because it would make me look paranoid, she'd say my suspicion about her judgement was 'interesting', and then defend herself against the accusation while pretending she was helping me explore my reasons for feeling that way.

Or maybe that's all a pile of negative rubbish and Estelle just wants to help.

Also, it's not like I have to be here – I pay *her*. That I

get supervision is a requirement of my profession, but I *could* go with someone else.

Or I could just admit that she's right – I am on edge today.

Estelle crosses her legs, drawing my eye to her fabulous knee-length black leather boots, which she's wearing with a long A-line skirt. She looks good.

She regards me steadily, a small smile parting her lips, waiting as long as it takes. For the first time I notice little lines around her mouth and wonder if she smokes. Estelle kicking back with a fag in her hand.

Eventually I say, 'She's got this child she adores, but she says she can feel herself losing her grip. Kass is prone to splitting: she talks in terms of good and bad. A thing is either good or bad, a person is either good or bad. It was dark in Kass's world and then Lewis brought light in, but now it's getting dark again – she said the dark stuff's coming back.'

'And you are worried about this happening?'

'Yes. She's got too much to lose. She's on her own – no support...'

'I thought you said she had a friend...' In an alternative universe, Estelle reaches for an ashtray, flicks her cigarette.

'She did say something about there being someone ages ago, but they moved away. I don't think the friendship was anything to write home about... I get the impression that Kass has been alone for a very long time.'

Estelle nods. 'She overcame the bad before, and she

was alone back then. Who's to say she can't do it again? And this time she has you, her counsellor – she didn't have that last time.'

'You really have a lot of faith in the power of therapy...'

Estelle smiles. 'I do. I've witnessed that power in action for over twenty-five years now. But I'm sensing you don't feel the same way.'

'I don't think I could do the job if I didn't believe it helped. But put a few sessions with me up against years of abuse... I just don't know. How will the good ever triumph? I know it's not that binary, but still...'

Estelle raises a salt-and-pepper eyebrow. 'You feel like she's at the mercy of past traumas. I've got an image in my mind of a huge army about to invade a little defenceless town...'

Estelle is all about *imagery*. Most sessions, she describes the images in her mind which my words seem to engender. This one works – it makes sense – but some of them are bizarre, and I'm left scratching about trying to find the connection between something I've just said and Estelle's internal picture palace.

I say, 'I *am* very worried that the dark is getting back in, and she is defenceless to deal with it. And you are wrong about her being alone the last time she overcame it – she was pregnant. What better motivation could there be to get better and stay better?'

'But she still has the child, it's not like he's gone anywhere...'

'Yes, but maybe all that initial maternal-preoccupation protective stuff kind of stuck around up till now. Up till real life finally ground her down again.'

'What are you worried is going to happen?'

'She talked about "not being in a good way" before Lewis. Back then she was looking for men to have violent sex with, with no care for her own safety, and she was cutting. God knows what else she was doing. Can you imagine the state of her mind...?'

'But she had good reason to, back then... She told you she was numb, she needed to feel, even if the only way she could feel was to recreate the trauma...'

'But that's so messed up – it's so the opposite of what she needs and what she deserves after what happened to her!'

'I agree.'

Then why do you look so calm? Why is what I've just told you not affecting you like it is me?

There is a tiny knowing smile on Estelle's lips.

'Do you think me cold, Jane? This is the job. We take others' pain for a little bit. We take it and we hold it, and sometimes we are able to hand it back in a better state than it was given to us, but mostly not. Kass brings her pain to you, you bring yours to me, and I take mine to my supervisor. We all have a job to do, and we all have somewhere to take the really difficult stuff. Remember when you had just started at the school? You would come here and offload all this pain. A fortnight's worth. You would cry every week – and then you got more used to it. You worked out what your boundaries were, you found your own ways of looking after yourself that meant you could be there for your young clients without it breaking you.'

She's right – every week in tears. That changed without me noticing it had.

'I think I'd forgotten. I mean, how it was at the start. I'd been counselling adults for years before that, but being alongside kids in *their* pain was a whole different ballgame.'

Estelle says, 'It was hard, really hard. But you got through it – you worked through it – and you got stronger. You became a competent practitioner. But we are never the finished article any more than we are the finished version of ourselves. We get affected by everyone we meet, and we hit walls…'

'You think I've hit a wall?'

'I didn't say that.'

'So what do you mean?'

'I mean that I know you pretty well by now. And I know you want to stop Kass from going back to old ways. But you can't stop her, you can't stop her doing what she's going to do, just like you can't fix the young people's problems. You can't make the world better for them, only that little bit of time you are with them, which is worth a great deal more than you seem to think right now. When you first came to supervision with me, you were full of belief in therapy, but I don't see that in you these last few months.'

'But she's got a kid, and if she goes down this path again, she'll lose him. She didn't have him to lose last time. I need to find a way to stop her from doing it…'

Estelle sighs, as well she might; I'm exasperating.

Now she'd be stubbing that fag out – stab stab stab.

'That's not your job,' she says. 'Your job is to listen to Kass, listen very carefully to what she is saying is wrong. And to what she's not saying.'

'I told you – she said she feels anxious, and she's worried the bad is creeping back in.'

'And what might she mean by this?'

Outside the snow has stopped falling and I feel the pang of loss which always comes when proper weather ends. Bright and sunny, dark and stormy, or freezing and snowy – inevitably give way to grey and uninspiring. But I keep this to myself because Estelle would have a field day.

'I think… I think she means that she is having complex trauma symptoms which she's not had since before her son's birth… For a while there, she had actually started to feel a bit safer in the world, felt part of it. She could sleep at night without nightmares, she wasn't hypervigilant – I mean she would sit and watch Lewis while he slept, but she wasn't always on high alert, thinking someone was going to come and hurt them. She was in charge – Mama Tiger. Things were good. But now… She didn't say much about what her symptoms are, but she got very distressed when I talked about family taking Lewis, and she's on edge – nervous.'

Like me.

'Okay. So, your job here is not, like you said, to find a way of stopping her from engaging in risky behaviour, because that feels to me like you removing her autonomy. Maybe you could try to think about what your job is?'

I sit with this one for a bit, turn it over in my mind, while Estelle eyes me over the top of her glasses.

'I don't know… To help her think about her symptoms and maybe try some of the stuff from my trauma training… I'm not even sure if she's ever tried anything like that.'

'Sounds like you have a plan. Talk to her about it. Tell her you heard what she said about the darkness returning, and how you want to work with her to find ways of reducing the trauma symptoms. But above all, just listen to her. As an abused child, she spent so long with no voice, but she has one now, and it is up to you to really hear it.'

I hold my face with my hands in the way I sometimes do to show myself what I'd look like with a face lift, though right now I'm just taking in what Estelle has said, containing her words inside my skull with the help of my fingers.

'I don't know if you realise it Jane, and I'm guessing it's probably because you see so many people, and the extent of that need must be so overwhelming for you – but, since you started seeing her, Kass is the only client you've brought to supervision more than once.'

She's right. Kass is different – she has Lewis, and he is part of her, which means he is my client too. Obviously not my responsibility, yet there is something in that idea… Something I can leave for another day to explore.

We sit in silence for a moment or two. It's not uncomfortable.

'I actually wanted to talk about Fraser...'

Estelle glazes slightly and I imagine her pulling open drawers in her mind, trying to find the one containing Fraser.

She smiles. She's got him. 'Ah yes, single mother with a health condition...'

I nod. 'Rheumatoid arthritis.'

'How's he getting on?'

'He's fine. But he's been using porn like a how-to guide and his girlfriend's accused him of being abusive.'

'Ah,' Estelle sighs. 'We've been here before, or hereabouts.'

'Yup. I'm *here* much more than I want to be. More and more I find myself lecturing kids, some of whom haven't even had their first kiss, about the intricacies of anal sex, the differences between porn sex and real sex, the misogyny, and all the other stuff porn throws up – it's a major part of the job now, and it's crap.'

'But you have to, because they bring it.'

'Yes. Usually it's girls who've started a relationship all starry-eyed, only to have Prince Charming unceremoniously shove their head onto his penis, like he's seen blokes do in porn, or tell them he'll go elsewhere if she doesn't want to go *all the way*. Sometimes he's emulating dangerous arsehole *du jour*, Andrew Tate... Though it's not just boys using porn as a template: yesterday I walked past a group of girls who couldn't have been more than fourteen, one of whom was trying to get the others moving by using the rallying cry, 'Come on spunk buckets!' So that was reassuring...

not.'

Estelle emits a little dismayed puff of air while shaking her head. 'Jesus…'

'If it were up to me, we'd all be talking about this stuff all the time, so that, like Fraser, kids would not just forget what they've learned in Sex Ed.'

'You're angry about this, aren't you?'

Yes, Estelle, I am fucking angry about this, and I spend way too much of my time with it sloshing around inside my head. I doubt any amount of supervision will be able to drain it away. I just get more and more full till it feels like I'm running over my own edges…

'…A few weeks ago, round at my friends Ross and Leila's house for tea – I've probably mentioned them before, old pals from school – Ross said that if he'd had internet porn when he was a teenager, he would never have left the house. We laughed about it, but then he said, "Seriously though, thank God all we had was nicked copies of *Razzle* and the bra section in the Kays catalogue."

He and Leila had both winced when I told them how frequently I get some kid in my room crying because their boyfriend has tried to choke them, pulled their hair, spat on them, or acted aggressively in some other way during sex. How they ask me if it's okay to smile during sex. If anal is supposed to hurt this much. About getting called vanilla if they resist this crap. And then there's all the kids being treated for anal fissures in the Sexual Health Centre… I can hear myself sounding like Mary Whitehouse, but I don't know how else to sound.

Things have changed so much in the last few decades...'

Estelle, with a slight purse of her lips, says, 'Can you say a bit more about what's changed? You're obviously comparing these experiences that your clients have to your own... Can you tell me a bit more about that?' She pushes up her glasses from where they've travelled down her nose.

Eros and Thanatos – the sex and death drives – are, if you subscribe to Estelle's favoured approach to therapy, at the heart of all human motivation. But I don't think I've ever spoken of my own sex life with Estelle. It's true that parts of our sessions may sound more like those of therapist/client than of supervisor/supervisee, but we rarely travel very far into the heart of me.

But she's asking, so...

'Internet pornography appeared on my radar in my early twenties. I used it infrequently as an aid to masturbation, but it never sparked true arousal for me.'

Estelle didn't expect that. She sits up slightly in her chair, sharpens her focus.

'Go on...' she says.

I take a deep breath, then go for it. 'I believe that for women, arousal can be a complicated thing, as much about the mind as of the body, relying less on the right-in-front-of-us visual than the patchwork fragments of our past sexual experiences and vivid fantasy of our imaginations. From puberty onwards, I was in the grip of roaring physical need. The kind of need that revealed itself in amorphous and brilliant wet dreams that weren't mentioned in any of the daft puberty books or awkward school talks of my teens. In the eighties and nineties, wet dreams, if mentioned at all, were purely phenomena that happened to boys – ha! For me, arousal and desire overlap but they are not the same beast. Desire has to have an object, a guy I'm attracted to, whereas arousal, though it may be a drive searching for an object on which to narrow its focus, exists primarily without one: arousal just *is*.'

Estelle nods. She likes it when I speak in psychodynamic language, and I'm not sure whether she's agreeing with me, or if she just wants me to continue, so I go with the latter.

'These days my body seems to beat when the sun starts warming up in spring, then curls in on itself in the winter, no matter whether there's a man about or not, or where I am in my cycle. I was well into my thirties before I noticed patterns – that the surge of oestrogen two weeks into my cycle when I'm ovulating fires me up like a rocket, as does whatever's going on with my hormones for those twenty-four hours just before I start bleeding, and then the utter drop in arousal halfway through my period.

'With desire, it's all about the mutuality in the conquest, imagining myself in the eyes of the other, wanting and being wanted, fiercely. Often now, in the times when neither arousal or desire are present, when there is just a…comfortable absence, I wonder if this is what it will feel like when the oestrogen runs out. And will I care? My own experience may just be mine and mine alone, but I see and hear matching accounts in other women's and girls' stories of their own sexuality. I also hear accounts which are nothing like mine.'

Do I sound like an idiot? I wonder what Estelle makes of what I've just said, her own oestrogen surely having run out long ago. Though it would surprise me not a jot if she were some kind of dominatrix on the side.

She just says, 'Go on, this is interesting. How does all this relate to young 'uns watching porn?'

I normally have no outlet for this stuff. All I see, all I read, all I hear, all burning below the surface – a woman without a platform from which to let rip. Why have I never brought it to supervision before? I mean, sure, we've touched on it… I glance at the clock. I've got fifteen minutes. Go Jane!

'Well… We know now that brains and therefore bodies can become desensitised to porn, needing more and more novel stimuli to reach the same levels of arousal. Young people, particularly boys, are most at risk of this desensitisation because their brains are still so plastic, still taking shape. Watching hardcore porn begets a need to watch ever more extreme content or to enact ever more extreme sexual practices in order to get the same feeling of excitement, the same dopamine hit. In my early thirties for a while I slept with a guy who, in order to come, needed his dick manually pumped by me so firmly and for so long, I'm sure I could have inflated your average bouncy castle with the effort I put in.'

I pause to see if I'm going too far, but Estelle lets out a throaty laugh, and says, 'And?'

'And I worried about doing him damage, but he insisted he was fine. He explained rather apologetically that it had been this way for years, as a consequence of his porn habit. In order to reach climax with a real live woman, intercourse was no longer enough. She, and therefore I, would have to replicate the almighty man-clench that he had grown to rely on to bring himself off while he watched ever more degenerate porn. The excessive grip was the physical manifestation of the need for visual excess. He was good in bed, attentive and unselfish, deriving huge pleasure from my pleasure, and it would have been rude not to reciprocate...'

'But...'

'Yes, but... *But* boredom and the first twinges of repetitive strain injury eventually put an end to our encounters. I can see now that this dysfunction was surely only the lighter end of the spectrum of harm that desensitisation to porn fosters. And yet it still ruined a good thing. This guy didn't come of age in the age of internet porn, yet it was still negatively affecting him. Anyway, I got older and smarter, and porn changed. I was never stupid. I had always known there was misogyny and exploitation in the industry, but now I saw brutality alongside the softer stuff, women were viewed as less than human, creatures to be overpowered through coercion and manipulation, to be used and defeated.'

Estelle nods, serious face back on.

'I see how it impacts the kids, and I feel hopeless – hopeless and powerless. Pornhub hosts thousands of videos depicting sexual violence, torture and gang rape, mostly directed by men against women and girls, which they defend by saying that sexual violence is in fact permitted if it is "role play". Sorry, what? How the hell do they know which videos are role play and which are not? The traffickers are not likely to announce themselves. And how many of these women are happily and consensually role-playing being kicked and punched, slapped and choked, pissed on and ejaculated on, sometimes by multiple men?'

I'm in full rant now and it feels fantastic.

'...How many of the kids sitting in the classrooms that I can see from my window have opened a porn site and clicked on one of these videos? How many watch them on a regular basis? What is this doing to their impressionable, susceptible, *malleable* minds? How many of them see people in porn as role models, like Fraser so obviously does? So many of the girls have social media feeds where they post sexualised semi-naked images of themselves, wet mouths pouting, open, because they have been sold the lie that to be a woman you first have to offer yourself as a visual possession to whoever may be looking. The same lie that tells them they must endure aggression and even violence in the bedroom. This is not progress; far from it. This is fucked.'

That's it, I'm spent. The snow's on again, I hope it lies.

'That's a lot to hold,' Estelle says, there being nothing else to say.

'It sure is.'

What I'm not telling you, Estelle, is that I like to imagine what I would say or do to the people who hurt my clients. These daydreams pass the time and give my anger somewhere to go. But how do I conjure up a revenge fantasy where the faceless paedophiles, people traffickers and porn companies who create this kind of evil get their just deserts? My psyche can't comprehend systems and networks so vast, so inhumane and merciless.

As if reading my mind, Estelle offers a lame alternative: 'I know of some people who have punching bags in their living rooms...'

Aye, very good Estelle, very good.

Beside the *Tradescantia* is a small glossy-leafed plant which reminds me of my *Psychotria* saplings on the window shelf in my therapy room at school; the saplings have come on so well that the leaf tips are pressing the sides of the bell jar. I must remember to bring them home.

Kass Session 4

It may have taken until the end of March but finally there is warmth and light in the world again. A forget-me-not blue sky reaches into my cupboard room and makes everything shine – from the stoor on the windowpanes (which must have been surreptitiously accumulating under my radar all winter long) to the bright typeface of the posters on the walls. My room is in the old part of the school that still has sash-and-case windows which, with a bit of fiddling, I should be able to open inwards in order to give them a good scrub. I must remember to bring in cleaning stuff. I took the *Psychotria* saplings home a fortnight ago, but the window shelf is now cluttered with on-their-way-out spring bulbs: rangy grape hyacinths clinging to their wilting bells, and papery narcissus, faded heads too heavy now to be supported by their own spindly stalks. The atmosphere when I arrived this morning was so temperate and heady with the over-sweet scent of flowers just starting to rot that I had to haul the window open before a headache set in. Now it's pretty much perfect.

Kass is thirty-eight minutes late for our session and hasn't emailed to tell me why. My mind is not at rest. There will be some innocuous reason for her absence, but if I let myself wonder what it might be, invariably my thoughts will slink into darker areas of possibility where, right now, basking in this glorious sunshine, I have no desire to go. And so, instead I'm writing a list for Arran.

In three days' time the second half of the spring term ends and the Easter holidays begin. Jessie has booked the pair of us, which includes the nearly cooked baby in her belly, plus her two kids (eight and thirteen) into a fancy-ass spa hotel on the Isle of Arran. We've not done anything like this since before lockdown and I can't wait. With Jessie being a high-flyer, the day-to-day childcare falls to Mike, a part-time tech support guy, who says he intends to spend the entire week playing video games in his pants, drinking beer and eating pizza; this holiday is for Jessie to spend quality time with her kids, which is apparently unthinkable without me present.

My list is fairly long because, for the spa I'll need much of the same stuff as I would for a holiday on the continent, as well as everything that a trip to the West Coast requires, such as a raincoat, wellies and jumpers. I'm wondering whether I should buy a new rucksack, when a figure darkens the door.

I call, 'Come on in, Kass,' and now she's entering my microclimate wearing a white blouse tucked into narrow high-waisted black trousers. The green puffer she's usually encased within is notably absent, and she drops a beige trenchcoat over the arm of her chair.

There's nothing of her: she could use a Mars bar or four.

Perennially I fantasise about looking chic and French in a beige trench, but on all three occasions when I've tried one on in the mirrored changing rooms of H&M or wherever, I just see Inspector Gadget staring back at me.

I remove my reading glasses and take a second or two to adjust focus; after years of twenty/twenty vision and then one day the back of a shampoo bottle withholding its ingredient list, followed by the packet of a cereal bar, and so on and so on, the glasses are a new addition.

'I'm so sorry!' Kass cries and dumps herself into the waiting armchair. I'm getting the impression of feast or famine with her: either she's slack and sagging against the upholstery, or perched lightly with neatly folded limbs like an origami paper lady.

Today, her hands clamping either end of the chair arms, she is more like an orangutan. She says, '...Wow, it smells like the hot house at the Botanic Gardens in here!'

'Still? I thought I fixed that when I opened the window. It smelled like a bin in a florist's shop an hour ago.'

'Oh don't worry, it's nice – like being on holiday. It's a good job you moved those psychedelic plants though, or we'd both start tripping!'

No we wouldn't; that's just nonsense. Besides, they were under glass.

She's very late – too late to have a session, really, and there's something up. Kass is usually too reserved, too wary, to feel relaxed enough to let her guard down and make that kind of crass joke.

I sit forward in my chair, gently ask, 'What's going on, Kass?' And, in a crap attempt at maintaining time boundaries, I add, 'We only have ten minutes, so we've not got long, but you look like you have something to say…'

The rushed, slightly manic demeanour falls away before my eyes, and I see now that it was concealing something awful behind it. Kass is frightened.

'I'm sorry I'm late,' she repeats, twisting the silver ring on her index finger. 'I almost didn't come, because I knew if I did then I would tell you what I'm about to tell you, and I wasn't sure if it's the right thing to do. I'm still not sure. But then I decided that I have to tell you, because I have to make sure he's safe whatever happens… Not that anything probably will happen, but I just can't stop thinking about it, and I know if I don't tell, then I won't be able to stop… Do you know what I mean?' The words spill out of her and lie in a discomforting mess around us like cornflakes from an upended box. I have no idea what she means but I can see how troubled she is.

Now she tugs the ring right off and holds it in her closed fist before returning it to its original place on her finger.

'Mm, sort of maybe? Make sure who is safe?'

'Lewis!' she blurts, as if this were obvious and I'm an idiot.

'Right, okay, of course. You need to make sure Lewis is safe.'

I know she's got a preoccupation with protecting Lewis, but this feels different.

'What is it that you need to protect him from, Kass?'

She suddenly sits so far forward on her chair that I worry she'll end up sprawled across the table.

'If I tell you, you must never bring it up again, unless I ask you to, okay?'

Her pleading pale blue eyes threaten tears, and I have to fight the urge to tell her I'll promise whatever she wants.

'Well...you remember the conditions of my confidentiality? Unless I believe you or someone else to be at risk of serious harm, then we shouldn't have a problem. Do you think we will have a problem, Kass?'

'I, I'm not sure... I mean I *am* worried about a "threat of serious harm", but it was made seventeen years ago, so it probably doesn't count.'

I adjust myself in my seat, 'Okay... Look, I can say that as long as whatever you tell me doesn't breach the conditions of my confidentiality, then I will endeavour to respect your wishes, which means that in future sessions I'll try to avoid bringing up whatever you tell me today.'

Kass nods, but I get the impression she's only half-listening to my assurances. Whatever's in there looks to be burning a hole in her mouth.

'I need to tell you who it was that abused me, because there is a big chance that if anything happened to me, Social Services would give Lewis to him.'

Here we go.

'Why? Is he Lewis's father?'

A vehement shake of her head, 'No – definitely not.'

'Then who is he?'

'He's Lewis's uncle – my big brother.'

Ah, of course. The sibling who is not a sibling. A

brother by blood, by genetics, but not in any other sense.

'Okay. How many years older than you?'

'Six.'

'And how old were you when he stopped hurting you. Physically, I mean.'

'Fourteen. He moved out of our parents' when he was seventeen, but whenever he came home, well, it would happen again. When he was twenty, he properly moved away. I never saw him after that – I avoided being at home most of the time, and if I knew he was going to be there I'd find ways of staying away for weeks at a time. I'd bombed school – my parents tore their hair out. They probably wrote me off as a black sheep in the end. I moved out as soon as I could, stayed in any shithole that would have me. It was probably a huge relief for them.'

I doubt very much if this is true, but it's a thread to pull another time.

She says all this while nervously chewing on the side of her thumb, something I've not seen with her before. She'll become aware of doing it if it starts bleeding down her hand.

So, it was her brother.

The bastard. No, that's not enough… The monster. The evil… None of these words are enough.

Focus, Jane, focus.

'And why, specifically now, are you concerned about something happening to you? I get the sense that this is more than just worrying about random accidents.'

Kass's whole body seems to vibrate and now she starts nibbling at the side of her pinkie. 'He knew by the time he left that he couldn't keep doing it. I wasn't quiet any more; I was wild, out of control, out drinking all the time – unpredictable. He told me that no one would believe me, and I was sure he was right – I'm still sure – but even so, he had no guarantee of my silence. Last time he saw me, he told me that, the next time, he would kill me.'

Her gaze, sparrow-like, flits around the room before resting on me. She needs encouragement to continue.

'Go on...'

She's working away at her knuckles now; I want to reach over and pull her hand from her mouth.

'I haven't seen him since. It's been seventeen years. He has a life and probably no interest in ever coming near me again, but ever since I started to feel low again, I've been obsessing over it. And, even if he doesn't ever hurt me again – what if I died some other way? My parents are getting on, whereas he's young and he's *somebody* – he'd be the obvious person for Lewis to go to.'

'Why does telling me now help this situation? I mean, don't doubt for a second that I'm glad you have, but what is it you'd have me do if anything *did* happen?'

She stops chewing at her skin and lets her hands fall to her lap.

All at once the storm is over. The thrum of anxiety beneath her skin ceases, and as still and serene as a bank of meadow foxtail after the wind has dropped, she replies, 'You could tell the police what he did to me.'

I slowly nod, drawing out the time I need to absorb her words. She tilts her head a little, eyes searching mine, wondering if I will agree.

Eventually I ask, 'Why can't we do that right now, together?'

She sighs, perhaps in frustration.

'Because I'd never be believed in a million years. He's a someone and I'm a no one.'

She shrugs and holds up her hands to illustrate the impossibility of my suggestion, like I'd proposed we join forces to stop the earth from turning. I see that I am supposed to accept her explanation without question.

'What sort of a someone?'

'What?'

'You said he's a *someone*…'

'Drop it, Jane,' she says quietly, pointedly. Disappointedly.

Fine.

'Okay, no more questions about who he is. Thank you for telling me about him – I know that must have been extremely hard. If one day something should happen to you, what is it exactly that you would like me to do?'

I've promised nothing but she looks to gather herself.

'Nothing more than what I said. I just want you to tell the police what you know. They'll have no problem finding him. Then he won't be able to hurt my boy. He'd deny everything, but surely with the suspicion hanging around him, Social Services would steer well clear.'

It sounds like a reasonable argument, but it doesn't

feel like one.

'He must have been only, what, twelve, when he started hurting you? Barely into puberty himself...'

She frowns, says, 'I suppose so. I don't remember him as young – he was so much older than me, but yes, he must have been about twelve when it started... I want to tell you Jane – I *need* to tell someone what happened to me, but' – she glances at the clock – 'time's up and I know how you feel about boundaries...'

I sense the sides of the therapeutic frame bending ever so slightly – what I'd thought was oak, is in truth something a little less robust: MDF or ply. That's okay; after all, I'm an experienced practitioner with thousands of hours of client work under my belt. I keep up with continuous professional development, I attend regular supervision sessions and, once a month, read *Therapy Today* magazine the same day it drops onto my doormat; a little bending is nothing to worry about. As long as the thing never actually snaps.

'Forget boundaries, Kass. We are here together right here right now, and no one is going to disturb us. But I totally get it if this doesn't feel like the right place to talk about this stuff, in the middle of your working day... Maybe you might prefer to work with a trauma therapist, or...'

But Kass, all the jitteriness from earlier forgotten, sits back in her chair and concentrates, centring herself and breathing into her silence. Regulating her emotions as best she can, in order to begin speaking the unspeakable.

1997

It's a bright summer's day and Jessie is behind me, pushing me toward an old grand-looking sandstone building with a big brass plaque next to the open front door. My back and shoulders are rigid and I'm trying to plant my feet firmly to the ground, but she has the advantage of being stronger than me. So, I pivot on one foot and veer off to the side, while she stumbles into air.

'Stop your nonsense and get your arse inside,' she snarls at me, defiant on the pavement. Sunlight flashes off the plaque and glints in her red curls.

'Your hair is blazing…'

'Get in.'

'It is though, You're really beautiful, Jess.'

'I know I am. But ever since you did the Pre-Raphaelites for your art exam you've been objectifying me.'

'What does that mean?'

'I'll tell you later. You're going to be late if you don't go now. *Come on,* Janey!'

'I can't,' I say, and I mean it.

Jess and the gorgeous morning helped get me out of the house, but now all I want to do is press my face against the sun-warmed pavement. People can just walk around me.

'Yes, you can.'

She has locked her arm in mine, and because I've used up all my energy fighting her off, I give in. She marches me up the steps, sails me through the front door and across an oval hall into a sunny and (thankfully) empty, high-ceilinged waiting-room alive with dust motes. It's now filled with the scent of Body Shop Dewberry perfume which every morning Jess sprays into the air above her head before pogoing into it like a nutter.

On the mantelpiece and surfaces are a collection of dying and dead houseplants, with soil so dry it looks like builders' rubble. Why doesn't someone water them?

'Lazy bastards,' Jessie says crumbling a lump of compost between her fingers.

Now she stands, hands on hips, in the middle of the room, thumbs hooking the belt loops of her moleskin trousers, surveying. 'It's not bad. Looks almost exactly like the waiting room at the Family Planning Clinic.'

Jessie knows what the inside of the Family Planning Clinic looks like because she's been on the pill for years.

'At least they've got water for the humans,' I mumble,

gesturing to the clear plastic jug and some assorted glass tumblers on a side table.

'See, that's better!' says Jess, pleased with my scintilla of positivity. 'But, no, you can't drink that.'

'Why not?'

'Germs, Janey; germs. That could've been sitting there for days. Pour it in the plants.'

I stare at the water in the jug and suddenly realise she's right. Jessie is the type to be nauseated watching someone drink milk straight from the carton, and she'd never eat a punnet of supermarket raspberries without first washing them. I'm used to it; I wipe the tops of Merrydown cider bottles before I pass them to her, let her go first on cigarettes. I know she doesn't mean that I can't drink the water because of what has happened to my parents – she means *no one should,* but it occurs to me now, watching dust dance and glint in the air like particles of gold, that I can't take risks any more. Clean; I need to keep clean. Inside and out.

A tall man with black hair and a black beard appears in the doorway. He wears brown corduroy trousers and a blue shirt with the sleeves rolled up. He reminds me of my art teacher, which bodes well.

'Jane...?' he says, looking hopefully at Jess.

Gingerly I raise my hand, 'I'm Jane.'

He tries and fails to hide his disappointment that it is me, plain old Jane, with whom he has an appointment, and not Lizzy Siddal over there.

'Hello Jane, if you'd like to come this way,' he says, smiling kindly as compensation.

I glance at Jessie, who raises her fist in a Black Power salute and grins at me. When I hesitate, she says, 'I'll be right here when you're done. Go!'

I follow the guy into the hall. There are stairs leading down to the basement and a spiral staircase of stone steps leading to the floors above. High above our heads is a round window which lets the light in through the spaces between the splatters of bird shit.

'We're just up here,' he says, and I trip-trap obediently after him.

My energy levels are permanently set to zero and I have no desire to be here, so this many stairs is hard and I'm panting slightly by the time we reach the third floor. He ushers me through an open door which he closes behind us. There is an old sash window that looks out onto the city, where the sunshine is burning through the last of the morning's haar. The wallpaper is embossed, cream and ancient-looking. There are two comfortable-looking armchairs and an ugly little table upon which sit a box of tissues and an alarm clock. In the corner is a massive hulking cheese plant trailing bare roots onto the rug below. The air smells slightly sweet – pot pourri or overripe fruit. It's very warm.

The man gestures to one of the armchairs, which I park myself in. The hems of his corduroy trousers ride up slightly as he sits down. Then, holding himself very upright, he opens a notebook. He looks like *The Joy of Sex* guy in that book my parents had, and also a bit like the illustration of Jesus in the leaflets the Jehovah's Witnesses sometimes put through the letterbox. He probably imagined having sex with Jess, because apparently men think about sex every seven seconds. Then, after, he might have fantasised about saving her soul.

The chairs are too close together. I can see his nasal hair from here, smell his coffee breath.

'Right, Jane, you're seventeen years old, good, good.'

Is it? How old are you, like?

'Have you had any kind of therapy before?'

'No.'

'Okay, well, no need to be nervous. Why don't you start by telling me a bit about why you think you're here?'

But I don't know you.

When I don't say anything, he gives a little expectant nod, to spur me on.

I ask, 'What's your name?'

'What?'

'I don't know your name…They just said I was coming for counselling.'

'Oh, yes. My name is Austyn. Now shall we get started…?' he says, and a muscle at the side of his jaw twitches. Should I not have asked?

'I don't really know what counselling is…'

'Don't worry about that, it'll work itself out as we go.'

What?

'So, why have you come for counselling today, Jane?'

'Because I was told to by the social worker.'

'Yes, but why did they think you should come?'

'I don't know.'

He contorts the beardy half of his face into a slightly hostile smile. He's gone from being disappointed to being exasperated, already. It usually takes people a little longer.

'Jane, I think an important part of the therapy is to speak it out loud.'

'Speak what out loud?'

'The thing that happened to you... An important part of the healing process is to voice your pain...'

'The healing process...'

'Yes... That's why you are here.'

'Right.'

'So...'

'So...?'

'Can you give words to what has happened to you?'

No.

Eventually I say, 'I'm sorry, I...'

I'm doing therapy wrong. Beardy guy sighs.

The jumper I'm wearing feels warm and scratchy where the wool touches my forearms and neck beyond the edges of the T-shirt beneath it. Apparently as a baby I was always hot as a boiled egg, my mother forever having to peel off layers of cardigan and babygro.

He looks down to his notebook then back to my face, but says nothing; just stares. I feel like something is squeezing my chest. I focus on the carpet, but when I look up again, he's still staring at me, and I don't know what to do.

He touches the hollow in the centre of his clavicle, strokes a finger backwards and forwards across the pale skin, the tuft of curling black hair sprouting from his open shirt collar.

'Jane, this is your time, and it's important that you can say whatever you want in here.'

There is nothing I want to say – nothing at all. Maybe he means to be kind, but all this staring is too much; it's like he's expecting something specific from me but won't tell me what it is.

I wish he'd stop rubbing himself.

I don't know what to say so I just repeat, 'My time…' and he nods, still rubbing the hollow – has he been bitten by an insect?

It's very warm in here – is there a radiator on? I look around but see none. I want to take my jumper off, but I can't remember which T-shirt I put on this morning. It could be the white one you can see my bra through, or the blue one that has a little constellation of hot-rock burns on the left side.

He's still staring at me, waiting. This is not okay – I don't want to be in here with him any more, not that I ever did in the first place.

He shifts in his seat, crosses his legs so that one of his feet in its shiny brown leather shoe dangles too close to my knee for comfort.

I can't bear the feel of the wool on my skin; why on earth did I wear a jumper on a day like today? I scan around the room, trying to find something to save me from his stare, but the room is nondescript. In spite of myself, my vision flits back to his face. He's still staring, but at least he's stopped the rubbing thing.

Still he says nothing.

Sweat prickles on the surface of my skin, against the wool that isn't even real wool from a sheep. *Some synthetic shite,* I hear my mother say.

I can bear it no longer; I pull the jumper off as he watches me.

My orange T-shirt, thankfully.

I shove the jumper down between my thigh and the side of the chair and wonder if I should have folded it or something.

He scribbles in his notebook. I feel like an animal being observed in an unnatural habitat.

He's back to staring. I'm glad of the orange T-shirt with neither see-through fabric nor evidence of my delinquency, but I still feel exposed. He just eyeballs me, but he knows what therapy is and I don't. He's the one holding the notebook with whatever important information it contains. He's in charge and I'm the one in a mess.

The silence is like being in a church tower where someone is ringing the bells with no intention of stopping.

Something; just say something – any old thing – to make this stop.

'I'm having trouble sleeping!' I blurt.

He nods, and says 'Good,' so I know that I've said the right thing.

'It would be helpful if you could tell me the content of your nightmares…' he says and clicks the top of his pen with his thumb, holds it poised over the open notebook.

'You know Freud called dreams the "royal road to the unconscious"...so...'

Did he, aye? I don't know who Freud is and I didn't say I was having nightmares.

The sweet scent seems to be getting stronger. I want him to open the window, but I don't feel like it would be okay to ask.

I don't want to think about my dreams, not in here with him. He's not getting anywhere near them. It is my waking hours, not my dreams that are the problem.

'Take your time,' he says with a tight, impatient smile.

I feel nausea rise as my heart hammers against my rib cage and my body is engulfed in more heat; my T-shirt and jeans sticking to wet skin feels truly unbearable.

He frowns and asks, 'Is there something wrong?' just at the moment that my stomach revolts and convulses, propelling me forward in my chair.

I vomit all over his shiny shoes, the patterned socks he wears pulled up high like stockings, the bottoms of his brown cords.

He actually screams.

Now he's up on his feet and out the room where I hear him yelling over the balcony banister, 'Miss, miss! Girl with the red hair, please can you come up here, NOW!'

By the time Jessie appears by my side the retching has subsided, but I'm still bent double, and I can't stop shaking. All over the floor is the stinking pink remains of the blackcurrant yoghurt and Coco Pops she made me eat this morning.

Jess grabs handfuls of tissue from the box on the table and gives them to me to wipe my face. She produces a hairband from somewhere and gently ties my hair back.

Crouching down next to me she says, 'You're okay, doll. Just sit for a minute, get your breath back, and then I'll get you out of here.'

Through my tears I can see Beardy over by the window, which he has finally opened, huffing and puffing, vigorously wiping at his own shoes with wads of tissue. I start to apologise but Jess cuts me off.

'Shoosh now, Janey.'

Turning her attention to him, she asks, 'What did you do to her?'

'What?' he says, forgetting his shoes and standing up to his full height, hot rage disfiguring his features.

Jessie stands her ground.

'She was fine when she came up here, nervous, yes, but fine. What did you say to her to get her in this state?'

'I didn't say anything. I just asked her about her nightmares, and she threw up all over me! Look at the state of me, my shoes are ruined. I hardly think I'm the one to blame here. It's obvious what kind of girl she is.'

'Excuse me?' Janey says, rising to her feet, matching his stance. 'What the fuck is that supposed to mean?'

'Well...' he stutters. 'She removed her sweater provocatively and she was kind of panting...'

Jessie gasps, 'Are you actually kidding me? She's ill! Not trying to seduce you! She's seventeen years old and came here for help. You were meant to make her feel safe. And I hardly think puking on you supports your theory that she was trying to be provocative, does it, genius?'

Beardy, spitting mad, clearly unused to anyone standing up to him, let alone a teenage girl, says, 'It also doesn't take a genius to see she's pregnant – why else would she have thrown up suddenly like that?'

What?

I get up out the chair, pull on Jessie's arm, 'C'mon Jess, let's go,' but she ignores me and takes a step toward him.

'You complete piece of shit. If a *man* puked on your shoes, would you assume he was pregnant? You're meant to be a therapist; how can you not know a panic attack when one is happening right in front of you? You stupid, useless, sexist dickhead.'

'Enough,' I manage.

I pull her out the door and we bolt down the three flights of stairs, across the vestibule and out into the street where we fill our burning lungs with fresh air.

'I can't believe I just vommed on the counsellor…' I say, feeling a million times better now we're outside.

Jessie snorts and says, 'I can't believe he thought it was a come-on!'

'I know… I just…the whole thing, it was bad. I'm not doing that again.'

'Agreed. What did he say to you?'

'Nothing really. I mean nothing that upset me. I just didn't know what to say, and it was so hot… But I did ruin his shoes. Maybe I should offer to pay for them?'

'Fuck his shoes,' says Jess. 'You're not giving that

tube a penny. And you're not to waste a minute more thinking about him... Right let's make a move. We need juice and Marlboro Lights pronto.'

I'm reminded of the water in the waiting room, of what Jess said and where it made my mind go.

I need to look after myself better.

'I'm desperate for a drink, but I don't know about the tabs...'

Even the breeze is warm, and the city will bask happily in the heat as long as it doesn't last too long – we aren't built for hot weather in Scotland. We walk to the park via the shops. The playground, hazy at the far end, with its recently installed pirate ship and climbing frame, moves with little bodies like an anthill in one of the nature documentaries I watch. Their bored mothers would get a fright if a giant anteater appeared like Godzilla and started scooping kids up by the dozen with its long tongue.

Boys older than us – probably students – are playing basketball on the court. Some with bare torsos have tucked their T-shirts into the back of their shorts, which looks casual but is as deliberate as low-slung jeans with boxers showing, or trainers with the shoelaces left undone. The air is filled with their grunts and shouts, rubber soles scuffing against the old tarmac, the basketball drumming the ground.

They check us out and we pretend not to notice as we walk by, feeling like we're in the movie *Do the Right Thing*.

'Alright, Red!' one of the bare-chested ones yells at Jessie.

No one ever calls Jess ginger. Dropping the pretence, she turns and locks eyes with the boy, which surprises him – he looks less certain of himself. He's tall and slender with a nice face, tanned skin, and short dark hair. Jess's face is unreadable but something about the neutral expression commands he hold her stare, which he does, but the bravado of moments ago is deserting him. Either he will break and mutter something about her being a slag to his mates – the classic boy defence for being bettered by a girl – or he'll hold his own.

He holds fast. The basketball lies still in the arms of his teammate as we all watch to see what will happen next. A breeze rustles through the line of rowan trees on the other side of the court and the sun beats down on our heads. There should really be tumbleweed bowling across the space between these two in their stand-off. Then Jess opens her mouth, throws her head back and laughs, and the boy's eyes widen at the sight. He presses his lips together and nods, pleased – he likes this bold girl.

The moment is over, his friends start the jostle and dodge of the game, their feet kicking up dust, but I know he's still got his eyes on Jess as we walk away and up onto the hill.

We choose a spot to sit among the daisies, looking out across the whole park, the basketballers, the kids and the pond.

'I bet he comes over.'

'I don't really care.'

'Yeah right – he's nice. Not all boys would react that well to having their power stripped away from them like that.'

Jess squints into the sun, 'You what?'

She pretends to be dumb though she's anything but.

'You're the one that did it!' I say. 'It was amazing. Don't deny it.'

Jessie plucks a daisy and uses her thumbnail to slice a hole near the bottom of its stem.

'I suppose I did stop him being so full of himself. It's just weird hearing something I did described like that – I thought I was just winding him up.'

She plucks another flower and threads it through the hole in the first until it's caught by the throat.

'How are you feeling now?' she asks, slicing a hole in the second daisy and plucking a third.

I take a long drink of juice before answering.

'Okay. Better. But I'm clearly fucked in the head.'

Jess frowning says, 'Don't be so hard on yourself. It's totally understandable.'

'Maybe…but I don't think there's a hope in hell I've passed my Highers. I'll have to stay another year and do them all again, and then what if I fuck those ones up too?'

Jessie turns onto her side, props herself up on her elbow.

'Look, you wouldn't have had a panic attack if that phantom had been better at his job…and maybe opened a window – I mean why was it so hot in there? You could have got someone decent… It was just bad luck.'

The way she bites her lip tells me she regrets having said that last bit – I mean how could my luck really get any worse?

'Story of my life…'

'Well, if that's true then your luck must be due to change pretty soon, eh? You'll pass these exams no bother. Why do you think Leila devised that punishing study schedule?'

I laugh at the memory of the study schedule which Leila had drawn up and photocopied, one for each of us – she even laminated them. No digression allowed; no excuses accepted. All of us – me, Jess, Leila, Ross, Neil and Angie – had to be in the school library, or in the designated house at the stated time, for serious study sessions round kitchen tables or on bedroom floors. I'd thought, yeah right, we would never be disciplined enough to actually sit and revise together, without someone proposing we ditch it to go do something more interesting, but weirdly the others had all got their heads down, so I had no choice but to follow suit. I hadn't questioned the study schedule, as Leila's always been bossy, but maybe Jess is right – they did it for me, to make sure I revised.

For a moment we are plunged into shade as a stray, lonely cloud slips across the sun, and then everything is bright again.

Jessie, watching the basketball court and threading her daisy chain, says, 'You're going to pass your exams, and then you're going to the art school to do the foundation year, just like you always planned. And if you *have* fucked up your exams, which I don't believe for a minute you will, then you get to spend another whole year with me. It's a win-win.'

Art school, then art college for a Fine Art degree in fashion and textiles, or painting and printmaking. This is the plan – this has *always* been the plan, but then that was before.

Everything was possible in the before. The scaffolding of my future all in place and secure, my family and friends around me like netting in case I should fall.

The basketball game has drawn to a close and another group is waiting to take their place. The boys are drinking from cans and chatting to each other, glistening sweat on their skin visible even from where we are up on the hill.

Jess's boy, T-shirt having travelled from the waistband of his shorts to over one of his shoulders, and a fully clothed friend, break away from the group and start making their way up the hill, exchanging amused but nervous glances which betray their swaggers. Silhouetted by the sun dipping at their backs, they match each other in height and physique. Slim, long-limbed, hard-shouldered, and slightly gangly, there is something about these boys that says they have grown up beside each other. Maybe not brothers – too dissimilar in colouring, but close, close friends. They seem just fully grown, like juvenile cheetahs. Male cheetah siblings remain together for the rest of their lives, forming a group called a coalition, which increases their hunting success and improves their chances against other predators. The duo approaching us could not be more of a coalition.

Up closer I can see there is something other than Caucasian in Jess's boy's gene-pool, and he is so gorgeous that she is studiously trying to look like she hasn't noticed. The other boy is pale with dark brown hair that falls to just above his shoulders; not as striking as his friend but still good-looking.

'Hi,' says bare torso. 'Would you mind if we joined you?'

'If you must,' Jessie says haughtily, but then her face softens into a genuine smile.

The hill makes it awkward for the boys to sit in front of us in a square, as they might have on flat ground. Jess's boy shrugs and drops down beside her, where they immediately start talking, which leaves his pal standing blushing above me.

'You may as well sit down then,' I say, feeling vaguely like I have the advantage since I was here first.

He mumbles something that might be gratitude and sits next to me.

'I'm Cam,' he says, and I catch a light lemony scent, with something else at the edge of it – cinnamon? No, nutmeg.

My dad used to give me hot milk with a grating of nutmeg on top when I couldn't sleep.

'Cam, short for Cameron?'

'No, not short for anything – just Cam.'

He studies my face, nostrils flaring slightly.

'Your parents just called you Cam – isn't that a bit weird?' I say, feeling emboldened, though I'm not sure why.

He frowns.

'No, I don't think so – most people just run with it... And, you know, some folk might call what you just said a bit rude...'

I didn't mean to be rude and now I'm embarrassed.

'Oh, don't mind me,' I say. 'I'm broken. I've already thrown up on a therapist's shoes today because I got so anxious, and now I've slagged off your name 'cause of nerves. Who knows what I'll do this evening...'

His lips curl in amusement.

'Right... Well, I look forward to finding out.'

'But you won't know...'

'Why not?'

'Because we won't be together this evening.'

'Not necessarily,' he says, still smiling. 'We might be best pals by then...'

I don't know what to say so I don't say anything.

'Would it be okay to ask *your* name?' he asks. Slight raise of an eyebrow.

I attempt to straighten the smile that's forming on my own lips. 'Go on then.'

'What is your name please?'

Again, nutmeg, warm and a little sweet; I want to lean in to get more of it.

'It's Jane, but my friends call me Janey.'

'Pleased to meet you, Janey,' he says, and laughs when I narrow my eyes at the presumption.

He holds out his hand, and though it feels like caving in, I take it.

The laughter is gone and something else is happening. His handshake is firm, but he looks startled and I'm sure I do too. We're holding on for too long. I have an overwhelming sense of recognition and relief. The feel of his skin on mine, our eyes locked, is like getting home after being caught in freezing rain. Like walking into a room full of strangers and seeing a face you know. It's like being in my father's arms, curling into his chest after warm milk laced with nutmeg. And it's more than that. It's too much.

I drop his hand. We look away from each other, pretending nothing happened. Did he feel it too? He looked like he did.

'So, may I also ask why you are broken?' he says, the jokey smile and breezy air reinstated, no acknowledgement of what just occurred – maybe it *was* just me. Although how do you put something like that into words?

I'm annoyed at myself for having said I was broken – hoped he would have forgotten. I've presented myself as some sort of intriguing mystery girl, which couldn't be further from the truth. I just meant that I'm a mess. As a warning, not a come-on.

This is all too much.

'No, you may not. In fact, I think I have to go…' I say, making moves to get up. The smile disappears from his face, and he looks alarmed.

'No stay! I won't ask again, promise. Sorry. Just stay

for a bit… It's really nice here.'

I hear my mother's voice telling me there is no excuse for anyone using the word nice in a sentence – not when the dictionary is full of alternatives – and then, as always, my father's with the counterpoint, in this case that sometimes it is more important to be kind than to be right. My mother is a total hypocrite – I mean how many times has she said, *oh my Janey-Jane, you are quite the nicest thing in the whole world.*

I look at Cam. I mean, really look at him, without whatever that was before getting in the way. He has an open, clear face with a wide forehead, long straight nose and hazel eyes. There is no air of mystery about him – he's just a person eager for life to happen. And he's right, *it is* really nice here on this hill in the sunshine, among the daisies, a circlet of which Jess, jumping up, now places on my head before returning to her boy.

I settle back down onto the grass.

'That's Sid,' says Cam, nodding towards his friend. 'Sid short for Sidney, but he hates it. He's my best friend. We went to primary and high school together.'

'Are you at uni together now?'

A slight shake of the head, 'No, that would have been pretty strange if we'd gone and done the same course together wouldn't it?'

I shrug, unsure of what is or isn't strange these days.

'No, he's a total nerd and a mummy's boy. He stayed here to do an engineering apprenticeship. I've just finished my first year of photojournalism in Brighton.'

Cam, who likes cameras. Whatever I say, he'll have

135

heard it before and I've already slagged off his name. Maybe later.

I think Brighton is in England and very possibly has a beach, but I couldn't tell you how I know this. What I do feel certain of, however, is that it is about a million miles from here.

I look at Sid, the open confident body language as he explains something to Jess, his hands forming shapes in the air, and can't imagine he'd love his friend's description of him.

'Do you like it?'

'Yeah, it's alright. Brighton's cool, it's got a great music scene. Are you at uni?'

'No – I've just finished fifth year.' Will you still want to talk to me now you know I'm only seventeen? 'And hopefully not going back. I want to do sixth year at art school.'

Cam, undeterred, beams – 'No way, I did that!' – and proceeds to tell me all about his time at art school, then ask me question after question about artists and designers I admire, places I'd like to work. He hopes to be a war photographer one day, but also thinks it might be quite fun to work on a fashion magazine. I can't tell whether it's the sun or his enthusiasm which deepens the green in his eyes.

He reminds me of me in the before, and I like listening to his plans, even though part of me resents the fact that his scaffolding is holding so strong. He is sure of his future because nothing that has happened in his life so far has so much as suggested that everything might not fall into place for him exactly as he wishes it to. I hope it stays that way.

'...Me and Sid are off to Indonesia next week – where Sid's grandparents live. We're going travelling for a month. I've never been, but Sid has, you should hear him describe it – it'll make you want to go immediately. My sisters are all raging.'

I suddenly feel stupidly upset that this boy I didn't even want to talk to twenty minutes ago is leaving for the whole summer, and then back to Brighton after that.

'How many sisters have you got?'

'Three, all older than me.'

'Do you get on with them?'

He tucks a lock of hair behind his ear. 'I mean, yeah, most of the time. I'm the baby of the family, which has its advantages, but I'm also the only boy, so sometimes when I was growing up, I felt like I was the odd one out...in a house that has a portrait of Emmeline Pankhurst above the fireplace.'

'Who is Emmeline Pankhurst?'

'Your mum's not a feminist then?' Cam asks, and immediately I feel a need to defend my mother, who may never in actuality have described herself as a feminist, yet the way we lived, the way my parents brought me up, was only ever in the spirit of equality, of humanity – and to have as much fun as possible. I've never really thought about whether she's a feminist, whether I'm a feminist.

'She's, I don't know...is a *humanist* a thing?'

I feel dumb, unworldly.

'Dunno,' says Cam. 'She's the founder of the suffragettes. Emmeline Pankhurst, I mean.'

Now I'm seeing *Mary Poppins* on the TV screen in our living room, my mum in blue jeans, marching in circles and singing along to 'Well Done Sister Suffragette!', hauling me, protesting, off the sofa to join in. Evidence of feminism surely.

'My mum's a feminist – both my parents are. We just don't have the founding, er, mother, above our fireplace; that's all – I don't think we *have* a fireplace, to be fair. Are you complaining about growing up with people who believe in rights for women?'

Cam grimaces. 'What? No, not at all… I'm just saying it wasn't always easy being the only boy. Just that sometimes I'd feel like I was the unwilling representative for nasty menfolk when I'd never asked to be, and I didn't like it; that's all – who would? Especially because I mostly agreed with what they said – I'm a feminist through and through. It's just not always that great listening to how terrible your kind are, and I knew if I ever slipped up – said or did something that could be considered remotely sexist – I'd get it in the neck.'

'Poor wee feminist you,' I say, and smile.

'Yes, thank you – some sympathy for my terrible plight is much appreciated and long overdue,' he says ,and makes a face, which makes me laugh.

'I bet you'd like my sisters. They're good value. You could join them in tormenting me.'

I like *you*, I say in my head. And I like how you are imagining me meeting your family.

In this moment, on this hill, I feel something different to how I've felt in great heavy slabs of bitter time. Something that isn't loss and isn't pain. Something that glows like the beginnings of a promise, that speaks of a possible future that isn't just grim. I don't recognise this feeling and I don't trust it.

I want to run somewhere quiet where I can sit by myself and think about Cam. Every little thing he said, and how he looked when he said it. But at the same time, I don't want to go anywhere. I want to stretch this afternoon out into the longest of days, like in the Arctic Circle in summer where it never really gets dark. I want to stay right here with the boy with the stupid name.

He reaches into his pocket, takes out a packet of Old Holborn rolling tobacco and skins, starts making a cigarette. The tobacco smells sweet in a wonderful way – the exact opposite of the therapist's room earlier today. Fuck, I haven't brushed my teeth since puking. Am I sitting here reeking of vomit?

'Want one?' He offers me the packet. His forearm is pale and the hair there is golden.

I reach out to take the tobacco from him, but now Sid is rising to his feet, saying, 'Come on Cam, time to split.'

What, why?

Cam looks equally disconcerted. 'Surely a bit longer?'

'Nah man, we need to get the car back to my dad and then get stuff sorted for tonight,' Sid says, looking pointedly at Cam. He wants Cam to go with him, but he doesn't want to say why, and something in his tone gives Cam no option but to comply.

Cam looks at me and all that ease of a minute ago is gone. Neither of us wanting him to leave but both too awkward to prevent it from happening.

He says, 'It was very nice to meet you,' offers his hand again and we shake for too long, our hands communicating what our mouths can't. If only you could pass phone numbers this way. I know I will regret neither of us being brave enough.

They walk off into the afternoon. He turns once, raises his hand in a final goodbye, but at no point does he come rushing back.

'Right. I'm hungry,' says Jess.

'What?'

'I'm hungry – let's get some grub.'

'Jess, why did Sid leave? Did you say something to him?'

Jessie twirls a ringlet round a finger. 'No, we just didn't click. Why, did you like his pal?'

'No… Yes… Yes, I really did. *We* clicked – I'm sure we did.'

'Oh what! Well, why don't you go after him, get his number?'

'I can't do that – it'd look desperate. He didn't ask for mine.'

'Don't be daft, Janey, he was probably just shy. Want me to go?' she says, getting up.

'No!' I hiss, and grab at the arm of the sweater tied around her hips before she has a chance to stand up. 'It'd be too embarrassing.'

'Okay then, whatever you say, doll. But you might be

missing a chance…'

I know she's right. I know I should go after him, but I just can't. If he'd liked me enough, he would have come back.

I'm trying to ignore how stupidly, ridiculously upset I feel, so I ask, 'What was wrong with Sid? I thought you'd like him.'

Jess takes a swig from the juice bottle before answering. 'There was nothing wrong with him… Just, you know when someone's *too* pretty…?'

'Hah, yeah, I've hung about with you long enough to know exactly how that feels.'

Jessie just shines brighter than anyone else. By rights I should be jealous. But how can I be, when most of the time her light is directed solely at me?

She twists the top back on the bottle.

'Oh, shut up, Jane. What a load of crap you talk. He was nice enough – there just wasn't any spark, you know? I was relieved when he got up to go.'

'Well, that's great for you, but I *liked* Cam,' I say, flopping backwards onto the grass.

She sighs, cocks her head to the side and pulls her face into an expression of sympathy which fails to mask the more pressing matter of getting her belly filled. 'I know, I can see that, and I'm sorry. But I'm sure you'll see him again one day.'

'Ha! Are you now? Well I'm pretty sure I won't – he's off travelling next week, then going to study in Brighton. I'll never see him again. One day I'll see his photos in the newspaper when he's a famous war photographer and then I'll try and find out everything I can about him and discover he's married to, like, Christy Turlington or something...'

'Good to have a positive outlook,' Jess says, and laughs.

Logan (S1)

Age 12
Referral from Head of Transitions
Presenting issue: low self-esteem
Falling asleep in class
Gets in trouble for walking out of lessons
Lost mum to breast cancer sixteen months ago
Often stays with maternal or paternal grandparents
Loves animals, wants to have a job like David
Attenborough's
'Sometimes Dad can't look after me'
Does dad have drink problem?
Child and Adolescent Mental Health Services
involvement
WHO IS NAMED PERSON FOR LOGAN?

Logan Session 4

'It's good to see you again Logan.'

'It's good to see you too,' Logan replies politely, warily.

Is he really twelve? He looks much younger. Little fine-boned person. He has the kind of crimson flush to his cheeks which waxes and wanes dependent on the strength of the emotion he is feeling. Adults will find this charming but other kids will tease him for it.

'So, last week you told me about the problem with that other boy...'

Stifling a yawn, Logan nods, then apologises for yawning.

'Don't worry, you can yawn all you want in here.'

'Is what happened still on your mind?'

'Sort of. Not really…'

He's yawning again. 'Logan, did you have a bad sleep again last night?'

More nodding. 'Like every night.'

'Because you couldn't get to sleep? Or you woke up after you did?'

'Both. It just takes *so long* to fall asleep, and when I do, I wake up again only a couple of hours later.'

'I'm sorry, Logan, I know we've had this same conversation quite a few times now, and I keep asking you the same questions. You've been trying all the sleep hygiene stuff Mr Benitez suggested?'

'Yes, I do it all. I'm not on screens or anything, and I don't eat before bed. I try to read the book he gave me but…'

'But…'

'But I can't concentrate…'

'You can't focus on the words? Are other thoughts coming in?'

'No, not really. I get… It's hard to explain… I don't like bedtime.'

In previous sessions Logan has managed to tell me that he can't sleep, but when it comes to the *why,* he has a habit of shutting the subject down by changing it to another topic – a tactic I should probably call out, were it not one which I frequently utilise myself in supervision, and therefore can't help respecting.

'Okay… Are you able to say a bit about why that is?'

'I don't really know… When it's lights-out time, I just start freaking out…' Across his cheeks the flush intensifies, like an internal dimmer switch turned up to full.

'Is it the dark? Loads of people are a bit scared of the dark. I'm not a huge fan myself…'

'No. I don't think so.'

'When you say you start freaking out…'

'It's like my heart starts racing, and I can almost hear it beating in my ears. I want to go to sleep, but I get this feeling like I mustn't.'

'What do you think might happen if you fall asleep?'

'You'll think it sounds stupid if I tell you…'

'Logan, I really bet I won't.'

He shifts his tiny self in the chair. This is hard for him.

'I start freaking out 'cause I know that it's time to sleep, and everyone tells me that I have to get a good sleep. And I know I need it 'cause I can't stay awake at school, and I always have to go to the loo to splash my face with water like you said to. And I know I'm supposed to go to sleep but if I do, then something bad will happen in the world and I will see it on the news, maybe not the next day but soon, and Dad or Granny will talk about it and I know they don't mean that it's my fault, but I feel like it is…'

'What kind of bad thing might happen in the world if you go to sleep, Logan?'

Tears well up in Logan's eyes. He wraps his arms

round his middle and brings his shoulders forward – every line of his body tight, tense.

'So much stuff. Like there was a pipe that burst in the Amazon and all this oil came out, spewing all over everything, covering all the plants and the animals for miles. I saw them on TV, all covered in it, trapped in this thick shiny goo… It gets in the birds' feathers so they can't spread their wings.' Logan holds his hands out in front of him, as if entreating me to see how he is trying and failing to contain the enormity of what he has seen. 'We watch videos at school too… Forest fires in Australia, and all this plastic for miles in the ocean, I…' he shakes his head, '… there is so much… But the worst is the wars.'

'What wars, Logan?'

'In Ukraine. Did you know the Russians dropped butterfly bombs? They look like little green toys. They chuck loads of them out of helicopters, and they flutter to the ground. Kids see them and think they can play with them and then, boom, bits of them get blown off…'

Tears stream down Logan's face. I have an urge to pick him up and put him on my knee, make everything better.

'Logan, that sounds very frightening and very evil. I haven't seen anything about this on the news. Who told you about the butterfly bombs?'

A tendon in Logan's neck flickers.

'My dad. He saw it on Twitter. He read it out – he was all upset. He doesn't let me go on Twitter.'

But he tells his already traumatised little boy about

bombs disguised as toys that maim children. What the actual fuck?

The urge *to do something* feels so strong in moments like this. I see my own fist banging on Logan's front door, can feel the words I will unleash on his father, when he opens it, crowding my mouth. But this will never be me, because I am a responsible counsellor in a cupboard with bills to pay, bound by the BACP ethical code, and not a fast-and-loose therapist in a BBC drama. Power-less. Sometimes I wish I'd trained in family therapy. Maybe that way I'd have a chance to ask parents why. Why on earth would you do that?

I've answered my own question. Logan's father is not in his right mind.

'Does he normally tell you scary stuff like this?'

Logan, wiping at his eyes, flashes me an anxious look, because he's loyal and suspects I'm questioning his dad's parenting, which is a no-go zone.

'No. He wouldn't... He doesn't... It was only 'cause...' Logan runs out of words.

''Cause he wasn't really himself that day?' I offer.

He just stares at me.

'Logan, I've got this idea in my head from our past sessions that maybe your dad sometimes drinks too much alcohol, which is understandable because you guys lost your mum and sometimes your dad will get very sad, just like you do, and sometimes adults will drink to try to feel better, but then it kind of doesn't really work... It doesn't make them bad people though.'

Logan holds eye contact like there is something to

lose if he looks away. Unsure whether to tell the truth or not, the conflict momentarily hardens his features. Then it's over. His gaze drops to the floor, and he says, 'No, my dad doesn't drink like that,' shoulders slumping in defeat. The rime from a thousand days of dirty necks greying the collar of his clean school shirt.

'Okay, Logan, but if you ever do want to talk to me about this again, you just say, okay?'

His head bobs.

'Now, do you want to tell me more about feeling responsible for the bad stuff that happens? Sometimes all the difficult stuff can build up inside us and turn kind of poisonous…and it can be really helpful to get some of that poison out by speaking it out loud to another person. You were saying wars were the worst…'

'Yeah,' says Logan, raising his head into safer territory. 'They bombed the hospital where the babies were being born, and that was only three days after I didn't get all the animals right.'

'What do you mean about getting all the animals right?'

'It's… I didn't I tell you this bit already?'

'No, no I don't think you did. So maybe you could tell me now…'

'Okay… At night, at lights-out, I have to list all the national animals of all the countries.'

'Which countries… Not all the countries in the world surely? I don't even know how many countries there are…'

'One hundred and ninety-five. And they all have a

national animal – sometimes more than one.'

'And you have to recite them all?'

'Sometimes it's only the ones from Europe, or one of the other continents.'

'So, when would it just be Europe?'

He bites down on his lip, says, 'I don't know. Just sometimes…'

'So, you think that if you don't say all the animals, then a bad thing will happen?

He nods, 'Yes, but it might happen anyway, just because I've fallen asleep.'

'Okay. You are doing really well, managing to tell me all this, to speak it all out loud. I know it's not easy for you. Have you told anyone else about these night-time fears, Logan?

He shakes his head, clasps his small hands tightly in a basket.

'Okay, that's okay. I'm wondering if I say something right now, will you really try to listen, not just with your head, but with your heart as well? Because I am going to tell you something that I am so sure about that I would bet my house, and everything I care about, that it's the truth.'

Logan stares at me.

'Logan, these terrible things that happen in the world – they have absolutely nothing to do with you. It does not matter what you do or don't do, they will happen anyway. The bad things don't happen because you haven't listed all the animals, or because you fall asleep – they happen because there are bad people in the world, and sometimes natural disasters...'

'But they're worse 'cause of climate change... And people make climate change.'

'Yes, you are right, that's often the case. But whether or not people make the bad things happen, those people are nothing to do with you. You are not making any of it happen. It's not possible that what you do, or do not do, at bedtime, or any other time, makes any of the bad stuff happen. Is there a part of you that understands this?'

Logan replies, 'I do understand it when you say it like that. It's just at night it's different. At night, when I start freaking out and my heart starts beating and I get convinced...'

I wish I could be with Logan at night. Fold him into my arms and sing him to sleep like my mother did with me.

'Logan, I think that something to do with night-time makes your body and your mind start worrying. When I say your body, I mean that something is actually happening in your body. It's starting to produce what we call stress hormones; they are called adrenaline and cortisol. Have you heard of them do you think?'

'Yes,' Logan replies., 'Like boys have testosterone...'

'That's right – that is a hormone. Good, so you understand that our bodies produce these chemical messengers that help us do stuff. Well, adrenaline and cortisol are what our bodies need to help us when we feel like we are being threatened. Have you heard of fight/flight/freeze?'

'Yes, like if a bear's after you?'

'Yes, exactly that! If a bear was threatening you, your body would produce the stress hormones you need in that situation.'

'But I'm not getting threatened at bedtime…'

'I know, but I think that something, probably something you are not even really consciously aware of, is making your body think that bedtime is threatening, and so it is pumping you full of fight/flight/freeze hormones which you can't use, so you start freaking out instead. Your body is telling you there is something to be scared of, but you don't know what it is, so your mind has to find some way of making sense of the fear. Your mind has made an association between bedtime – the time when we sleep – and bad things happening in the world. It is your mind's way of making sense of what your body is doing.'

I can tell Logan is concentrating hard. I add, 'What I've just said is really quite complicated – not very easy to get your head around…'

Chewing on the inside of his mouth he says, 'No, I do sort of get it, I think. But I still don't understand why it happens at bedtime and not at other times.'

I sigh. 'That I don't know. There's probably something about bedtime that we haven't thought of yet. It could be as simple as bedtime is time alone, time to worry about the things you care about, all the animals and the people… Do you ever get the freaking-out feeling at any other times?'

'I got it in Social Subjects a few weeks ago…We were

watching this video about Afghanistan. Do you know what's happening there?'

'Yes, I do. It's horrific.'

'They were saying about the women and the girls. Did you know the primary-school girls can go to school, but the high-school girls aren't allowed? If we were in Afghanistan, all the girls in my class wouldn't be there. And women can't go to work any more – if they leave the house without a man from their family they can get in trouble. They can't really do anything any more, and I don't understand why.'

He looks to me like I might have the answer, but any of the explanations I can think of are too terrible to make sense, and I won't explain them well, so I just say I don't know either, because I really don't.

'So, watching that video made the freaking-out feeling happen again?'

'No, watching the video made me cry.'

A new flush of shame blooms on his pale cheeks like red ink dropped in milk.

'It was at break, after Social Studies, when some of the boys from the class started having a go. They'd seen me crying… They asked why, so I told them…'

'You said you were upset about the women and girls in Afghanistan…'

'Yes, 'cause I'm an idiot,' he replies, the last word almost a shout. 'It had *really* upset me, and I couldn't understand how it hadn't upset them. I'd imagined how it would've been for *my* mum, how she would have hated to live like that – maybe they weren't thinking about it like that, 'cause they've all still got their mums. But it was the worst thing I could have said, saying I was upset about girls, 'cause they called me things… It's bad enough I don't want to play football, and that I don't know about any of the teams. And I'm always picked last in PE – well, not last: third from last; I'm in front of the only girl who chooses basketball over dance, and a boy with massive thick glasses, and he gets extra help with stuff, you know? Anyway, they always say stuff, shove me in the corridors. Most of the time they do it kind of quietly, so teachers don't hear, but sometimes, like after the video in the playground, they get right up in my face and that's when I start freaking out.'

'So, most of the time it's kind of subtle but still very hurtful, and other times they openly confront you…'

'Yeah, and after the video when I said what I said, one of them said 'What's wrong with you, gay boy?''

'And what did you do?'

'I didn't do anything. I just froze. It was like I couldn't think, and my heart felt like it was going to burst out my chest. Then someone came along, and they backed off. I couldn't concentrate for the rest of the day, and when I got home my dad knew something was wrong, even though I tried to hide it. I ended up telling him, even though I knew it would end bad.'

'Why did you think that?'

'Because it always does. He says I need to toughen up, stand up to them – that if I throw the first punch, they'll never do it again. He says I should get into football, so I can join in their conversations. He says it's how men talk to each other, like a special language that helps you make friends. But I don't like football at all. I don't like any of that stuff and I don't like them. And he gets so frustrated at me and I know I'm disappointing him, but I can't fight them. It's not that I don't get angry – I get so angry, and I want to hurt them, I want them to hurt – but when I'm freaking out, I can't do anything but stand there, while they say all those things about me, call me gay. They laugh at my face, and I know it's getting redder and redder, and they joke that my head is about to explode.'

Tiny gentle boy. I'm not sure whether my anger belongs to him or me. Am I just feeling the rage he has passed to me to hold for as long as we are in this room together, to take and to contain, and to hopefully hand back to him in a more manageable form as I was trained to do? Or is it my own fury at the world we live in which boils my blood? I want to ask his father if he realises that it will be *his* voice that Logan hears inside his head, now and for as long as Logan lives. It will be his voice saying *toughen up, never show weakness, be better, be something you are not.* His beliefs which will calcify inside Logan's little heart and likely make him do the same to his own child. Does dad not get that? Do parents not get that?

Easy for me to say.

'Logan, when you were freaking out, that was your body responding to threat, just like how it does at night, but this time the threat was very real. The bit of your brain – I can never remember the name of it –

anyway, the bit that controls thinking and language and decision-making, sort of shuts down, goes offline, as it were, and the primal bit, called the amygdala, which is responsible for fight/flight/freeze, is activated. Whether we fight, run, or freeze is not under our control any more. You froze, just like most people do, and you had no choice in it.'

'My dad thinks I have a choice...'

'And it sounds like he's trying to help you as best he can, but maybe he doesn't know so much about the amygdala and how it works. But you do now, so I need you to understand that it's not your fault – you literally cannot fight, and anyway, even if you could, fighting can end pretty badly.'

I always get this rush when I explain trauma responses to kids, like I'm imparting this incredibly useful knowledge that will free them from self-blame and help them understand themselves a little better. Then, generally, they say something that shows me my grandiose moments, my tiny triumphs are just a piece of nonsense.

Logan frowns, 'It doesn't matter if I know about the *ambilala* – my dad would never believe it. He'd think it was an excuse for me to get out of being tougher. Even if I said *you* said it, he'd just say that he'd suspected it was you who put "this stuff" in my head.'

'He knows you're coming to counselling though, right?'

Kids can come to see me without their parents' consent but I'm fairly sure it was discussed with his dad in the child planning meeting last term.

'Yeah, but he doesn't like it. He says men should be able to sort their problems out themselves, like men, without talking to someone who doesn't know them and doesn't understand their lives, so I try not to talk about coming here.'

Wanker dad.

Something in my face maybe? Because Logan says, 'My dad isn't bad – he's just not very…he doesn't know stuff like this. My mum was much better at it. When she was here, she got him to listen, and he was softer. He was happy and sometimes acted daft. In all the photos he's smiling… But I just think he sort of lost the soft part when she died… He doesn't smile now. I don't think he likes himself any more, and I try to make him better, and sometimes I do, when he's himself, and not…but when he's not himself, then he gets mad at me, says the world is a hard, hard place and there's only a place in it for hard men and I need to wise up and have a word with myself. And then I feel like I hate him, but I hate myself more because I can't make him better. I can't do what she did…'

Oh, Logan.

He said more than he intended. The shame is too much, and for a moment he closes his hands over his face. Now he's swiping roughly at his tears with his sleeve.

Sometimes I can't bear it, the way kids feel responsible for saving their parents, like they have any power at all. The way they think they are always failing because they never succeed in making it all better. It's survival – they need that parent to be well again so they can be looked after properly once more. And it's love – they love their parents no matter what, no matter what that parent has done to them. They might have been physically, sexually, emotionally abused, and part, if not all of them, still loves that parent. It makes me want to scream.

It's why my heart sinks when I see I'm to be working with younger ones – the urge to try to *do something* to help is just too strong, their pain and my helplessness too hard to hold.

'Logan, your father needs help, but you are too young to be the one who helps him. You can't be the one who is responsible for him...'

I'm saying it wrong. I feel useless; I can't help. I know this is *me* feeling what Logan's feeling – the countertransference of powerlessness, helplessness, anger, not being good enough – but the knowledge doesn't make me feel any better. I want to scream – to do something to help him, instead of just...sitting here.

'Logan, I am so sorry your mum died. I am so very, very sorry.'

He looks up at me, clear green eyes, fringed by wet, brown lashes, a whole world of pain visible in his gaze.

'She must have died in the night, because when I woke up, I could hear the baby pigeons whistling on the roof, and I ran through to tell her, because she loved the pigeons too, but Dad and Granny were there holding her hands and Granny said she was gone. They'd been up all night, but they didn't wake me. Why didn't they wake me in the night? So I could've said goodbye...'

This will haunt Logan for the rest of his life – I don't doubt that. But saying goodbye is a gamble. One I wish I hadn't taken. I would envy Logan this absence of memory, this empty space in place of what might have been the worst, the most unendurable moment of his life – if only the loss hadn't stolen his sleep from him.

Phone call with Child and Adolescent Mental Health Services (CAMHS)

'Thank you so much for calling me back.'

'Not at all. Have you had trouble getting to speak to someone?'

She has a lovely Geordie accent, and there is genuine concern in her question.

'Just a bit of back and forth. Logan's doctor gave me the names of the two mental health community workers who have been working with him, but it seems to be someone different now...'

'Ah yes. Logan is on the waiting list for clinical treatment soon, but you know that could be quite a while away. Sorry, can you give me a moment?'

She sounds a little stressed, like someone in the room is mouthing information at her while she's trying to focus on me.

'Sure.'

She puts me on hold to the clamour of discordant fairground music, both whimsical and eerie, and so loud I have to hold the phone away from my ear. Who chose that?

People ask if my job got harder because of the pandemic, if more kids than usual have mental health problems now. At first I'd reply that the pandemic has only highlighted the mental health crisis in young people, not caused it. That CAMHS waiting times were still averaging eighteen months before the pandemic, as opposed to three years nowadays. But lately I've been witnessing the damage the lockdowns have done. Young people without each other, locked up with parents at precisely the stage in their lives when the opposite should be happening. The radio news told me teenagers were flouting lockdown. I understood that many people found this upsetting and no wonder, but we also needed room for empathy. These kids got lonely, craved connection. I was nostalgic for my own youth, wanted the same for my clients.

My pals and I were the tail end of Gen X. They 'came in' for me as you did in the days before phones. Evenings, weekends, school holidays we'd be shoulder to shoulder on bedroom sofas, sharing bottles of juice or horrible Bulgarian country wine (depending on how flush we were), often straight from the neck. Once driving tests were passed, we'd be squashed together in Nissan Micras, off into the hills, huddled close around fires. Never distanced, socially. Not holed up with our stressed-out families. Not lonely. We were lucky; for so many of the teenagers I now see, for so long, there was no 'shoulder to shoulder', no sharing of bottles, no 'squashed together' or 'huddled around'. To touch was to break the law – a dystopian precept and an invisible barrier to the easy intimacy teenagers need to maintain healthy minds. They had too much time alone inside their own heads, time for disordered thinking to develop. Too much easy access to websites that would encourage and amplify their darker thoughts. We're told that since the lockdowns, referrals to CAMHS for eating disorders have risen 100 percent – a heart-breaking statistic that mirrors the frequency of new kids, mostly girls, with eating disorders who find their way to my room. But how many of them actually get seen? It's another of these CAMHS Catch 22s. If you aren't thin enough to get treated as a priority, you don't get to start treatment. The organisation that states early intervention is critical inadvertently incentivises girls to get sicker. The healthy part of these kids knows they need professional help, but then they are told that, to get it, they have to be more successful at having an eating disorder.

Logan is already in the system, yet still he must wait many months between appointments, never quite getting the help he needs.

The music stops abruptly; she's back.

'Hi, so sorry about that…so I was saying Logan's on the waiting list…'

'Yes. Can I ask what that means? The clinical treatment – who will he see?'

'It will be a psychiatrist,' she says, matter of fact.

Why is he to see a psychiatrist again? Logan needs care and understanding, not a diagnosis and medication.

'Oh, okay. I know you can't say when it will be, but I would really like to speak to that psychiatrist before they meet Logan. It's just I'm concerned they might treat Logan for generalised anxiety, when I think he's suffering from trauma from the death of his mother. On top of that there's the school bullying he's dealing with on a regular basis, and his unsettled homelife. I'm not sure Dad is coping too well. I'm really keen for his care to be more joined-up and transparent, by which I mean working with the family in light of what has happened to them, rather than treating Logan as if there is something wrong with him.'

I know I'm firing words at her, machine-gun style, but this is the only chance I've got. So I continue '…I mean there is something wrong with him – he's traumatised and grieving, and he needs support – but it's a natural response to his mother dying and his father being depressed, not anything pathological. I'm worried he'll be given anti-depressants, as he was told last time that this might be an option…'

'Of course,' she says in her milky-soft tones. If she were a dessert she'd be rice pudding. 'I'll make a note on the file for the psychiatrist to call you, when they get round to seeing Logan, though as I say, that might be a while…'

Months or years? Who can say? What odds would the bookies on the high street give for the psychiatrist phoning me back at all?

'Thank you for doing that, it's much appreciated. Now what I'm actually phoning about is the possibility of Logan being prescribed some melatonin to help him sleep. I wouldn't be asking for this if I didn't think it was necessary. It's not a question of sleep hygiene – Logan is not staying up looking at screens. He is a very traumatised twelve-year-old and can't get to sleep because he feels frightened. His mother died at night. He's getting weekly therapy with me, but not for much longer, and waiting for support from you guys, but none of that is enough right now. His GP and I agree some melatonin over a short period could give him some relief so that he won't be struggling to stay awake in school. But the doctor told me he isn't allowed to prescribe melatonin without CAMHS permission, and that I would have to go through CAMHS, which is why I'm speaking to you now.'

She makes a noise like she's suppressing a sneeze before saying, '…Okay, I understand, and I see what you're saying. Problem is, I'm a clinician and not a medic, so I can't do that for you. What I will do, is leave a note for one of the medics to get in touch with Logan's doctor.'

'That would be great – thank you!'

Fantastic! I mean the fact the GP is not allowed to prescribe melatonin to Logan seems crazy to me but at least we are getting somewhere. Melatonin wasn't a thing when I was desperately needing sleep, but if I had a pencil and a sheet of paper I could still draw the label of the bottle of antihistamine I used to glug from right now, from memory.

'…Only problem is we don't have any medics at the moment, so it may take a while…'

Kass session 5

During our last session a fortnight ago, after she disclosed that it was her brother who had hurt her, Kass decided she wanted to tell me the physical nature of the abuse she suffered. What she was able to tell me took a monumental force of will and undeniable courage. I stressed beforehand there was no expectation for her to tell me anything in particular, and that she might choose somewhere more private, certainly away from her work environment, and not necessarily with me. She listened, and then told me some of what happened to her.

Last night, the school emailed all staff and parents to tell us the building would be shut for the day due to an electrical fault which has left it without power. Soon after that, I received an email from Kass, asking if I might consider having today's scheduled session in the park, since last time I had implied sessions didn't always have to be in the counselling room.

Did I imply that? I can see how she might have got that impression, but it's not really what I meant. But what did I mean? I wasn't clear when I said she may not want to disclose abuse at work, and so now I am in a pickle. I would never normally meet a client outwith the very contained therapeutic space. But then...

Kass, bundled in her green puffer, which is a better shout than my light raincoat on this sunless grey day, is looking bored at my attempts to explain, unnecessarily circuitously, the importance of boundaries in the therapeutic relationship. I'm feeling guilty for having stretched the therapy frame to incorporate the park. We got lucky that it's so empty, but I keep expecting Estelle or one of the members of my supervision group to jump out of the bushes and reprimand me, bashing me over the head with a copy of *Counselling: Best Practice*. I could always pretend this is my first foray into wilderness therapy, though the tatty little playpark, with its empty cans of Monster energy drink littered about, wouldn't be anyone's idea of actual wilderness.

Get it together, Jane.

Behind our bench, a bank of glossy, dark green rhododendron bushes, their showy blooms long gone, rub shoulders with the dramatic crimson flower tassels of an unexpected amaranth, known commonly as love-lies-bleeding. Amaranths crave light and warmth, so this spot must be a suntrap on a good day. The velvety trails of tiny bright flowers pour down from the tall pale foliage with the air of sorrow I always attribute to them, but Kass hasn't noticed. They dry well; I'll nick some before I leave.

Lewis, who was already playing by the time I joined his mother on the bench where we sit, is in among the sea-themed playpark, a splodge of colour weaving between massive steel octopus tentacles, chipped paint like a necrotising blight on their suckers.

Now I know why Kass suggested the park. She failed to mention she would be bringing her son. Part of me respects her for this, the other is put out at having been tricked. I would have said no, and she probably knows it.

'I know about boundaries,' she says. 'I just… He's had the norovirus – don't worry he's fine now, they just don't let them back to school until forty-eight hours after the symptoms have stopped.'

'What about you?' I ask, not altogether altruistically. We are sitting awfully close on this small bench.

'I had it first. I'm well past forty-eight hours; don't stress yourself.'

She smiles and snorts gently, which makes me smile.

As a counselling student in an agency, I saw a young woman who, without pre-warning me, brought her baby to our second session. She was a refugee who had been accused of witchcraft in her own country and fled when it became clear that she and her baby were no longer safe there. As she unfolded her story before me in more-than-adequate broken English, I came to understand just how precarious her situation was and marvelled that she had got to Scotland at all, let alone found her way to a counselling agency. I never got to know her, because she came only twice, and I had no means of finding out why she didn't return after that second session. But I remember how her features contorted with distress and longing as she looked at that baby in its carrier at her feet, sucking away on its mittened hands, and how it took me longer than it should have to realise what was going on. But when I did, I said, 'Would you like to breastfeed your baby here?' and her relief transformed the energy in the room as she pulled up her top and her child latched on like a limpet. Determined to keep my focus firmly on her face, I caught only a glimpse of one large, dark-brown, long-lashed eye, swivelling in bliss. That is the only time I have attempted counselling with an adult with their child in the room.

'I still don't think we can really *do counselling* though,' I say. 'If I know wee kids, pretty soon he will come over saying he's hungry, and no matter how many times you tell him you need peace to speak to *this nice lady* – she being me – he'll be wanting another dubious need met.'

Kass starts laughing and says, 'Well maybe we don't *do* counselling then. Maybe we just sit and chat. Breathe in the fresh air…'

She's making a joke. We are both ignoring the reek from the local sewage works which sometimes likes to make its presence known, even this far into the city. I have a magnet on my fridge providing a number I can call to complain, but I always forget.

'Seriously though, I do appreciate you taking the time to come and see me like this.'

'I got the impression there was some urgency. But you seem okay now. That wasn't a complaint – I'm glad you're not upset – it's just a noticing.'

A little shake of her head. 'I wasn't good last night, but today is a better day.'

Days of norovirus. First her, then her kid. What must that have been like, doing it all by herself? But today she is smiling, whatever darkness visited last night gone, however temporarily.

And now the splodge is running towards us and taking on the shape of a boy. All knees and elbows and shoulders. Close up, the trace of shadow hollowing his eyes tells of recent illness, and the flush in his cheeks the song of his joy at being outside again. And of course, just like in his photos, he has his mother's pale blue eyes and soft, mouse-coloured hair. If I touched those cheeks, they would feel cold. If I got close, I imagine his skin would have that fleeting mineral smell that rises from cobblestones just before a thunderstorm. He is even lovelier than his photo.

'Hello!' he says, bold as you like. Curious, he looks around, trying to locate the kid I must surely have brought. Someone to play with, maybe.

'Hi,' I reply. 'I'm a friend of your mum's. My name is Jane, and it's just me I'm afraid.'

'Don't you have any kids, Jane?' he asks, my name round and perfect as a blackcurrant in his mouth.

I shake my head, 'No, no kids.'

Kass, embarrassed, is about to tell him to stop being so nosey, but before she can, he says, 'Don't worry about that, you can watch me! Today you can pretend I'm your kid too.'

Permission to pretend he belongs to me. Just another exhausted mum sitting in a playpark.

I don't know why he's got to me, but he has, and I'm thankful for the moment to compose myself as he and Kass rifle through her bag for one of the snacks she has brought.

Now he's running off with the Tupperware tub she

gave him. Climbing up the tentacles to the flat space at the top of the octopus's head. He is hyper-real against the grey backdrop. I'm sure he would be this way against any backdrop.

'I'm sorry about that,' says Kass.

'Don't be daft. He's lovely. He really is. He was being kind.'

'Yeah,' she laughs, 'he clearly thinks that getting to watch him crawl about a playground when you should be relaxing at home, enjoying an unexpected day off, is some sort of great honour that he's bestowing on you.'

You don't know the half of it.

'Well, he's impressively fast and agile!'

Kass looks towards her son. 'Yeah, he is. He never crawled, that one. Just went straight from bum-shuffling to walking – it was the weirdest thing.'

'Were you there when he took his first step?'

'I was!' she says proudly, '...phone in hand of course.' She takes her phone from her pocket and after a minute or so of searching finds the image for me.

The camera has captured Lewis, jaunty in a candy-striped babygro, mid-stagger. His face a picture all of its own.

I look back to him munching his snack. He sees me watching and waves enthusiastically. *Today you can pretend I'm your kid too.*

As she's about to put it back in her pocket, Kass's phone rings. She touches the screen to accept the call, answers, 'Yes, hello? ...One second please...' then puts her hand over the receiver and mouths *'Gotta take this, back in a minute, will you…?'*, gesturing to her boy.

I know she just means keep an eye on him. But he's already invited me into his world.

I leave the bench and walk towards the octopus. Lewis's small face lights up as he scrambles towards me.

Crouching on a tentacle just above my eye level he waits for me to say something.

'Permission to climb aboard your octopus, Cap'n?'

'It's a squid.'

'No it's not.'

'Yes, it is!' he yelps.

It looks nothing like a squid, though I don't suppose it needs to be anything other than what he wants it to be. Yet still I can't help myself, because now I say, 'Honestly, it's an octopus…'

From his crouch position he shrugs and says, 'Potato tomato…', and I have to bite my lip not to laugh or correct him again.

He unsquashes to his full height, offers me a small pointy hand reminiscent of a raccoon's paw, and leads me up and over the tentacles towards the flat of the creature's head, where he gestures to me to sit.

There is enough room on the cold steel for us to sit cross-legged, facing each other, so this is what we do. Lewis reaches into his pocket and produces a new pack of strawberry Hubba Bubba which he rips open in a practised manner with his raccoon hands. Now he removes the individual wrapper of the first piece and instead of eating it himself holds it a hair's breadth away from my lips. The smell instantly makes my mouth water. I open up and he drops it in. The Covid implications are not lost on me – this manky climbing frame, his germ-ridden little kid fingers (no doubt he licks his palms to get purchase on the monkey bars) – but the gum tastes like 1986, and for once I don't care.

We watch each other chewing, swallowing the first brilliant bursts of strawberry juice, moving the gum around our mouths, both determined to be the first to have a go. He wins only because I let him, blowing a huge bubble which collapses across his freckled face.

'My mum said you're a teacher.'

'Did she now?'

'Yup. Do you go in the staff room?

'Not really – it's miles away from my room.'

And I'd have to talk to people.

He nods, holds one end of the gum in his front teeth and, with two fingers, stretches the other out in front of him before doubling it back towards his mouth in a folding motion. Then he asks, 'Do you know Mr Huntley?'

Casual as you like, pulling me up short.

Why is Kass's kid asking me that?

'Yes, I know who he is. Do you know him?'

Lewis gives an exaggerated shake of his six-year-old head.

'…But you know *of* him.'

A solemn nod.

'How?'

'Mum says he hangs around the office like he's got nothing better to do.'

'He does, does he? What else does he do?'

'Sometimes he asks her if she wants a lift home.'

'And does she take one?'

'No. She says he's a clown.'

She's not wrong. A clown with an agenda. At least she's not falling for him; I'm not sure I could've handled that. But what is he up to, and why's Kass not mentioned it? Odd to tell Lewis about Huntley hassling her, but then again, if not Lewis, who? Apart from a few work pals, she's got no one. There is some reassurance in the word 'clown' though – that's not a name you give someone you're worried about.

'Are you worried about him? I mean is that why you asked if I know him?'

Lewis glances across at his mother still on the phone, 'No, not really. I just thought 'cos he's a teacher and you're a teacher…'

'I see.'

I wait to see if there's more to come.

Lewis works away at the gum in his mouth, a dribble of vermilion juice escaping from one corner of his lips. 'Mum pointed at him once, when we were on the bus, and he was in the street with his family. She said *that's that clown Huntley*. But it was fine, he doesn't look like one of the bad ones.'

Doesn't he? I suppose that depends on your definition of a bad one.

'What do the bad ones look like, Lewis?'

'They have lighter hair like mine, and they are taller than Mr Huntley. They don't have his beard.'

I thought we were making generalisations, but I realise now that Lewis is talking about a specific type of man.

'Where do you see this kind of man, Lewis?'

He shrugs, 'They can be anywhere.'

'But why do you notice particular men who look like that? And why do you think they are bad?'

A flick of his surprisingly long tongue and he's dealt with the escaping juice.

'Because those are the ones Mum's scared of. When she sees one that looks like that, she gets frightened, and we have to go. She says if a man like that ever tries to speak to me, I have to run away as fast as I can.'

Always ready to run.

Here's Kass, finished her call and on her way to join us, smiling, I assume, at the prospect. I only ever see her move from door to chair and back in the counselling room, never across a space as she is now. People have distinct walks and hers is liquid, with perfect posture and grace infusing every step, gliding lightly over the surface of a hostile world. Maybe there were dance classes once; maybe there was ambition. Aspirations, dreams, *hope* – for more than just safety – once upon a time. Expectations for her life left unspoken, extinguished before they'd even properly formed along the edges of her awareness. What's more bearable – to know what it is that you want, and to feel as if every step ineluctably takes you closer, only for it to become impossible, or to never have had the chance in the first place?

Lewis waves her up, the subject of our conversation forgotten at the sight of his mother.

'Room for one more?' Kass asks, scaling the octopus as nimbly as her son did; this is not her first rodeo.

We shuffle over and, yes, there is just enough room for three. In fact we are a perfect fit, like sides of a triangle. Lewis tries to tell a terrible joke which Kass has obviously heard more than once, but both our laughs are genuine because the boy can barely speak, so lost is he to the giggles that bubble up every time he attempts to deliver the punchline.

On a different day I am this woman's counsellor, and Lewis only an extension of her, abstract and unknown to me, but right here, right now, we are all something *other* – here we sit on our bums with our knees touching, here we chat rubbish about nothing, and laugh about everything because it's all suddenly, stupidly funny, and I feel puffs of Lewis's hot breath on my face as his fingers clasp my neck for once again insisting that the climbing frame is in fact an octopus.

'Stop strangling Jane!' Kass bleats, her voice ringing in the pearly air, clear and high as a bell.

My mother insisted she'd coined the phrase *one's company, two's a crowd, and three's a party,* to describe us, but Dad said bollocks, it was Andy Warhol, and then she said who the hell cares as long as it fits, yeah? And she was right, it definitely fit.

After giving his mother gum – this kid is thoughtful – Lewis bisects his fourth and penultimate piece by ripping

174

it with his teeth, before solemnly handing me one half and then watching to see what I will do. I carefully stick out my tongue and, showily, ceremoniously, place the fresh half upon the sorry masticated pink lump which lost its flavour ages ago. Now I close my mouth and eyes and start to chew, arranging my features into what I hope looks like an approximation of ecstatic bliss. After all, I am honoured.

I don't know what this is, but it's definitely not a counselling session.

George (S6)

Age 17
Referral by Head of Senior School
Parents divorced
He and younger brother live half/half with book-
keeper mum and lighting engineer dad
Amicable split, parents still friends
Mum has new partner who is 'alright'
Dad does not
Presenting issue: sleep problems
George is trans boy (physically female)
Dysphoric as long as he can remember
Describes parents as supportive, yet mentions that
they still often use his deadname, and when his
mum is drunk on a Saturday night, she gets very
emotional, cries and says that it's all her fault
that he is the way he is, then begs his forgiveness
George says she's just talking shite and finds it very
embarrassing
Other times she talks of him in the past tense,
using his deadname, as if they were a dead child
she has lost, as if he, George, is now a completely
different person
This he finds less embarrassing and more shocking,
much harder to take
Binds his breasts and looking forward to
transitioning one day
Has boyfriend but doesn't know if boyfriend will like
his body once he transitions
Boyfriend doesn't know either

Says he needs not to be in his body any more
Described to me some of the worst abuse from people in the street/school/online that I have ever heard
Gets to sleep but wakes up after a few hours and can't nod off again
Says inability to sleep leads to panic attacks
Tried sleep hygiene, though hard not to stay off his phone when he's wide awake in the middle of the night
Very attached to dog, Tina

George Session 3

George's perfect oval face, with its spattering of brown freckles, reminds me of an egg. His skin looks chalky next to his black oversized school hoodie. He did exceptionally well to tell me so much in our last session and I'm wondering if he's going to pick up where he left off.

But he doesn't.

'I feel like I can't get enough air in,' he says, a note of panic present in his voice.

'When did you start feeling like this?'

'I don't know...I think maybe I've been like this for months, but it's kind of crept up.'

'Any other symptoms?' I ask, being my GP.

'Yes. I feel this tiredness in my legs, like I don't have any energy in them. I mean, I'm fine right now, but trying to run, or climbing the stairs to my house – I feel like my legs can't do it.'

When George first came to see me, he was very wary, bad experiences in the past having leached his trust in other human beings.

Teenagers exist in a time of flux and change, trying out different identities, seeing what fits and what doesn't – they need space to explore and room to grow. What we decide about ourselves when we are fourteen may hold true all our lives, or it may be something that changes dramatically in the months and years to come. For some kids, questioning their sex/gender is a phase like any other teenage phase, for others it is a fundamental need and the start of their personal liberation. Young people come to school counselling with strong ideas and feelings about themselves – often conflicting ones, so counselling should be a place where they can think about some of it with someone who won't judge them, who will accept and respect that this is where they are, and how they feel, right now, without giving an opinion one way or another. Sometimes I mess this up, but I think it's going okay with George. George isn't questioning his identity; he knows who he is, but his body doesn't match. He told me that, for as long as he could remember, he has felt this way, and that, as an older child, for many years he'd engaged in a kind of magical thinking: 'I'd look at myself…no, not *myself*, because I didn't recognise what I saw there as myself… I'd look at *my body* in the mirror, and I kind of had the idea that if I stared at it long enough, wished hard enough, that it would change. When I was really low I imagined making it disappear completely. But of course it never did. The prospect of puberty was terrifying, and I was unlucky – I started early, though I suppose maybe I got lucky that I never got big boobs or anything… I never got that curvy.'

With George I feel like the work, if I do it well, could be in some way reparative, heal some of the hurt he's been forced to endure. That's the hope anyway.

'George, I want to try something if that's okay…?'

George nods enthusiastically, swiping at his fringe which flops over his eyes. He reminds me of River Phoenix in some brat-pack movie I can't quite pin down.

'Sit back in the chair so that you are comfortable, arms loose by your side.'

I realise as I'm saying this that, for a kid who has spent the last five years with his shoulders hunched forward in an attempt to ease the *discomfort* of his dysphoria, what I've requested is an oxymoron. But he does it anyway, perhaps because I'm modelling it for him by doing it myself, and I've just closed my eyes.

'Okay, we'll both do it together.' I say, keeping my eyes closed. 'Now place one hand on your stomach and take a big breath in… Now breathe out.'

I open my eyes and George is breathing out, his hand still on his stomach.

'Okay, I'm wondering, when you took the big breath in, did your stomach move under your hand? Did it fill with air, do you think?'

'Uh, I'm not sure…' George says, looking confused.

'Try it again,' I say, 'and this time I'll watch you.'

George, hand on his stomach, inhales deeply and I

watch his shoulders rise, his flattened chest expand.

'No, my stomach didn't really do anything' he says. 'Maybe sucked in a tiny bit…but not much more than that.'

I feel excited. I know what's wrong with George – I just have to convey it in a way he will understand, and not sound like some crystal-wielding, New Age hippy. Do young people associate deep breathing with that stuff? Has he already been lectured on belly-breathing by the mindfulness brigade?

Shut up, Jane. You have every respect for mindfulness – it's just the word you hate.

I contain my glee and embody my GP again.

'George, when you breathe, your shoulders rise, and your chest inflates.'

'Doesn't everyone's?'

'Nope. It means you're shallow breathing, and the oxygen you're inhaling isn't getting to all the parts of your body it needs to reach. When you feel short of breath, it's because you are hyperventilating – breathing too fast and not deeply enough. Rapid, shallow breathing. Your legs get tired quickly because you aren't getting enough oxygen to them.'

Mystery solved: I can't help but smile.

George just looks confused. 'If that's wrong, how *should* I be breathing?' he asks.

'From your diaphragm. This bit,' I explain, running my hands across my stomach and all the way around my back. 'All this part of you should be filling up with air. It will be hard at first, because you have to retrain yourself to breathe properly. You weren't always breathing from your chest… If you watch toddlers breathe you can see their little tummies rising but their shoulders are perfectly still…'

'I didn't know you had kids…'

'I don't.'

'So where do you watch toddlers breathe?' he asks, innocently enough.

Everywhere. I watch toddlers breathe everywhere.

It's hot in here. I need to find something bigger than my roll-on deodorant to jam the window open. I usually have trouble, what with all the assorted crap on the narrow window shelf, but there's more space now that I've moved my *Psychotrias* home and into a bigger terrarium.

'I saw a YouTube video about it.'

'Oh, okay. It's funny, I can't really imagine you watching YouTube…'

He means because I am so old. At forty-one. There is no guile on the perfectly oval face. No offence meant, no recognition of any caused.

I glance at the clock. I just want this session to be over. Which means I have to double my efforts to be here for *this* child, George, who can't breathe properly, because one of those times that someone said something foul to him triggered a trauma response. Or maybe an accumulation of all these times has created a tension in him, a feeling that he is no longer safe in the world, and he, now, even when calm, breathes in air as if he were still being threatened. The world is a terrible place, and we are not endlessly resilient creatures.

But we can train ourselves to breathe as we once did. I know because I had to.

'So how do I get my breathing right again?' George asks, sitting forward in his chair.

I sit up straight and gently clap my hands together.

'Well now, it will take a bit of practice and patience but don't worry, we'll get you there.'

At the end of the session George stands and thanks me, just as he has in previous sessions, with a deference that has, I feel, more to do with my status as counsellor than my age. It's a moment of the formality that some of my older teenage clients affect at the hour's end. It returns the dynamic from collaborators back to young person and adult-in-authority, and marks the ending. When the older boys stand up, I become conscious once more of their height, their physical difference, that was not so apparent while they reclined in the armchair. George is not particularly tall, though he is taller than me, and physically female, yet I feel that same sense of physical disparity, and it is this I am thinking of as he slings his schoolbag over his shoulder and slopes off down the hall.

By the end of our session, George understood the concept of diaphragmatic breathing, getting to grips with it impressively quickly. He had also seemed serious about retraining his body to breathe this way unconsciously and using it as a tool for tackling anxiety. So in that sense, the session went well. What

I'm grappling with right now, as I return to my room, and from my window watch him stride across the quad to his next lesson, is what happened to me during our session.

George, one hand on his stomach and the other on his shoulder, after performing a perfect belly-breath, looked up at me and grinned, seeking confirmation of his success, his fringe once again flopping across his eyes, having to be swiped away.

I smiled and nodded in acknowledgement, we continued practising and talking, but I was working mostly on autopilot, because I was experiencing a sudden and strong countertransference that either wasn't there in previous sessions or had only just surfaced from my unconscious. George was reminding me of – no, more than that, unwittingly conjuring for me – a boy I knew. Someone I loved and had to give up. Not River Phoenix – a real boy, though River Phoenix was also in the mix, catapulting me back into the nineties, and as I talked with George, I was trying to ignore seventeen-year-old me who was seeing the boy she loved, at the age he was then, for the first time in twenty-four years.

I did not expect that to happen today.

Countertransference – the reactions therapists have to their clients – can be very useful to the therapy. For example, if I feel frequent irritation while listening to my client, it may be that this is a feeling the client often engenders in other people, which might be a source of distress for the client. Gently sharing these feelings with the client can result in greater self-awareness and ultimately be helpful. Or it may be that the irritation doesn't even belong to me but is an unconscious communication from my client – they are irritated, but rather than experiencing the feeling themselves, they are projecting it into me, and I am experiencing what we call the projective identification.

Again, if I recognise this feeling as not really mine, not belonging to me, and convey this insight sensitively, it can prove helpful for them. Similarly, if George reminded me of a good friend of mine, and I thought some aspect of this could prove insightful for him, then I might share my countertransference.

However, I simply cannot see how telling George any of what just happened to me would be anything other than creepy and weird. This is my stuff, not his, and right now I am steeped in shame, run-through with the absence of people I have lost, and I really miss my mum.

Jojo (S3)

Age 13
Referred by nurse for anger management
Lives with parents
Support worker mum
Dad does something in an office
No siblings
Presenting issue: anxiety, keeps turning up at
nurse's office after walking out of class
File reports talking back to teachers and swearing
in class, occasional skipping school
Self-harms – cutting
Non-binary, fine with she/her pronouns
Intimidated by groups of boys. Bullied, especially
in PE, where boys ask her why she is so shit at
everything. When she walks through the quad, boys
shout at her that she has no tits, and that no one
will ever want to fuck her.
Hates being powerless
Hates being a girl
Says father is traditional
(EXPLORE FURTHER. WHAT ABOUT MUM?)
When she speaks up, she gets called a feminazi

Jojo Session 5

This last fortnight my *Hoya* decided to produce flowers
for the first time since I bought it five years ago. I knew
this might happen one day, but I'd resigned myself to
the idea that it might never bloom, and that was okay.
Then two tiny clusters of green buds appeared and grew

and transformed into waxy white stars which today burst open, revealing fragrant pink centres. When I walked into my room and saw them this morning, I did something I seldom do these days, despite all the horrors I hear – I started to cry. But now I've got over myself and I can't wait for someone to notice them.

The fetid, slightly sweet stench of an overflowing bin behind the dinner hall has carried on a summer breeze all the way across the quad and into my open third-floor window. Jojo wrinkles her nose. Her hair is held in place at the nape of her neck with a scrunchy; are they a thing again? Thought they went out with culottes and snoods.

Jojo is so small you could probably fit two of her in the armchair. She removes her black school trainers, places them neatly under the coffee table and tucks herself into a cross-legged position. She takes each corner of the blanket I've used to cover the grotty upholstery and folds it around herself like she is the filling in a knitted filo pastry parcel. I wrap the blanket from my own chair over my knees in solidarity, even though it's not cold in here. Her small face, plastered in curdling orange foundation, an awful match for her light olive skin, is livid. And she's close to the tears which, previous sessions have told me, will fall in opaque milky drops, leaving pale vertical streaks down her cheeks and an almost camouflage effect.

'Looks like it's not been an easy morning…'

She bites at her lips, says, 'No it hasn't.'

'Do you want to say a bit about that?'

She stares hard at my *Hoya*. 'Is that plant fake?'

'No. It's real and those are its new babies.'

'Oh.'

Not the right audience.

'You look pissed off, but I may have got that wrong...'

Jojo's referral was anger management, whatever that means. I've not yet met the anger management referral kid who didn't have plenty to be angry about. I now understand the 'management' bit to be about managing the irritation and expectations of the grown-ups around these distressed and snarling little darlings.

She pulls the blanket tighter so all I can see of her is her head, and says, 'Everyone always underestimates me.'

I catch the faint scent of Imperial Leather soap which always accompanies Jojo. As a kid I thought only posh people had Imperial Leather and have associated the fragrance with luxury ever since. Jojo is not posh, and the smell seems incongruous.

'I don't,' I say, then immediately wish I hadn't, because she glares at me and says, 'Everyone else then.'

'How do they underestimate you?'

'Last night at tea I told my parents I wanted to be a surgeon in the army. They thought it was hilarious – had a big laugh about it.'

'They laughed at you?'

She scowls, thinks I'm trying to catch her out, which I'm not.

'Well, no, maybe not laughed,' she says, the scowl softening slightly – clearly she's decided to give me the benefit of the doubt. 'But they smiled at each other, then Dad said, 'How about getting into nursing?' And Mum said, "Yes, you can do a proper degree in that now, and they *pay you* to do it. Same with social work." Then they looked well pleased with themselves.'

'How did it make you feel?'

'It made me feel like they hadn't heard what I said. Or worse, like they'd heard it and thought it was the stupidest thing in the world, like there was no way I could ever be good enough. It made me feel like I wanted to pick up their bowls of minging carrot and coriander soup and pour them over their stupid, patronising old heads.'

We sit with this image for a bit. Acquiescing to the heat of the room, she lets the blanket fall to her sides and swigs aggressively from a bottle of Seven Up that she's taken out of her schoolbag. Her white shirt rides up, revealing a faded patch of old cuts on the soft skin of her stomach – she's the only kid I know whose self-harm resembles a noughts-and-crosses grid. Even on a taut belly like hers, I don't know how she gets the lines so precise. Good to see no new scabs.

I say, 'I have this idea from previous sessions that maybe your mum is a bit more…let's say open-minded than your dad…'

'Eh?' Jojo slowly enunciates this nothing-of-a-word with utter disregard, while giving me evils that would instantly turn a lesser mortal to stone. Not me, though. Jojo is a challenge that I am well up for.

'I dunno why you think *that*. My mum is a woman

who spends half an hour each night before bed *layering serums.* Do you know what that means?'

She doesn't give me time to answer. Must have been a rhetorical question, as, given the state of my face, it's clear I've never *layered a serum* in my life. Only joking – I don't really think she meant that.

'She's forever scrolling fucking Instagram, and it makes her buy all these wee expensive bottles of what basically looks like water, which she has to slather on her face one after another, 'cause she thinks it'll stop her getting wrinkles.'

'And does it?'

(If it does, will it send out the wrong message if I ask the brand?)

Jojo scratches the side of her face then says, 'Does it fuck. I tell her to go get some Botox if she's that bothered, but she says Dad won't let her. And if I say who gives a fuck what he thinks and she doesn't need his fucking permission, she says he likes her *au naturel,* though he doesn't seem to have a problem with the amount of slap she trowels on every day of the week – even the weekends when we're doing fuck all and not even leaving the house, so he can't really talk can he? And then she just says I should be starting my *serum routine* now, as a *preventative measure.* I'm thirteen years old!'

I'm suddenly sad, not at her protests – she has every right to rant and rave – but at her little orange face. Some of mum's ethos is finding a way in.

Slap and *trowels* – these words do not belong to a

189

thirteen-year-old. Is this what mum accuses Jojo of doing? Even though Jojo is only following her lead. At least the fashion for heavy contouring and highlighting is over. For a while, every second girl who sat across from me looked like a Thundercat.

'Then what happened? I mean, after they'd trampled on your hopes for your future?'

'Then they started talking about something else.'

She stares at the wall for a bit before saying, 'It must be so easy for them.'

She reaches forward and pulls a tissue from the box even though she's not crying. Perhaps she's about to blow her nose.

'Who, your parents?'

'No, boys.'

'Ah.'

I'm distracted by the tissue in her hands. Isn't she going to use it?

'Your parents started talking about something else, and now you have started talking about something else.'

'It's connected,' she says, with a glare. 'I bet there is no boy in this school who gets told he looks "like a little bird" on a regular basis, or that his balls are too small, or that he couldn't be in the army, or that he should go and be a nurse. No one underestimates them. I hate them, I hate them all.'

'And you envy them.'

Maybe Jojo hasn't considered that her hatred for boys is fuelled by a blistering jealousy, because she takes her time to think about my statement, her eyes narrowing slightly.

She dislikes being underestimated, so rather than keeping my thoughts to myself, I'm going to share them, and see what she thinks.

'See that bloke with the beard in that picture?' I ask, pointing to the black and white photo-postcard of Freud I have on my wall.

'Yeah...?' she says, scrunching her nose at the lack of obvious relevance an old beardy man has to our conversation.

'That's Sigmund Freud – the guy who basically came up with the idea of counselling, which he called his 'talking cure'. He helped loads of people, particularly women. But then he also came up (pardon the pun) with his theory of penis-envy, whereby he thought women are jealous because men have penises and they don't.'

Jojo's 'Riiiiight....' brims with scepticism, which it should.

'...Anyway, he had this female student called Karen Horney, who brilliantly argued in a paper entitled *The Flight from Womanhood* that it is not men's penises that women are envious of – but their freedom. Their personal and professional freedoms. And that this envy leads them – by which I mean us – to reject the feminine, by which she meant female gender roles.'

I pause, to see if she can bear any more, and am encouraged by a nod of her head and a 'go on'.

'Though not completely discounting Freud's theory,

Horney proposed that women and girls are not in fact, as Freud and his followers believed, in a state of unconscious penis-envy, soft and fragrant ladies on the outside, craven and bitter within, walking wombs with an axe to grind, forever condemned to be inferior to men, on account of lacking a willy. Far from it – we just want to be treated equally. And I'm saying to you that this envy you feel is not really because these boys are any better than you – it's more that people and systems treat them differently because they are male.'

Jojo chews on her lip a little before saying, 'Well, she was right, that Karen Horney, but she had a fucking terrible name.'

'Yeah, I suppose she did.'

'Can you hate someone and envy them too?' she asks, looking suddenly younger than her thirteen years.

'Definitely,' I reply. 'I think the two often go hand in hand.'

She sits with this idea for a moment or two.

'You mentioned getting called a little bird... Do you think your life would be better if you weren't so...so petite?'

'Well,' she says, and to my horror, with her squoval nails, she tears off a small piece of tissue and drops it onto the floor. The cleaners never seem to find their way up here, so it's always left to me. At least she hasn't blown germy snot into the tissue and *then* dropped it.

'I might not get picked on so much. But it's not really about my size. It's my size *and* that I'm a girl.'

I do not query why Jojo refers to herself as a girl,

when she has told me she identifies as non-binary, and I'm not entirely sure why I don't. I'll need to think on this later.

Then she does it again with the tissue... And again. Quick little rips with her slender little fingers.

'I know for a fact that small boys get picked on by other boys.'

'Maybe, but they wouldn't say the stuff they say to me to a boy.'

'No, maybe not. But I don't suppose it's so great for boys either. Life can be hard on them too. All that pressure and expectation to be strong and not show their emotions. It can't be easy.'

Jojo looks vaguely annoyed at me, unsure if or why I'm defending her tormentors.

'Yes, I know that,' she says. 'That's why I'm non-binary – I just don't want to be either. Don't want people to think they know who I am when they haven't got a clue... Don't want to be underestimated any more.'

I want to say, but you can be a girl and be anything and anyone you want to be, if you'd only stop caring so bloody much about what people think of you, just get through your adolescence, get out of this shithole, go be yourself with people you want to be with, and stop tearing up tissues and dropping them on other people's carpets!

But I don't, because I did that with Vaishali, and it didn't land well. I can't keep foisting my own stuff onto the kids if I want to fall on the right side of history. Not that that's the priority.

'I'm wondering what it would be like for you to *not be* underestimated by your parents and peers for once?'

I wonder what it would feel like not to underestimate myself. To know that I was capable of doing something which might actually make a huge difference to another person.

She takes another angry swig of her water and says, 'You're always fucking wondering, you are.'

Supervision with Estelle
Session 76

Estelle says, 'We've been here before…'

'And we'll be here again.'

She smiles. 'It would seem to be a major theme of high school counselling.'

'And not of normal therapy, do you mean? That's interesting.'

Estelle's silver hair gleams where she's brushed it back into a neat chignon – the only bright point in this dull room, in this dull building, in this dull afternoon. Even the sky outside the window is dishwater grey. She looks good today, different… Maybe she's taken a lover, like Shirley Valentine.

Estelle adjusts her glasses on the bridge of her nose. 'That's not what I'm saying. Of course, my other supervisees bring anger at times, but with you it's a recurring subject. Could you say something about why you think that is? It might be a good idea to express some of that anger here, rather than carrying it about…'

'Ha. You think if I let it out in here, I won't still be carrying it about?' I say, taking cover behind a flare of indignation.

Estelle can weed the anger from me like a dandelion from a lawn, but never quite manages to pull it out at the root. She is not a miracle worker, so why am I being such a bitch?

She makes a little snorting noise. 'That's not what I meant and you know it. You're being very combative today and I can't help but think that it might be a good use of your time to get some of it out.'

'Fine.'

'Good. I'll even put up with you glowering at me.'

I smile despite myself.

Isn't everyone angry all the time? Except Estelle and Costas, or whatever he's called. Fuck, that actress was probably closer *to me* in age than Estelle.

'I think it's quite obvious why it's a recurring subject...' I say. 'I mean, I'm dealing with kids. They have no power, and their parents do despicable things to them, which makes me angry.'

Why am I not telling her that I know who abused Kass? Why have I made no mention of Kass's last two sessions? I go to start telling her, but something stops me every time. I fill up our fifty minutes with other clients and leave no space for Kass. Estelle hasn't cottoned on, mind you. It's perfectly normal not to mention clients in supervision – there isn't the time to think about all of them. Besides, mad as Kass's situation makes me, it's only one among others, and her brother hasn't been near her in nearly two decades.

'Mmm,' she says, '...but it's not just their parents, is it? You talk about other kids hurting them, about siblings, about teachers even. And strangers. And then of course social media, pornography, etc, etc. Society – all of it – hurting them. Don't you think it's possible you are projecting your own anger at your own parents into your client's parents? Might you be defending yourself against feeling anger at your mother and father by instead feeling it about the parents of these children? And this powerlessness you feel, is it really about them? Or could it be about your inability to change what happened to your parents?'

Oh fuck off, Estelle.

'Why would I be angry at my parents?'

'Because they left you when you were still in your teens.'

'Not on purpose.'

'No, not on purpose. But they still left you. And you might feel angry about that.'

Might I?

After an age I say, 'Maybe. But you are wrong about feeling powerless to bring about change – I feel powerless to get revenge.'

Oof, now there's a carrot I had no intention of dangling today.

'That's interesting. Maybe you could say a bit more about what you mean by "getting revenge"...'

Or I could just not. Always trying to get to my shadow-side, aren't you, Estelle? Wouldn't you like to know the things I do in waking dreams, the rights I wrong? Kass's brother, Logan's bullies, Jojo's parents, the men who sexualise Vaishali... The list goes on. Who wants to wait around for karma when retribution is on offer right now?

Except it's not on offer, except in *phantasy*. Freud used that term (fantasy but with a 'ph') to describe the act of imaginative fulfilment of frustrated wishes. He believed phantasies could be both conscious and unconscious, which I thoroughly agree with, losing myself in mine more often these days than I ever have.

'Poor choice of words,' I say, eyeing Estelle, wondering if Ms Psychoanalytic will let me get away with it. I will bamboozle her with words and make her forget I said anything about revenge.

'What I *meant* is that I see more and more girls rejecting their femaleness because the world makes it so unbearable for them to *be* female. From all around them, right from babyhood when they are praised for being pretty and placid, they are bombarded with the message that being a girl means they have to be a certain way, to fit into a narrow, constrictive definition of femininity. And having one woman in a cupboard – i.e. me – tell them that all these messages are wrong and don't matter – just a pile of performative nonsense designed to keep women powerless, and that they can and should be anything they want, while still calling themselves girls, that they don't have to reject their girlhood – well, it's not enough. They are bullied and abused and oppressed and exploited precisely because they are girls. No wonder they want to fly off somewhere else. And the ones that are trans, who've always felt like their body isn't right – when they take that huge step to come out as trans boys, they are rejected and bullied just like the girls. Then there's the boys like Fraser and Logan – completely different problems, but both soaked in misogyny.'

'So, are you saying you don't believe girls should be trans or non-binary if they want to, need to…?

'No, of course I'm not saying that. Oh god, I don't think I'm expressing myself very well... I suppose I'm saying that there are so many reasons why someone might no longer want to be a girl. I just wish one of those reasons wasn't a world that shits on them because they're girls.'

Estelle smirks in a *don't we all, Jane* kind of way, but I can sense she has little interest in further exploration of my feelings on gender discrimination – she'd much rather take me back to that big juicy word *revenge*.

I feel a diversionary bitch about CAMHS coming on, but Estelle has unexpectedly doubled back to where we began the session – with little angry Jojo.

'Why do you think she cuts?' she asks.

Always an interesting question.

'Well, I don't know if you can ever affix self-harm to one reason. Every cutter I see – or biter, burner or hitter – seems to have a different reason for doing it. I suppose the most unifying element is that they don't like themselves very much. For many it gives a sense of control; not just control – *ownership*. In a world where everything they do is prescribed by other people – parents, teachers, dominant peers – the slide of a blade through skin can be like the planting of a flag, something that's theirs and only theirs. They know their pals do it, they see people doing it on social media – no wonder they assume it is a useful thing to do. For Jojo, I think, cutting relieves overwhelming frustration. The worst for me, though, are the girls with eating disorders who cut as punishment, for having 'given in' and eaten. It's like the modern-day version of hair shirts and flagellation.

Estelle winces, as she should. Then she asks, 'And why don't you tell anyone about it? Jojo's cutting, I mean.'

'Like who?'

She shrugs, 'I'm not sure… But surely this is the kind of thing that should get a kid onto the CAMHS waiting list, no?'

It wasn't even me that brought CAMHS up! But why is she asking me this? Sometimes I wonder if Estelle is actually listening to me at all.

'I don't tell anyone because it's enough that she's telling me. The wounds are pretty superficial and she keeps them clean. If I was to tell someone, I'd completely betray her trust and she'd never talk to me again. Besides, she'd have to be cut to ribbons, slicing really deep over old cuts for CAMHS to put her on a priority list.'

I take a drink from my plastic water bottle.

Maybe Estelle does listen after all, because she throws the end of her silk scarf over her shoulder with intention, like she's buckling up, sensing where I'm about to take us.

'CAMHS are a mythical unicorn.'

'How do you mean?'

'What I mean is, I meet so many parents who believe that once their kid is taken on by CAMHS, that's them sorted. That suddenly a system will kick in, give their kid the care and expertise they need to get better. I don't blame the parents at all. It's a hopeful thought,

CAMHS being the light at the end of the tunnel. The long waiting list gives people the idea that the wait must be worth it – like waiting three years to get a table at one of these posh London restaurants, when in reality the wait is just the consequence of a broken system, and you might still end up eating something that tastes like McDonald's. The problem with mythical unicorns is that when you finally meet them, you realise they are just ordinary horses in fancy dress.'

'That's a whole lot of metaphors. Could you explain what you mean a bit more plainly?'

Oh, for fuck's sake Estelle – I thought you liked metaphors. How many hours have you spent interpreting people's dreams?

'Plainly, okay. How's this: once a child gets seen, they will be allocated a practitioner or a team of practitioners, who are just ordinary people, and, like any other large group of people, some are brilliant, and some are not, but all are under huge pressure and chronically under-resourced. The model, as far as I can see, is deeply flawed. Social workers joke that if they finally manage to get a kid and their family a meeting with CAMHS, said family is much more likely to leave the appointment with some photocopied pages from a parenting book called *The Incredible Years*, than they are an arrangement for psychological therapy.'

'Fascinating…' says Estelle, and I have a strong desire to slap her. Then she adds, 'Might it be possible that you are projecting your own feelings of powerlessness into CAMHS? That slagging off CAMHS gives you an opportunity to feel righteous rather than inadequate? That, like Jojo's cutting, it gives you some relief? Because to be fair to CAMHS, you only ever seem to hear the horror stories, you only notice the flaws in the system, you've never met the people whose lives they've saved…'

Oh my God, Estelle, what an absolute bitch of a thing to say. Why can't you just agree with me and let me rant?

All I manage in response is, 'Huh, yeah, maybe…'

'What would you do?' she asks, 'I mean, to fix it…?'

'I dunno… Burn it all down and start again.'

I'm so pissed off I can't look at her. And I know if I did she'd be regarding me like the petulant child which right now I very much am.

It didn't help to get it out. I walk out of supervision and into a beautiful afternoon feeling humiliated by my own impotence. I bang on about it being the kids who have no power. Ha! I pontificate from armchairs, but when do I actually get to do something real? Something which will make a real difference? When do I get to do that?

1998

Leila, standing over us with her hands planted on her hips, is complaining that she doesn't look like Kate Moss at a music festival, and Ross points out she doesn't look like Kate Moss *anywhere.*

'You do, however, look like *you* at a music festival.'

'That meant to be a compliment?' she asks, squinting into the sun.

'No,' says Ross, oblivious that he's missed the opportunity to pretend otherwise.

'Dick,' says Leila.

'Eh?' says Ross, looking to me for clarification.

'Just tell her she looks nice.'

'Leila, you look lovely.'

Leila plucks a long thread from her denim cut-offs.

'Oh, shut up. I'm off to get beers. Are you coming?'

she asks him, not waiting for an answer.

Ross gets up and trots off after Leila, in her green B&Q wellies with her waist-length brown hair swinging.

Angie, cross-legged on the grass, is using her long tasselly skirt as a kind of saggy table on which to skin up a joint. She's wearing a vest top the wrong shade of light pink against her pale arms and chest, reminding me of that one in the Spice Girls who's meant to be good at singing.

Neil and Jess are playing poker with a tatty deck of playing cards. Yesterday was mostly a wash-out because it drizzled for most of the day, the others couldn't find any drugs and the band we all really wanted to see cancelled. But today started brighter, warmer, and we've seen all the acts we wanted to see. Groove Armada are playing on the main stage soon.

Neil, incredulous that a triumphant, cackling Jess has just trumped his pair of aces with three sevens, having been convinced she was bluffing, slides a hand down the black stubble which has sprouted on his cheeks and throat literally overnight, then pushes her by the shoulders so that she topples back onto the grass.

Before she has a chance to get up, he's on her, pinning her to the ground.

Jess hoots, 'That's not very sporting of you!'

He holds her there for a moment, her burnished halo of curls splayed around her beautiful freckled face, eyes glittering with humour, with mischief – she's enjoying herself – before saying, 'Ach you're not worth it,' and releasing her.

204

Jessie gets up. Kneeling down behind me, she reaches over to her bag and fishes out her hairbrush. She works away at my tangles painlessly (which had always seemed impossible for my mother, who met my yelps and squeals of protest with a hilarity that enraged me) and begins deftly plaiting my hair, the familiar action of her fingertips separating and tugging the sectioned strands, picking up more from either side and adding it to the braid. I close my eyes, trying to block out all other sensations but the feel of her hands and the heat of the sun.

For years now, Jess and Neil have been like this. Competitive, physical and fighty – never far from, and often on top of, each other. It would make sense if they got together, but they never do, both stubbornly insistent that they are just very good friends. After the summer they are off to study and work at opposite ends of the country, and I feel like they should say something now, before it's too late. But then, of all of us here, it's only me that's learned what too late feels like. They still think they've got forever. This unsolicited knowledge is the only area in which I supersede Jessie: how she knows herself – has *always* known herself – is unfathomable to me. She even knows *me* better than I know myself, frequently buying me the exact food I didn't know I was craving, making me mix-tapes of favourite songs I haven't stated a preference for. Tells me things I never knew about myself. Where does that come from?

Leila and Ross return with beers, a cider for me

and a bag of pills they've acquired from somewhere. Everyone immediately takes one, washed down with beer – everyone except me. They all know I've got a thing about pills of any kind, recreational or medicinal, but I don't mind a smoke, which is why Leila doesn't offer me an E but Angie hands me her joint. I screw up my eyes and draw just enough smoke into my lungs to make me feel something.

An hour and a half later we are wending our way towards the main stage. Bass vibrations from every tent we pass take fleeting occupancy of our bodies, moving through and leaving again to make way for the next, and the next. Neil buys me a yin/yang pendant on a leather cord from one of the tat stalls and ceremoniously places it around my neck. Gurning slightly as his pill takes full effect, he says, 'Light in darkness, Janey, darkness in light,' as if this is supposed to mean something to me. I say, 'Cheers Neil,' and he kisses my cheek before trotting back off to Jess.

As we traverse the multitude of festival-goers, I'm enjoying looking down at the pendant sitting prettily on my chest, the tight feel of the fishbone braid, and the bare skin on my neck and shoulders drinking up the warmth of the sun. Angie tugs on my hand because I've stopped to look at a guy on a unicycle.

'Come on, we're gonna lose the others.'

We set off after them, taking slugs from our plastic pint glasses and pointing stuff out to each other as we go. She's done her own hair in lots of little twists all over her head and looks like a blond Björk.

We stop as the ground slopes gently downward, opening out onto the main stage field where the restless, sunburnt, buoyant crowd, looser at the edges, becomes ever more packed the closer you get to the stage. Technicians are setting up – it won't be long now. Jess has Neil in some sort of headlock while Ross kneels down to tie his bootlace – he'd wear his Docs in a desert – and Leila opens a pack of Juicy Fruit. I close my eyes for a second, watch black stars spin away into a white gold universe.

'How far are we going in?' asks Angie breathlessly, accepting a stick of gum from Leila.

Neil, having escaped Jess, his face flushed, rearranges his hair. He looks wired – they all do. Leila, bouncing on the spot, says, 'The front of course,' as if any other answer would be ridiculous.

'Right then, me and Janey first...' Angie says, grabbing my hand. 'Keep together,' she barks, and we embark on the journey to the heart of the crowd, the others following behind. I feel warm and light and alive as we thread our way through all the other revellers.

We are quickly swallowed up by a jostling, noisy, sweaty sea of T-shirts and vest tops and flashing sunglasses, bare skin and beaded hair, the sweetness of hash and the sour tang of beer mixed with Calvin Klein Eternity, patchouli oil, chemical toilet fluid, poppers and the churned-up grass beneath our feet. The buzz of anticipation as excitement grows with the hum of an amplifier being turned on, and the sudden discordant screech of a microphone being set up.

We are as close as we are going to get, and Angie brings us to a halt in a little pocket of space with enough room for dancing. I feel Ross's hands on my shoulders, inserting himself on my left side to keep me away from the skinny, bug-eyed, bare-chested guy who's chewing his ecstatic face off next to me. Harmless though. When will my friends stop being so protective of me? And what am I going to do when we all go our separate ways in the autumn?

A roar erupts from the crowd. I can't see enough of the stage between the heads and shoulders of people in front of me, but I know the band must have come on, and now we are straight into a rocking, soaring banger of a tune. We dance towards each other, towards the music, like the coiling tendrils of those delicate plants that look like they're reaching for the sun.

We dance and sway to tune after tune, Angie on Ross's shoulders, me, Jess and Leila moving in sync, the press of their tacky suncream skin on mine. Most of the beautiful girls at school manage their mystique with some clever sleight of hand – the sheen is glossy, but the core hollow – but these two are the real deal and I love them with everything I have. Neil and bug-eyed guy bounce in unison, arms draped across the other's shoulders, their free hands drumming the sky; all my friends' faces bright and happy, off their tits.

I raise my face towards the sun, close my eyes. My body, which for so long has felt rigid, inflexible – as if all the sorrow had seeped into my muscles, hardened like concrete around my bones, taken permanent residence in my anatomy as well as my psyche – seems to open, to release. My limbs loosen and my shoulders relax – the heaviness gone, at least for now, and I am a light thing, a thing of light, connected to everything under this enormous sky.

I doubt any of us will remember this moment, but that doesn't mean it won't stay with us. Somewhere deep and treasured.

Then the music stops, and for a few seconds there is just the crowd, and beyond and above the stage the setting sun, where deep-blue tiger-stripe clouds streak across a sky filled with fire.

Until it erupts again as the first synthesiser strains and slow beats of 'At The River' break, followed by the languorous, dreamy trombone refrain which we all know so well. This song is ours; other generations will have their own anthems, but this is one of ours and it belongs to us and us alone.

I've drifted. Angie, Neil and Jess are a few bodies in front, Ross and Leila are snogging, which is new. I close my eyes again, elation rising, the crowd sings *if you're fond of sand dunes and salty air...*

...when suddenly I'm banged into from behind.

A familiar voice – one I've longed to hear – says, 'Sorry, sorry... Someone pushed me. Are you okay...?'

I turn and look up at the owner of the voice- and everyone and everything else around us falls away until his is the only face I see. The shoulder-length hair has gone, replaced by a shorter cut with a too-long fringe, but I know him, even though the last time I saw him he didn't have the tanned skin that greens his hazel eyes.

He should've been braver that day in the park. Maybe I should've too, but I was a mess whereas he knew where he was and where he was going. Meeting him just to lose him again had been more pain for the pile which I hadn't realised was possible, and right now rage courses through me, entwines with the elation of moments before. With both hands I shove him hard in the chest because he deserves it, but he barely flinches. So, I shove him again, and again he just lets me do it, and mouths 'Janey…' because he hasn't forgotten my name, even over a year later.

I honestly don't know what I'm doing, so I go to shove him a third time but this time he grabs my wrists, immediately releasing me when I stop pushing. He's not sober but he's not wasted either. He's locked on me like his eyes are telling him a lie he can't resist, like he's seeing some mythical creature for the first time – a mermaid or a fairy. My vision trails slightly as the air around us takes on a cinematic intensity. Instead of dropping my hands to my sides, I raise them up and around his neck, drawing his face down to meet mine, his mouth to mine.

He tastes of cider and cigarettes as his tongue flickers and slides around mine. Stubble rasps lightly against my skin, but I just want more. Dropping one of my hands from his neck, I let it travel under the short sleeve of his black T-shirt and up and over the warm skin of his bicep to his shoulder. He holds me tighter in his arms and we kiss deeper.

'At The River' has morphed into a high-energy techno beat, with the crowd cheering and clapping along, by the time I stop kissing Cam. A kiss that will be remembered.

'Hello,' I say, my nose against his, still firmly in his embrace. Panting, he breathes, 'Hello,' breaking into a smile. He's going in for more, but I pull back properly this time, draw his attention to the five people staring at us.

'Erm, these are my pals. Pals, meet Cam. Cam, meet pals.'

*

I don't know how long it will last, because I'm suspicious of those things which feel like they should naturally continue forever, but there *is* something more powerful than grief, and I think I've found it.

Part of me is certain that Cam is meant – not just meant but fated – to be for me. The other part can't conceive of why this older, brighter, better person, who's got his shit together and never has to reassemble the fragments of himself, patch himself up on a regular basis, because he is perpetually *whole,* wants to be with me. Yet he does.

Cam's family home is the top two floors of a Victorian tenement, accessed through a gate with peeling black paint, then along a path with small, neglected front gardens either side. An overgrown bush with dark green leaves spills lemon-scented flowers over the fence and the sporadically backlit intercom system buzzes slightly.

Since the age of seven, Cam tells me, his bedroom has been in the attic. The rest of the house has high ceilings, cornices, fireplaces with mantelpieces and other features I'm unused to, having grown up, and still living, in a house built in the 1950s. Cam's parents are on holiday in France, and he's just shown me round every room in their apartment, including the study – they have a study! – leaving his bedroom till last.

I'm not sure this could be described as an attic conversion because little has been done to change the red brick walls or the unvarnished floorboards, though the sloping ceiling and woodwork look like they've been freshly painted white. Everything is clean and tidy which, as Cam explained as we were ascending the narrow staircase, is because his mum invades his privacy every time he goes back to uni. A large window at the gable end and a skylight under each eave flood daylight into far corners which must get very dark at night.

I realise I've never been in an attic other than the ones in books. Heidi in the attic of her grandfather's house in the mountains; straw on the floor and a patchwork quilt drawn up over her knees as she gazes up at the stars. More recently, ultra-creepy and totally brilliant incest-fest *Flowers in the Attic*. Cam's bedroom resembles neither.

'What do you think?'

He's standing awkwardly, shoulders hunched, hands plunged deep into his jeans pockets, and I realise that he's nervous, embarrassed even, to be showing me his childhood sanctuary. 'My room in Brighton has got most of my actual stuff, I mean this is more a kid's bedroom...' He trails off.

'Shh,' I say. 'I love it.'

I move around unhurriedly, taking in Cam's life. Below one sloping eave, a small wooden chest of drawers squats – fine for a child, or a man who spends most of his time elsewhere. Adjacent are large shelves with what must be upwards of two hundred records, and a turntable. The opposite gable end without a window, next to the trapdoor we've just come through, is lined with shelves full of treasures. Rows of children's books, the bright colours of their spines muted with age, Cam being the youngest sibling of four, and novels – adventure stories and space operas, bookended at either side by flat piles of *National Geographic* and photography magazines. Jack Daniel's and Southern Comfort bottles on their side make a small pyramid, capless mouths revealing empty bellies. A mountain of plastic *Star Wars* figures, some missing a limb or two, lie rigid in undignified poses – worth something now, I'm sure. There are a couple of broken trophies, both for football, and the paraphernalia for various pursuits – snooker cue chalk, sex-wax for surfing, the metal bits off the underside of a skateboard, the deck of which is covered in foot-worn stickers and propped against the far wall, a heavy-looking dumbbell ensuring it stays put. A jar full of poker chips and beside it a pack of playing cards with a naked woman kneeling on the front, which I pick up and turn over in my hands.

He grabs the deck off me, blusters, 'You weren't supposed to see them – they're a joke!'

The woman pouts at me from his fist which fails to cover her large pale breasts.

'Hand them over,' I say.

'No way – you'd get the wrong idea,' he says, wincing, pushing his flop of fringe away from his eyes.

'You should get that cut.'

'I was going to, but I've just changed my mind – it's good for hiding behind.'

'Oh come on, give them to me.'

'Why d'you want to look at them?'

'I just do. Now hand 'em over.'

He snorts with laughter, intended to hide his embarrassment, as he reluctantly gives them to me and says, 'Fine. Think what you want. I bought them at a flea market in Berlin, AS A JOKE.'

I turn the pack on its end and the cards fall into my hand. The back of each has a bright yellow border and a different picture of a naked woman. I want to see them because they are so unlike the pornographic images that scream down from every newsagent shelf. The boys I know all seem to have copies of *Loaded* and *FHM* kicking about their bedrooms. They aren't top-shelf porn, but they aren't far off. The pictures in these magazines make me feel uncomfortable; the women all have huge, perfectly spherical breasts, tiny waists, flawless faces, and immaculate, glossy tresses. All have zero body hair but for the tiniest millimetre-long flat triangles above their privates, and apart from the pneumatic tits and arses, they are thin.

But *these* women on *these* playing cards, photographed with a soft-focus lens, don't look like that – they are still beautiful, but the lines of their bodies are less angular, softer, and much more like mine. Their silicone-free breasts, of all different sizes and shapes – rather than projecting outwards, firm and solid as mangoes – sit cushiony further down their chests, suggesting they'd yield to the touch.

These images don't intimidate me – they have the opposite effect. As I turn each card over, I think of the zillions of times Cam must have held one in *his* hand, and his dick in the other. Does he have a favourite or favourites? Which one is she? I like that they look more like me, how different they are to the girls in the lads' mags who make impossible rivals. If Cam likes them, then maybe he'll like me.

'They're from the 70s…' Cam explains unnecessarily. I know he's rattled, desperate to know what I'm thinking. Am I some prude, right now changing her mind about being with him? I doubt he has any idea what's really going on, how the thought of him wanking over the pictures is turning me on.

I assume he's done it before, lots of times – he's at uni after all. My sexual experiences are not extensive. Technically, I suppose I've lost my virginity, if a bit of painful penetration and some bumbling chat, never to be repeated, counts. But I've never met anyone I liked this much before.

Since the snog at the festival three weeks ago, that

night spent in my tent after chucking Leila out (she was fine, starting something that's still going with Ross) where we talked and kissed and talked and kissed, fully clothed but wrapped around each other under unzipped sleeping bags, keeping the cold out, still stupefied from having found each other again – since then, we've been engaged in a very strange dance. I know the fault is mine; I can't trust that he's real, and I keep thinking he'll disappear. Which makes me retreat every time we get close to each other. We meet and we talk and within minutes are glued by the mouth, powerless to resist the overwhelming urge to sink into each other, despite my friends saying how disgusting we are. When we're alone he tells me he can't believe he's found me.

He strongly implies a desire to seal the deal before he returns to Brighton, circling around making it official, and I wonder if he's worried about coming across as too keen. Or because he's still unsure he wants me; I don't know. And I'll reciprocate, show every indication of wanting him just as much, but then feel myself pulling back, retracting the affection of moments before by changing my tone, creating a big ball of distance which spreads between us like oil dropped in water, pushing us apart and changing the intimacy to sudden and excruciating civility. It comes unbidden and I can't stop myself. I leave him alone and bewildered and I hate myself for it.

My friends take turns to talk me out of it – to shake off what Jessie knowingly, after reading every column inch ever written by *Cosmopolitan*'s agony aunt, Irma

Kurtz, calls my self-sabotage – sending me back to Cam love-struck and horny once more.

And he keeps taking me back, maybe sensing I'm mad but not bad. He's taken me to his parents' house because I refuse to have anyone back to mine, yet. And this is the first time we've really been properly, quietly alone, somewhere we won't be disturbed.

'I like the cards,' I say, placing them back on the shelf.

'You do, do you?' he says, but it's not really a question.

I turn back to him where he stands illuminated by a shaft of sunlight slicing across the room, and smile. 'Yes I do, as a matter of fact.'

He raises an eyebrow, sensing he's got away with it. More than that – maybe there's an unexpected consequence he'll profit from.

I nod towards the single bed under the other eave. 'I see you've got a bed.'

Inclining his head slightly he returns my nod. 'It would appear that I do. Would you like to continue your tour over there?'

I bridge the gap between us in two paces, stepping into the light where I reach up and draw him to me. The faint nutmeg and citrus scent of aftershave combines in the dust-mote swirling heat with the salt of his sweat and the vanilla of the Lynx Africa deodorant that all the boys seem to use.

He's a good kisser. I put the idea that he's good because he's kissed so many girls before me out of my mind. I will not think of that. The eagerness of his mouth on mine shoots a bolt of desire down through my body. We pull back from each other and I tug at his T-shirt, which he immediately removes cleanly over his head in one motion, in that way that hot boys in movies do. His body is slender and lean and strong. His shoulders and chest gleam white beside his tanned arms, and the muscles of his torso appear finely traced on his skin. Wiry dark hair sprouts up from the waistband of his jeans, narrowing to a seam before meeting the sprinkling of finer brown fluff across his chest.

He is perfect. Nerves rip through me, equalled by excitement, by the demands my body is making. His skin is soft and warm but everything beneath is tight and hard as a drumhead.

My dad read me stories of selkies, the beautiful seal-women who always seem to be victims. The female selkie sheds her skin on a rock to walk as a human on land for an evening, minding her own business and troubling no one, then some arsehole man comes along and steals and hides the skin, coerces her into living with him, *forever.*

But the guys, the male selkies, always handsome bastards, are primed and ready to take advantage of human women – seducing them, then luring them into the sea, again *forever.* Neither of these scenarios reflect what is occurring between Cam and me, but I bet male selkies' bodies feel just like Cam's does as I run my hands down his front and grip the top of his jeans.

'First you,' he says, meaning it's my turn to take my top off. I dutifully raise my arms above my head, let him lift my T-shirt, which he does so slowly that I'm reminded of the scenes in films where the groom lifts his bride's veil – something about the way he does it feels ceremonial. His eyes go the pale green of greengages as he drinks in the sight of my boobs in the lacy white bra Jessie chose specially from Topshop.

He lifts his hand and strokes my collar bone, left to right and back again, so gently, like there's a risk I might shatter at his touch. He traces from my throat down to the space between my breasts, and with his thumb follows the curve just above the lace on each. He does no more than that, though I want him to – just pulls me back to him, kisses me hungrily. I yank at his belt, undo the buckle which is easier than I thought it might be. Now he's unbuttoning my jeans and pulling them over my hips as I do the same to him. His mouth is on my neck, my cheeks, my shoulders as we stumble over to his bed.

Through the skylight, heavy dark clouds have seen off the hazy blue of the late-summer sky and the first of the rain is spattering the glass, thunder rumbling not too far away. I can't imagine ever wanting to be anywhere else but right here with him.

After, when our breath has slowed, when we can do little more than just grin at each other in disbelief at the strange good fortune that's brought us together, I sit up and take a drink of water from the glass on the bedside table. And then, because unaccountably it feels like the right moment, I tell him what happened.

It can't take longer than three minutes.

He listens, and when I'm finished, he draws me

towards him and holds me in his arms until the rain stops.

The next day he comes to meet me with a buzzcut, and I discover I quite like the shorn Marines look.

Autumn Term
Late August – mid-September

Kass Session 7

In our second session, Kass told me about falling in love with her baby. I remember thinking *bring back the clients with post-natal depression*, because, for me, their misery was easier to listen to than Kass's outpourings. But now I feel like I'd do anything to hear Kass talk that way again.

In our fourth session Kass started to tell me about the abuse. She said she felt like she needed to, and it seemed important to her that I hear her, witness her. And maybe it was, but later that day she had to deal with a brutal flashback in the office with the harpies. Are our sessions really the right place for her to be recounting the abuse in detail? But if not here and now, where and when?

A few minutes ago, she came into the room in the kind of trauma-induced psychological and physiological state where she sees everyone as a threat – something she is experiencing more and more these days. A return to how she was before she discovered she was pregnant with Lewis. In this state she can be angry, fearful, hypervigilant and always steeped in shame. Frequent night sweats and nightmares don't help. I have no idea how she is getting to work *and* looking after Lewis when she is like this. My plan is to use something I've recently read about called polyvagal grounding and calming techniques – mostly deep breathing stuff – whenever she seems in a triggered state like this.

At least she's still managing to come to work. But her hair, once so perfectly straightened and shiny, hangs dull and limp about her face. She puts all her energy into keeping it together for Lewis, but she's going through the motions, and it scares me to think what she does at night. I know her babysitting options are limited, so she can't be going out very often. But she finds other ways to hurt herself.

I want her to get better. No, I *need* her to get better. Why can't I bear seeing her like this? The states I've seen people in, why not her? Is it even her that's the problem? Sometimes I feel like a bookshelf packed too tightly – so crammed with other people's stories that I just can't take another…

'You don't look so well today.'

'Thanks for that,' she snaps back.

'You know what I mean.'

She doesn't respond, her mouth a tight line on her pale face. She's so angry, and I know her rage will be directed at me, but that it's herself she hates.

We sit in silence for longer than I can cope with. Why am I so bad at this?

'You know Freud called it the *return of the repressed*. When we bottle up and repress our trauma for so long, for years, but then one day it all starts bubbling back up again.'

Kass, whose gaze has been glued to the carpet, turns her white-hot attention to me.

'Do you know what I do not need right now, Jane?' she spits. 'What I do not need right now, is you telling me what some bearded German weirdo said a hundred years ago, like you and he have any idea how I'm feeling. Like your pseudo *psychoeducation* is going to make any fucking difference. Do you really think I don't know what is happening here? That your interpretation is going to help me in some way? Like I didn't notice the smug tone in your voice as you remembered something from your training?'

Bitch. Though she's right – I'm agitated and failing to contain her pain. Yet still I hear myself say, 'Austrian.'

'What?'

'Freud – he was Austrian.'

Kass stares at me, incredulous. Then turns to address my framed reproduction photograph of Freud in a black suit and his daughter Anna in white lace, taking a stroll on a summer's day. 'Please accept my humble apologies,' she says sarcastically, and turns back to me with a filthy look that makes me laugh.

She shakes her head and smiles for the first time this session. And, just like that, our connection is back. A warming relief as equilibrium is restored.

'I'm sorry,' I say.

'That's okay,' she says. 'Me too.'

After a while she speaks again. 'Everything is tatty…'

'How do you mean?'

'After Lewis was born, the flat and everything in it was like our nest. Yes, it was all cheap, second-hand, but it was ours and we had everything we needed. But now it all looks old and tatty. There's not enough room to swing a cat. I see what other people have and realise that in comparison what we've got is shit. What I'm providing for my son is shit. And he deserves so much better.'

As if to illustrate how disgusted she is, she takes the clumps of lank hair which hang by either cheek and shoves them back behind her ears.

'I get what you are saying… But I'm wondering, if you were not depressed, if you weren't having to manage the sleepless nights and the flashbacks that have started coming back these last few weeks, would you be seeing the world in the same way? Because I think if you were feeling better, you might remember that children don't need *stuff* – they need love. There are plenty of kids out there with PlayStation Fives who would give anything for their parents to spend time with them…'

Kass makes a little snorting noise. 'You would say that.'

'Yes, I would! Because I'm a school counsellor and I meet them every day.'

Kass looks like she's biting the inside of her mouth.

'Our fridge is in our living room next to the sofa,' she says, determined not to be swayed by rational argument.

'My washing machine is in my bedroom,' I parry.

Though the shift from believing I could never leave my family home, to deciding that I must, was one of the hardest decisions I have ever made, the move in my late twenties from my parents' bungalow, in its family-centric neighbourhood, to my small second-floor flat in the bustling anonymous centre of town, was, mostly, emancipating. Not least because the flat was so much easier to clean. But swapping a large utility room for a washing machine in the bedroom still rankles.

'It is not.'

'Yes, it is.'

She snorts again. 'Why don't you move somewhere bigger?'

'I would, but all my money is tied up in Switzerland right now.'

Kass's eyes widen, and then she says, 'Oh, shut up, Jane! What's with your cheek today? You're a therapist. You're supposed to be serious, respectful.'

'Ah yes, sorry, I forgot for a moment.'

'Stop smiling!' she says.

'You stop smiling!'

'Sometimes I hate you…' she says, almost shouting.

'Good.'

'Why good?'

'Better me than yourself.'

She's stumped. But so am I.

She sits back in her chair, studies the wall to her right.

Shit, I completely forgot about the polyvagal techniques.

'Kass, I wanted to talk to you again about getting your doctor to refer you for trauma treatment…'

She shakes her head. 'I'm not doing that.'

'But I'm not a trauma therapist. There are people who are trained specifically to support folk with complex trauma.'

She looks at me now, 'Jane, is this because we've switched to lunchtimes after six sessions? I've been wondering about that – are you seeing me in your own time now?'

'No,' I lie, because this is not the reason I want her to go for trauma therapy. It's because I feel out of my depth. Inadequate.

'It's because there are experts out there, better able to help you…'

'Jane, you made me laugh.'

'Yes, but that's not therapy.'

'Isn't it?' She raises an eyebrow.

'Okay, I'll leave off hassling you about trauma therapy. But I do think we should try some polyvagal techniques…'

'Some what?'

'It's all about balancing your parasympathetic nervous system with your sympathetic nervous system, to help relieve trauma symptoms…'

'How do you do that, then?'

'Well, one of the main things is breathing techniques…'

'No.'

'Why not?'

'Because focusing that much on my body right now is not a good plan, Jane.'

I feel stupid; of course it's not. 'Right. No.'

She regards me steadily, says, 'I don't need you to try and fix me, Jane.'

She keeps saying my name and it feels like a good

thing, like she's taking power back, but also because it shows familiarity. We are far from strangers; we are in relationship.

Suddenly my mother's face is in my mind.

'I'm trying to help you…' I say.

'I know. But I just need you to just be you. I can handle your obsession with old dead men, but I don't need you to practise trauma therapies on me. I've got a laptop – I can do that myself.'

'Trust the process…'

'Exactly, Jane.'

But I'm so frightened for you, Kass. You need to get better, because if you don't, you will lose your little boy.

There is a person out there, somewhere, a breathing, walking, talking, *living* person, who is responsible for this. I know very little about him other than he is her older brother, and he lives far away, Kass's disclosures coming with the caveat that she would not welcome questions. But I have questions all the same.

How is he doing right now? Has he, like Kass, regressed into a state of arrested development from which he is trying and failing to claw his way out? Is he stuck, trapped, unable to escape an onslaught of trauma that simply will not quit? Did he think he was finally free, only for it to return like a cancer, like a curse he thought reversed? Does he live a life suspended?

I imagine not. I imagine he is just fine. Tip top, top-of-the-morning-to-you, and tickety-boo. Successful – wealthy, even. She said something about him being powerful, but then of course she sees her abuser that way.

What punishment befits a man who did what he did? A man who is still, though he may not have come near Kass for years, an ever-present threat. In a country that rarely jails its rapists, what retribution is there, really?

This line of thought does not help Kass. So, I pull myself back into the here-and-now. I'm just a woman in a cupboard after all.

Supervision Group

In attendance:
Jude, Facilitator, 60s, short-haired, gentle,
intelligent, and measured in a way I will never be
Very person-centred
Mother hen

Daniel, early 30s, tall and thin with designer
stubble
Rudolph Steiner school counsellor
Bit of a virtue-signaller but makes his own amazing
granola and brings me bags of it
The only non-Scot among us
Has clients in common with (and works near) Raya,
which makes them very chummy

Raya, mid-to-late 20s, slender and stylish, knows
her Taylor Swifts from her Demi Lovatos
Texts very quickly using both hands
Works in young persons' community health and
wellbeing clinic, has nursing background
When she speaks, her switched-on-ness and
sheer obvious potential put me in mind of just
how ignorant, lost and flailing about I was at a
comparable age
By the time she reaches her forties she will be
running the show, we just don't yet know which
show

Niamh, mid-50s maybe?
Art therapist for an organisation that puts
therapists in schools
Works in the middle of an extremely deprived
housing scheme
Looks exactly like an art therapist should, big
earrings and knitted things, but sexier, like Susan
Sarandon

Elaine, a new person who Jude has just introduced
to the group and looks to be somewhere in her late
40s
Slim, with shoulder-length, expensive buttery
blonde hair

We all work with teenagers – when we say *kids,* we
mean young people between the ages of eleven and
eighteen – and we mostly get on. Mostly. Knowing
each other well enough to be comfortable speaking
our minds results in lively debates. Jude does her best.
Every four weeks, on a Wednesday evening, we occupy
the third-floor antechamber of one of the main lecture
theatres up at the university, an impressive Victorian
building but stripped of most of its original features
inside. There are plug sockets under flaps on the floor,
and ugly strip lighting. We are lucky enough, however,
to have a huge round window that looks out onto the
city like a giant eye; the kind of thing you see in movies
with a steampunk aesthetic.

We have all arrived on time and taken our seats

making the circle, even if we are placed further apart than before the pandemic started. Though we have been back in this room for a few months, this is the first time all five of us have been able to attend, and something about the full house makes me, despite having felt unusually tired this week, feel a little giddy and unfettered. I once had a bipolar client, who, in the first stages of a manic phase, would be so alert, so full of energy and sort of effervescent, that we came to use the word 'fizzy' as shorthand: I'd say you look fizzy today, and she'd agree. I'm not manic, but right now I can feel bubbles rising, as violet light from dusk falling beyond the round window suffuses the room.

As she always does, Jude smooths the folds of her long skirt with her hands and looks around at each of us intently, the way she might watch water settling in a measuring jug, judging our readiness. Are we calm, tranquil, present enough to begin? Or are there ripples of agitation, an undercurrent of disquiet – something needing to be addressed before we commence? I sit still and arrange my features to neutral. Satisfied that we have met the former condition, she smiles brightly and says, 'Okey dokey, nice to see we are all here today…'

She pauses, scans our faces again, the smile still playing on her lips. Just as I'm convinced that she's about to give a little speech about the symbolism of the occasion and her gratitude that we have all got to this point where we can be together again, she looks to think better of it and instead gives a little, slightly stunned, can't-quite-believe-we-all-made-it shake of her head. Now she's opening the dog-eared orange school jotter she uses as a notebook and running her finger down the page.

'Right, folks, can I remind you that we all agreed we weren't going devote too much of our time to complaining about CAMHS this week...'

'Why are you all looking at me?' I say, holding my hands up.

Raya says 'ha', and I make a face at her.

Elaine looks lost, so Jude explains rather generously that I'm not always CAMHS's biggest fan.

'Now, Elaine, we usually set a rather loose agenda. Each time we meet, two of our group will have an opportunity to bring client work, or really whatever they want, as long as it pertains to some aspect of practice, and if anyone has anything particularly pressing or troubling, they should say so at the start, so that we can make space for it.'

Elaine, sitting nicely, hands-in-a-basket, smiles the rictus grin of someone who feels thoroughly outside their comfort zone. I wonder if she's new to therapy.

Jude continues. 'So, Elaine, it's completely up to you if you want to share anything today. But you might want to tell the group a bit about yourself and where you work.'

Is that a twinset? Being worn non-ironically? Oh, stop being such a bitch, Jane.

'Yes, okay,' Elaine says brightly. 'So, I'm a psychosynthesis coach...'

What the fuck is that?

'…and I'm the school counsellor at ＿＿＿＿ College.'

Which just happens to be one of the most expensive private boarding schools in the country.

Daniel asks, 'Is that co-ed?'

'Oh yes,' replies Elaine proudly. 'It's boys *and* girls. And every day I feel very privileged to be working with the young people in my care.'

I chance a glance at Niamh, who is smiling politely but looks like she needs the loo.

'…And I'm very happy to have found a supervision group of other like-minded people,' Elaine continues, grinning pointedly at Raya, eager perhaps to emphasise her kinship with the Black community.

Raya, startled, darts a look at me, and I cannot stop my nostrils from flaring in an attempt to quell the laugh rising inside me.

'Great, thank you Elaine,' says Jude. 'And would you like to bring any client work today?'

'Well,' says Elaine, 'I was wondering where everyone stands on whether or not it's okay to make our young clients a cup of tea?'

New to therapy then.

'There are just so many pros and cons to consider. Like what unconscious message am I giving if I offer them tea? What does it say about me if *I* have a cup of tea? Does it look like I'm maybe hiding behind it? If I have a cup of tea and they have, say, a water, does that say something about the power imbalance? I suppose I just wonder what you guys do…?'

'I offer the kids a hot chocolate or a water,' Niamh

says cordially and looks at me to go next.

'Em, yeah, so, I don't have a kettle. I have to use the one in the office down the stairs so it's not really feasible for me to offer tea, but I've always got one for myself…'

Raya and Daniel aren't offering anything, so Jude says, 'Raya? Daniel? Thoughts on tea?' Elaine, straight-backed, does her expectant grin thing.

Daniel says, 'No, I don't offer anything. I always bring a Starbucks in the morning for myself…'

Admitting to patronising a big multinational! Is he feeling alright?

Raya says, 'There's a table in the waiting room with jugs of water and bottles of cordial. They can make their own.'

'Oh, that's a great idea!' says Elaine. 'Thanks, Raya! Thanks everyone.'

Raya nods.

Thank God Elaine resolved her tea dilemma – she'll sleep tonight.

'Okay…' says Jude. 'Now, whose turn was it?…' She consults her notebook. 'Daniel, who or what are you bringing today?'

'Yup. Today I'm bringing God.'

'Excellent,' says Jude. 'As long as we are mindful to be respectful of others, then this sounds interesting…'

Daniel strokes the designer stubble which looks longer than usual. Is he attempting to grow a proper beard?

'I'm curious how often God comes up in your sessions with kids, and in what ways,' he says. 'Because to be honest, I'm getting a bit creeped out by how often I'm hearing a young person describe God or religion being used by a parent or care-giver as an excuse for abusive behaviour.'

There is a murmur of recognition from everyone bar Elaine, who is frowning.

Daniel says, 'Right, it's not just me then. So, I work with a fifteen-year-old boy, so that's S4, who is the youngest of four kids. Let's call him Paul. Paul was an "unexpected surprise". His siblings are much older and don't seem to be in the picture much. Anyway, his parents are members of an evangelical church. The parents don't get on, and Paul's evenings are spent listening through the walls to them fighting.'

I ask, 'Does it get physical?'

'Occasionally – hasn't happened for a while. Paul described trying to intervene one night, years ago. He saw his mother slap his father and then his father punch his mother. Ever since then, he's had the fear, understandably, that one of these arguments is going to end up with one of them killing the other, which has led to him being hypervigilant. He thinks he has to stay awake to listen for escalation, that it will be his responsibility to intervene or call an ambulance.'

Raya says, 'Poor kid. What do they fight about?'

'Everything, judging by what Paul says. They sound like they have fundamentally different views on just about everything, except their religious beliefs, although that sounds like a bit of an oxymoron, doesn't it? How they are still together after four kids... Mind you, maybe they changed over time. They had a baby they hadn't planned, and it all got too much...'

'So, where does God come in?' asks Niamh, fiddling with an earring.

'Well, the family is very involved in the church community. Mum, who works for a charity, does some sort of volunteering for the church, and dad, who owns or part-owns – I can't quite work it out – his own bike shop, also has something to do with it. Paul says their solution to everything is not to talk but to pray. If he tries to speak to them about their arguments, their response is that they should pray as a family for Paul to find peace. They don't talk about anything; just pray. So nothing ever changes. It's like some weird form of avoidance, of denial.'

'It's gaslighting, is what it is,' I say.

'I agree,' says Daniel. 'Paul gets up the courage to speak his mind, and they somehow twist the situation to make it about Paul being unhappy, the solution to which is prayer. They don't acknowledge or take any responsibility for being the cause of his distress. They don't sit down and talk things through. They make it *his* problem and pretend to be supporting him as a family through prayer.'

He vigorously shakes a metal bottle before taking a drink, which leaves a spot of white liquid on his cupid's bow. Is he drinking straight oat milk? Is that normal?

'That's some dark shit,' says Niamh, sounding and looking even more Susan Sarandon than usual.

Elaine is staring at her shoes.

'Child protection, surely?' says Raya.

'Yeah, well, you'd think so. But it's complicated. The physical stuff was ages ago. On the face of it they are a fully functioning family. Two parents in employment, steady income coming in, regular churchgoers and involved in the local community. We could argue emotional abuse, but we all know what the police or social work department are going to say about that...'

Elaine – who obviously doesn't – looks around at each of us.

'Very hard to prove,' Raya explains.

'And Paul is fifteen, nearly sixteen. He's not a little kid, and it's not too long before he can get out. If he can hold on, and we as a school can support him emotionally and get him through his exams...'

I know this one so well. Not this exact story, but the one where the abuse is real, the trauma is evident, but there is little to be done other than supporting the child, encouraging them to look to the future when they can escape, when the power dynamic will shift. If they are lucky, the Great Escape from hostile parents can happen in their late teens. For others it will take longer to financially extract themselves from the family home.

For so many kids, school is their safe place, which is why it is vital that every person working in a school setting, from the senior leadership team down to the cleaners, is aware that there will be many kids in their care in this position (I can see Vaishali in my mind, saying 'Dream on, Jane...'). The problem with the Great Escape is that not all fare equally. Some young people revel and thrive in the newfound freedom which escaping their parents gives them, while others are forever caught at the checkpoint, trapped inside disturbed minds, true freedom denied because the damage done in those early years was too severe.

Daniel continues, 'He's very clear he doesn't want me telling anyone. I'm troubled by this, but even though he's clearly traumatised – as I said, he's hypervigilant, and he freezes a lot – there is a strength in him that I'm hoping will get him through. And he has a good friendship group.'

Jude nods and says, 'And what about *you* Daniel? You started today by talking about God. Why is this aspect of Paul's story the one that troubles you most?'

Daniel cocks his head and looks up towards the ceiling, thinking. He takes his time, longer than would be acceptable in most other peer groups. But we are therapists. We all had different training, but we have all learned to sit in silence.

As a baby counsellor, your therapeutic education will most likely commence with yourself, two facilitators and the other new recruits sitting in a circle for thirty whole minutes, with no agenda and no requirement or expectation that anyone speaks. At first it can feel almost unbearable: the exposure, the awkwardness, the where-to-look embarrassment of it. But over time you get good at silence, you see the point in it, you might even say something, or respond to something someone else has said. I have sat in circles where no one has uttered a word for the full half hour.

Leaving silence in the therapy room gives space for the client. Learning to resist the urge to fill it, or not even feel the urge in the first place, is an art in itself. In my experience, most teenagers find silence excruciating. And then there are some who use it well. It's a matter of gauging what the individual can tolerate.

Every now and then I meet a young person who needs the time and space that moments of silence in the therapeutic encounter gives them. So I am always attempting to offer a silence long enough for them to use, but not so long that it makes them feel uncomfortable. I'm much better at this than I used to be, but I still mess it up sometimes. Now and then I find myself wondering when I'll be a proper therapist. It's like that other question – when will I be a proper adult? Then I remember Carl Rogers, who reckoned that we are always in the process of *becoming,* right up until the day we die.

Eventually Daniel says, 'That's a very good question. And I'm not sure what the answer is. I think I've seen so much crap parenting. So many parents projecting anger or failure or fear into their kids. So much inter-generational trauma getting handed down. So much emotional abuse. But it's only in the past year that I've seen God used as a get-out tactic, like with Paul's parents, or as an excuse.

I've worked with two clients who have family members who've basically told them that in the eyes of the Lord it's okay if they hit them because they've *been bad,* and that it is appropriate punishment. I guess I thought – naively as it turns out – that what with society becoming so secular, and most parents now being Gen X or younger, we wouldn't have these problems.'

We sit in silence until Niamh says, 'I find that very upsetting to hear. I'm a Christian – I mean, not practising, but I still believe – and I know that, throughout history, atrocities have been carried out in the name of religion, but I don't usually hear of it happening like this, like what is happening to Paul. These people, his parents, they are not Christians.'

'Thank you, Niamh,' says Jude.

'I've got a kid,' says Raya, 'who goes to her local church youth group: Christian, but I don't know what denomination. She's lovely; very sweet girl. She's maybe not bullied as such at school – more that kind of subtle bullying where no one really says or does anything overtly, but she's treated as a bit of a joke by all the other kids. She struggles with the academic side of things and gets Support For Learning, which is good because they've got a decent SFL department at her school, and she can hang out there at breaks. Her mother died years ago, and her father is pretty neglectful. She's very overweight, her clothes are often dirty, and she smells. I mean, so bad I have to open the windows in my room.

'Anyway, like I said, she goes to the youth group at the local church, and frankly, I don't know what her life would be if she didn't. When she talks about her time there, and the people, she glows. She goes twice a week. Once after school, and on a Saturday. They go on trips and do activities and things. They sound incredibly kind. They did a play, and she was really involved – she loved it. So, you know, I'm a complete atheist but I can see the good these people are doing.'

Niamh, looking more and more upset, says to Raya, 'You make it sound like they are the exception to the rule, like an oddity.'

Raya, taken aback, says, 'I didn't mean it to sound like that at all...'

'Well, it did,' says Niamh.

I like Niamh, but she's got a very sensitive streak and can't seem to give others the benefit of the doubt.

'I'm sorry if I offended you...' Raya says, slightly more forcefully and not sounding very sorry at all.

Niamh snaps, 'You didn't offend me; what you were implying was offensive. There's a difference.'

Real tension in the circle. Common when I was in training – great for waking you up if you've got a bit sleepy – but not so much in this supervision group. We are a bunch of lefties who are generally somewhere on the same page.

Raya says, 'I don't think I was implying anything. I think you've imagined something that isn't there, and I'm interested in why that might be...'

Great, a bit of passive aggression cloaked as therapeutic enquiry.

'Well, I don't think that's true,' says Niamh. 'I think you're being dishonest and trying to make this about me when really you were implying that these "good Christians" you have found are an anomaly.'

'That I've found? I didn't find them anywhere…'

Elaine looks appalled. Daniel looks like he's thoroughly enjoying himself, as am I.

Jude interjects, 'I'm wondering if we've gone a bit off-topic, perhaps even mirroring Paul's parents a bit…'

That's a tenuous connection worthy of a psychodynamic purist like Estelle, less likely to be said by Jude, who couldn't be more person-centred if she tried. Any port in a storm.

Time to save them from drowning.

'I've got something to say on this subject,' I say. 'But it's not a subject I find particularly easy to talk about, so, uh…'

'That's okay, Jane,' says Jude. 'Take your time.'

Where do I start?

Aiden. I start with Aiden.

'I don't know why I find it hard to talk about this client. I mean, he's fine now, at least as far as I know. Off living his best life…'

Niamh and Raya have stopped glaring at each other and turned their attention to me.

'His name is Aiden. He was sixteen when he started coming to see me. No one could figure out what was wrong with him. He was coming into school but couldn't seem to concentrate in classes and wasn't doing any work. When teachers asked him why he hadn't handed in work, he'd be rude to them or burst into tears. His Head of Year spoke to his mum who said nothing was happening at home and blamed his hormones. When he came to my room for the first time, he looked at me with such a hostile expression, like he thought I might be dangerous, and I realised he was completely traumatised, but no one knew why.'

'Tricky,' says Niamh.

'I tried to put him at ease. I made it very clear that he could leave any time he wanted, and I was encouraged by the fact of him not scarpering. But he simply would not respond to anything I said. He wasn't interested in trying my thing-bowl, or—'

'Your what bowl?' asks Daniel.

'My thing-bowl. It's a bowl of random stuff – toys and feathers and what-not. Little objects. You ask the client who's struggling to talk to pick something to represent themselves, then you ask them to pick for family members. It's a way of opening things up. You can ask them why they picked the objects they did, get them to place them on the table, then talk about why they've placed them where they have.'

'I'm going to try that. Thanks, hen...'

Daniel appropriates the Scots language intentionally, to annoy, and it works. It makes me cringe, but it also makes me laugh, so he gets away with it. I'm guessing he does the same with the kids in the school where he runs therapy groups. Collective mortification at the English counsellor embarrassing himself would give the anxious, self-conscious group members an immediate route to identification with one another. In my mind's eye I see a circle of wincing kids and Daniel feigning obliviousness.

Now he reaches for one of the three ballpoints which

sit officiously in the breast pocket of his shirt, their red, blue and black lids gripping the perfectly pressed hem in an orderly fashion, before using it to write something on his left hand – 'thing-bowl', presumably.

He should run summer camps.

He probably does run summer camps.

I continue, 'The younger ones especially like a thing-bowl… Anyway, Aiden wasn't up for any of it, but he didn't leave either.'

'What did you do?' Elaine asks, speaking for the first time since her tea poll.

'Funnily enough, considering your question earlier, I told him I was going to make myself a coffee and asked him if he wanted one. He refused. I wanted to leave him alone so he could get a sense of the space without me in it, look at the posters on the walls.

'When I got back, he was standing by the window looking out at the sky. I remember thinking he looked older than he was because he was so tall. Then I saw he was crying. It wasn't until later that I realised he must have seen the little transparent LGBTQI+ rainbow sticker on my window.'

I stop to take a drink of water. The others wait for me to continue. Beyond the glass of the round window, a gold and pink sunset scorches the sky. As far as I know, Aiden's Great Escape is going strong, and goosebumps prickle my arms thinking of him.

'So, he started talking. His family was Christian fundamentalist. He knew when he was growing up that sex outside marriage was wrong, as was contraception, and the big one – homosexuality was the worst sin of all. That gay people would be going to hell. This threat felt very real. In Aiden's family heaven and hell were real places, and the idea of going to hell was extremely frightening.

'Aiden's upbringing sounded very traditional and very rigid. Women stay at home and look after kids; men go out to work. Girls should be caring, boys ambitious etc etc. Narrowly defined gender roles. As a child, Aiden had always felt like he didn't fit, but couldn't explain why. Aiden's mother sounded very loving, and he clearly felt loved by his father also, but it always felt dependent on Aiden being a certain way, a way which he was finding it harder and harder to be.'

'His parents' conditions of worth,' says Niamh. '*We will love you as long as you fit the definition of who we want you to be.*'

'Exactly. And maybe all parents, unconsciously or otherwise, give their kids conditions of worth – I don't know… Some are definitely more aware of trying *not* to do it. But Aiden's parents… He always said they were good people at heart.

'When he hit puberty, he started to feel very low. It sounded like he was having episodes of depression. His father encouraged him to go to a church youth group. Aiden was pretty resistant at first, but he found that when he went to one, it was a small group – only three other young people and a facilitator – and they were actually really friendly and good to talk to.

'The young people were encouraged to bring a

problem each week, and then the group would pray together. Aiden said at first, he wasn't sure about this. He worried that what he said wouldn't remain confidential, so he brought little problems like not getting into the first team at school football. But after a while he grew to feel very comfortable in the group. The facilitator was a man named Magnus, who had seemed very kind. Aiden felt it was easier to talk to Magnus than his own father.'

Daniel shudders. I think he knows where this is going. Why did I start talking about this? I normally entrust this one to Estelle. I feel like I've committed to telling a story I may not be able to finish. What happened with Aiden was big and shocking, and I'm clearly not done processing it.

But I've started now.

'Bolstered by the love and care he felt from the group, and from this guy Magnus, one day Aiden decided to bring his big secret, that he was gay. It felt risky, but he had faith he would be accepted after listening to Magnus's rhetoric, week in, week out, about how everyone was welcome and everyone was safe. He told me about coming out to the group, his first experience of doing that anywhere.

'Just imagine – the first time he ever told anyone, after years of struggling with a feeling that he didn't fit, that he was bad, sinful – the courage that must have taken. The other three young people looked to Magnus to see how he would respond. Aiden said the relief was overwhelming when Magnus thanked him for telling them and told him he was very brave for having done so. The prayer, led by Magnus, was that God would help Aiden *find his way,* and Aiden remembers feeling utterly elated. The next week he went, Magnus asked him to start coming to "counselling sessions" with him, and Aiden felt so lucky to have this adult in his life who was willing to talk though all these feelings he'd kept bottled up inside for so long, who would help him become the person he wanted to be.'

Raya says, 'But it wasn't counselling…'

'No, and it lasted nearly three years.'

Elaine asks, 'So what happened?'

'Well, Magnus pretended to be on his side, told Aiden he understood that he felt this way, but that he was really worried about him, and that he was going to help him. Magnus was very manipulative, very abusive. He told Aiden that the only life out there for queer people was one of shame, loneliness and destitution.

'When Aiden talked about queer people he'd seen at school or on TV or social media who seemed to be doing well, Magnus told him they were lying, and that it was all part of a huge conspiracy to harm young people, a conspiracy led by the devil himself, to lure them into leading lifestyles which would secure their place in hell. And if this sounds ridiculous, remember Aiden had grown up in a family where this stuff was as real as anything they might see on the news. Magnus told Aiden that the Lord had brought him to Magnus, so that Magnus might save him.'

Elaine looks appalled, like somebody's just slapped

her. Am I a total freak for deriving pleasure from her reaction?

'These sessions were torturous for Aiden, but he still believed Magnus was helping him. When Magnus told him he must have been abused physically or sexually, which was why he thought he was gay, Aiden knew this wasn't true and said so. But Magnus insisted something must have happened, even if Aiden couldn't remember it. And when Aiden insisted nothing like that had occurred, Magnus just glossed over this fact and moved on.

'Magnus convinced Aiden that his ideas and feelings about his sexuality were sinful, but that he could change them through prayer, which they would do together and in the prayer group. Magnus was very clever, in that during prayer group time with the other young people, he never explicitly referred to Aiden's sexuality as sinful, just asked that they pray he would *find his way*. He must have known how the rest of the group might view what he was doing, so he didn't want them to witness it.'

Niamh shakes her head, 'How awful…'

'Yes, and when it became clear that Aiden could not change who he was, and that the prayer was not working, Magnus changed tack. He said Aiden must suppress the feelings and live his life in obedience to God – i.e. root his identity in Jesus and live in accordance with the beliefs his parents taught him.'

'Christ,' says Raya, shooting a guilty look at Niamh, who ignores her.

'Quite. So, you can imagine how that played out.

248

Aiden was broken by the abuse. Totally traumatised, and as he told me later, frequently suicidal. Someone referred him, and he managed to open up to me.'

'What happened?' asks Daniel.

'It was Child Protection. Completely blew up. What Magnus was doing was clearly emotional abuse. The police and social services got involved and his parents were told. It was awful for him. The parents were hugely ambivalent. I think if it had just been his mum, things might have been different... But Aiden just couldn't stay at home any longer.

'The school was good: they got in touch with the Rock Trust, who gave him a place to stay, and somehow, against all odds, he managed to pass his exams. I think maybe studying was a distraction for him, an escape. Doesn't usually work that way with traumatised kids, as we all know.'

Though it did for me.

Fuck a duck, I'm dissolving. Just get the last bit out...

'He ended up going to college in another city. I got a note from him a few months ago saying he was doing well and had made friends. It didn't say much more than that, but it did say "I'm finally getting to be me".'

I'm crying. I don't like crying in public. I take another drink of water. Fuck me; must compose myself.

The group sighs, shifts in their seats.

Raya gets up and gives me a tissue, places her warm hand on my knee.

Breathe.

In through the nose for four, out through the mouth

for six.

And I'm okay again, back in the room.

'What happened to Magnus?' asks Daniel.

'Em, not much. There were no witnesses to their "counselling sessions", so it was Magnus' word against Aiden's. Magnus was arrested but the charges were eventually dropped. He argued that Aiden was a very confused boy who was having a crisis of identity and that he was providing gentle pastoral support, helping him explore his feelings and find his way back to God. He was very good at obfuscating. He didn't outright deny that he was trying to eradicate the gay from Aiden, but he couched it in terms that were very vague. He talked about his guidance being reparative, and claimed that Aiden had *wanted* help to – what was it he said? Ah, yes, he said Aiden had asked him to help him *transform*. As far as I know, he got kicked out of that particular church. But he could very well be doing the same thing somewhere else.'

Saying all this out loud, for the first time in a good while, was perhaps not such a good idea. I did it on impulse, because it tied into what Daniel was saying – I should have given consideration to the consequences. I'm long-acquainted with the anger that simmers away inside me; I know how to keep it at bay. But lately it's been rising, spitting black and bitter as bitumen. This time for Magnus Mackay. For the people who didn't fight hard enough to get him locked up.

'Well…' says Jude. 'What a terrible, terrible story that was. Although it's cheering to hear Aiden is doing so well despite all he went through... Now, shall we check in? How are we all doing after listening to Jane? Elaine, how are you doing, this being your first time here...?'

Elaine shakes her head, says, 'I, I really haven't heard of that sort of thing...'

I genuinely want to hear what Elaine makes of it, but she just sort of gives up, purses her lips together and retreats.

'Okay. Raya, how about you?'

'Yeah,' says Raya. 'I've heard about this before, but maybe done more subtly, and without the religious aspect. Kids coming out to their families and being told they will end up as prostitutes, or that they will never get to have children. Pressure put on them to "change their minds", when of course they can't and shouldn't have to. It's toxic stuff, and I feel for Jane. She told us about Aiden, but she said very little about her part in it all.'

Raya now speaks directly to me. 'What you had to do after Aiden's disclosure, the report you wrote, all the other agencies getting involved, trying to wade through a broken system... The disappointment you must have felt when the charges were dropped, and you knew there would be no justice for Aiden. I can only imagine how that must have felt. Fighting for Aiden and offering him the containment he so desperately needed... I've been in a very similar situation – different story but similar outcome, and I know how hard it can be. I want you to know that I heard what you *didn't* say, as well as what you did.'

'Thank you, Raya,' I say, and I mean it. 'But I did a lot of supervision at the time, and I think I'm more at peace with it now.'

Liar.

Jude says, 'Niamh, what about you?'

Niamh shifts in her chair and says, 'Yeah, dreadful story. I mean this guy, if not put in prison, should at least never get to work with kids again. What a monster. And though I disagree completely with what he did, it brought up something I've been thinking about recently...'

'Okay...' says Jude.

Niamh continues, 'Jane said that Magnus told Aiden that everyone who identifies as queer has been sexually or physically abused as a child...'

'She did, yes...'

'And of course, this idea is completely wrong, absolutely abhorrent. But it made me think of something my partner, Kay, who as most of you know is a psychologist, has been talking about recently.'

She looks nervous, how big a bomb is she about to drop?

'So, Kay works in a clinic for victims of domestic abuse and sexual violence. She says that every week, more social workers are approaching her to talk about the traumatised kids they are working with. Kids who have been through unimaginable abuse, and are suddenly identifying as trans. The social workers are anxious because on-high are telling them that they should just affirm the kids without exploring the trauma which is clearly behind it.'

BOOM!

Daniel says, 'Sorry Niamh, I don't quite get what you are saying…?'

'I'm saying that I think there could be a link between sexual abuse and trans identity. Not all trans identity, obviously, but some. I mean Kay is hearing about this happening so regularly… Can it really just be coincidence? And remember, Kay is on the board for a trans rights group. She has always fought to protect trans rights because she knows they are one of the most discriminated groups in society. She's not saying that all trans people have been abused, but she *is* saying she thinks that for some there is a link to abuse. I know this all sounds pretty controversial…'

Raya tucks a stray hair behind her ear. 'It really does. I mean you say this, but what *is* the link?'

Niamh takes up this question with enthusiasm, clearly happy to have a platform from which to try out her theory. 'Well, we all know that kids who are sexually abused can become sexualised far too young, which can lead to all sorts of horrible problems for them, such as being sexually inappropriate with other kids, dangerously promiscuous as teens and adults etc. And people who have been abused as kids often dissociate from their bodies, often hate their bodies, as, in their eyes, their bodies are the objects which caused the abuse. Most kids are sexually abused by men. Victims try to get as far away as possible from the body that caused the abuse, the body that the man fixated on.

'You can see why children would reject their own genitalia and bodies so completely. They do this by self-harm, bathing in the dark, drink/drugs, risky sex, avoiding intimacy, etc etc. Rejecting your gender, the gender that was so attractive to the abuser, particularly in a climate that is more open to people changing their gender than ever before, makes complete sense to me.'

I think of Kass, who doesn't fit Niamh's argument. She hated her body for a long time, for the reasons Niamh gives. But she didn't reject her gender, or her sex, or whatever it is. I get so confused with this stuff. George doesn't fit the argument either.

Fuck it.

'I'll buy that,' I say, '…at least for some.'

'Well I won't,' says Daniel.

'Me neither,' says Raya. 'I think it's a leap – and a dangerous one. Jane's just explained how this is a key argument in conversion therapy, yet still you are making it…'

'Just because it's used in conversion therapy doesn't mean that there isn't some truth to it,' says Niamh.'It's complicated.'

'And Kay saying she is seeing this *more and more* is just anecdotal. It's hardly an evidence-based study,' says Daniel.

'No, that's true, it's not,' I agree. 'Niamh, I will accept that it is possible that some trans people are trans because of rejecting their gender as a result of being sexually abused. What I want to know, is why are those trans kids who *haven't* been abused rejecting *their* bodies?'

Raya says, 'Why are you making being trans all about people rejecting their bodies? It's not just about their bodies, it's about the gender they were assigned at birth being wrong. Why should they be made to live with the wrong gender?'

Niamh counters, 'But we aren't assigned genders, we are born a particular sex. Gender's just a made-up thing… It just means stereotypes.'

'I don't know how you can say that,' says Raya. 'You are a woman who has, I'm sure been discriminated against because of your gender. How can you say it's made-up?'

'I'm discriminated against because of my sex.' Niamh's eyes flash.

Raya says, 'We'll agree to disagree on that point, Niamh. I just think it's hard enough being trans in this world, without people saying you must have been abused… I think it's dangerous…'

'I think it's dangerous to deny the reality of some young people because their experiences don't fit with the larger narrative…' says Niamh.

Aaaaargh! I can't stand any more.

'Well, *I* think it's all just more evidence for Karen Horney's theory of The Flight from Womanhood being just as relevant today as it was when she wrote it in 1926,' I say cheerily. I like to mention Karen Horney's work at least once in every supervision session; we all have favourite theorists and, despite what Kass calls my love of old dead men, Horney's mine.

Niamh and Raya both glare at me.

Daniel sings, 'Jane and Karen up a tree, K-I-S-S-I-N-G', which is probably the right thing to do because Niamh bursts out laughing and Raya smiles.

Elaine, however, looks utterly horrified, so I ask her if she's okay.

'I just… None of this stuff you've all been talking about bears any similarity to my practice. I work at a very exclusive school. In fairness I haven't been qualified for long, but even so, I don't think I'm likely to be dealing with cases of abuse, or any of the things you have all been talking about…'

'Why not?' asks Daniel.

'Because…because the children come from good homes…'

HAAAAAAAAAAAAAAAA!

'Gosh, well…' says Raya. 'Thank goodness for that!'

Jude shoots Raya a warning look.

Niamh says, 'Elaine, I have worked in schools up and down the land for the best part of thirty years. I have worked in semi-condemned dumps in the middle of massively deprived housing schemes, and I have worked in places that look like fairy-tale palaces with former prime ministers among their alumni. What I've learned from my time in them, is that money and privilege do not guarantee "good homes". They do not inoculate children from abuse and neglect. You will learn this too – if you are open enough to listen.'

If you are open enough to come back, which I think we all know you won't.

2002

Cam, applying for a job that requires a varied portfolio, insists his university portrait shots are shit and can't be used. So we are in the studio he has hired from his old college for the afternoon. I've been in photographic studios before but never one quite like this. It's a large space with a high ceiling and, from where I'm standing by the door, having just arrived, appears to be missing a far wall, as the room rather disconcertingly disappears into white nothingness.

Everything in here is black, white or silver. An enormous domed lamp is suspended from the ceiling by a sturdy zigzag arm. Other smaller umbrellas on stands are dotted around the room, alongside huge white blocks and towering partition sections which look like they are made of concrete but can't be, because Cam is moving them around the room with ease. Opposite the disappearing wall is a sheet of black fabric on a frame which I assume is used to provide a dark backdrop. Two of the high black partitions form walls on either side, and there is a stool in the middle, waiting for someone to sit in the darkness within.

Cam sets up his laptop on a little table while I investigate the white space with the disappearing wall. I see now that the effect is created by the chalky white floor. Rather than ending at a sharp right angle against the wall, it curves upwards in one smooth swoop to meet it. It's a space that makes me feel playful and self-conscious at the same time – just me in all this brightness.

'Jay, can you hop on that stool for me?' Cam says, using his pet name for me.

I climb onto the stool while he sets up his camera on a tripod in front of me and pulls across the enormous light from the ceiling. I'm blinded by a flash I wasn't expecting, and then another and another.

'Have we started? I didn't realise we'd started.'

'Yeah, I'm just making adjustments…'

I don't know how to sit or what to do with my face and feel increasingly uncomfortable.

Cam laughs. 'Relax, woman. You've gone all stiff and mental-looking.'

'I don't know how…'

'Just think about something else. Here, tell me how it feels to have finished art college with a big fat 2:1…'

'Terrifying – it feels terrifying!'

'Why's that then?' Cam asks, moving between laptop and camera, giving just enough of his attention to the conversation to keep it going and no more, while flashing away.

'Because now I have to find a job.'

'You've had jobs before; you've got a job.'

'I don't mean bartending. You know what I mean – a proper job in fashion.'

'What's so scary about that? They'll be falling over themselves to hire you...'

'No, they won't. There are a zillion graduates like me going after a handful of jobs and I've not even started looking, not really.'

Cam looks up from what he's doing. 'Seriously? I didn't realise you were so worried about this.'

'Well, I suppose I was just so focused on getting it done – I hadn't really considered what happens after. Which in hindsight was stupid of me, because lots of the others did. Did I tell you Elsa already has an internship on a magazine? It's just a local monthly guide to the city, but she's doing the fashion section – isn't that amazing?'

Cam leaves the camera and comes over to me, holds my face in his hands. 'You need to stop worrying about what other people are doing. You'll find the right fit for you, even if it takes time – so try not to stress so much about it. It'll all come good.'

He leans down and kisses me. It is meant to be a reassuring, comforting kiss, but as so often happens with us, even after four years, the most innocently intended moments of physical intimacy act like a touchpaper and we end up fucking in inappropriate places. But I draw the line at doing it against a dazzling white backdrop in a room with an unlocked door in a busy college.

'No, not here,' I say, drawing back. Cam makes a face, gives me an *oh go on* tilt of the head, the green in his eyes now more prominent than the brown. He is less boyish than when we first met; recently I've been catching myself seeing the man he is becoming.

Cam is kind – I mean, really kind. He's forever thinking of ways to make me happy. I don't mean big, showy gestures, but little things like screwing a hook in the wall and filling it with hairbands he's bought me because I'm always complaining I can never find any. Like when I find him scrubbing the grass stains out my jeans after I've been helping Angie in the community garden she runs. Like, on my bad days, gently stroking his fingertips up and down my back, along my arm and up my neck for as long as it takes until I fall asleep. Like holding me close and telling me everything will be okay when I wake up screaming in the night, my heart hammering in my chest because I'm sixteen again and have lost everything, begging the shoddy social worker to let me stay in my home (which they eventually did).

And these times are not infrequent. Cam is stalwart, devoted, unwavering. He is good and funny, handsome with a long, lean body that always smells good. He loves and is loved by my friends, and I adore him. But I'm not going to have sex with him right here, right now.

'No. Behave yourself,' I say firmly.

Cam, sighing in capitulation, says, 'At least you don't

seem as anxious now. It wasn't quite the vibe I'm going for.'

'What *is* the vibe you are going for?'

'I dunno... Now I'm thinking sexy girl next door...'

'Ah okay, shall I take my top off?'

'Really?'

'No.'

'Right, sorry. Well, how would you like to be photographed? How would you like to look?'

How do I want to look? How do I want people to see me? I feel like I don't even know what the words mean.

'I suppose I just want to look normal...but also extraordinary...'

'Okay then; easy brief,' Cam mutters, shaking his head.

'Well, I don't know! It's weird all this...' I say, making exaggerated gestures to all the kit around me, the crazy walls and odd spaces.

Cam, who has been snapping away, now looks at the images he has just taken and laughs. I jump up from the stool and go over to the laptop. I look like a loon.

'Right. Delete them, and sort this out. It's your job to make me look good, not the other way around.'

'Okay, okay, don't sulk. Sulking's on a par with stressing. But you're right, my darling, it is my job, not yours. Let's talk about something cheerful – how about our plans for the future now we've both graduated?'

Cam likes a plan, and he's the sort of person who always knows what he wants, but we've never really talked about long-term plans, as I always said I needed to get my degree first – which at times has seemed the most unlikely of outcomes – and making plans might have jinxed me getting it.

Now there is nothing preventing us from discussing our future together, other than my fear of life changing. I like the way things are right now, I've no wish for any of it to be in any way different. I suppose he might suggest moving in together. Could I do that? Could I live with him? I mean we practically live with each other as it is – ever since he came home from Brighton, he's stayed between his parents' home and my house. But I like when he goes; I give the place a deep clean, get rid of all those toxins we both bring in from outside. What if he wants a pet – a cat or a dog? I couldn't cope.

Cam places a white block about a metre long at my feet and hands me an enormous silver disc which he instructs me to hold just above my thighs in order to reflect light up and onto my face. He returns to the camera and directs me this way and that, turning my body to the right and then left, tilting my face up, then to the side, while he snaps away, and I try not to blink at the flash.

'Okay then,' I say. 'You first. Future plans…'

But Cam is back at the laptop.

'Come look, Jay. Some of these are great. I gotta say it's fairly easy to take a good shot with you as my subject.'

I join him in front of the screen. Some of the images are awful – I really don't know why he thinks it a good idea to get me to talk while he's taking pictures – but there are a few that are actually pretty good.

'Now, over here,' he says, gesturing to the dark space with the black backdrop. I do as he says and perch on the stool between the black partitions while Cam sets up lights that, rather than being bright, give a much more muted, goldish glow.

'Lift your chin a little and look over here,' he says waving his left hand in the air. 'The way I think of it…' he says, peering down into the camera on the tripod, 'You know how you have an idea in your mind of your plans for the next few weeks, and also a kind of structured picture of your past? Do you know what I'm talking about or is that just me?'

'A kind of mental representation, you mean…'

He nods. 'That's exactly right. So, I have something similar for the rest of my life. I know that sounds a bit full-on, and anything could happen. I'm not saying it's detailed, but there are some elements of it that are kind of fundamental to what I want. It's hopeful. What I *hope* will happen, I suppose.'

'Okay…What is it you hope will happen?'

'I *hope* I will have a brilliant career, like Don McCullin.'

'Or Lee Miller…'

'Or Lee Miller. I want my work to be important to people, to be instrumental in holding the bad guys to account. I want to go everywhere, see everything – I want to have adventures.'

He sounds like he's ten years old. I think of the stacks of books around his room in his family home: John Buchan, Joseph Conrad, Patrick O'Brian, George

MacDonald Fraser and Rudyard Kipling. Not a Brontë in sight. And of the scouting uniform his mum brought out to show me one Christmas when she had all her children back together for the holidays. The teal green shirt covered in badges, his sisters gently mocking him, his father smiling absent-mindedly before returning to his book.

I have been welcomed into Cam's family like some wondrous curiosity. I can sense how intrigued they are by my past, and how they are prevented by their own kindness from asking the questions they long to ask. Cam's mum spent years teaching in India and cooks the most delicious dahls and curries which, on the first few occasions I went there, she would watch me eat as they all chattered around me. As an only child of parents who liked to eat out – a fish supper in a chippy, or some fancy new restaurant in town on pay-day – or else cobbled together teas from whatever was in the fridge, eaten in front of the television, I was unused to these kinds of big noisy family dinners where everyone takes turns to pontificate on whatever issue they have buzzing in their bonnet. Everyone except me. I've known Cam's family for four years, but never quite managed to feel comfortable with these clever, funny, intellectual people, even though I wish with my whole heart that I did.

'…But obviously, I want all that while being with you,' Cam continues. 'I know photojournalism means working away, but you will be busy in your career too, and I think that while we are young that could work pretty well. We can get a place together here, or I suppose it might be in some other city, depending on where you get a job... London is probably the best option for both of us.'

He frowns suddenly. Something has occurred to him that he hadn't considered. 'But we'd have to come back here, to Scotland, to have our kids, to be near Mum and stuff. I'd like our children to have the same sort of upbringing I did. And I know you'd want to be near your friends when they're all having kids too. I guess Neil will probably stay in London, but the rest of them will return here, don't you think? Jessie definitely will – she's always desperate to get back to you. And Leila and Ross have never left... Anyway, yeah, we build our careers, always coming back together, and then in a few years – late twenties, early thirties time, we'll start a family. We'd share the childcare of course – you know I'd never expect you to give up your job or anything. Who knows, we might both jack in our jobs and take the kids off somewhere else for a couple of years before they have to start school – we could go live on an island or take them travelling... We'll have to settle down a bit while they're at school, but no living in the suburbs or any of that crap... and when they leave home, we'll be free again, at least until we have grandkids...'

He says it all without looking up from the lens.

Snap. Snap. Snap.

I wonder what the images will show. There is a scene in the disaster movie *The Day After Tomorrow,* where the pilots of a helicopter flying over Scotland realise the temperature has dropped so low that the fuel lines have started to freeze. The camera travels across the interior of the helicopter, capturing the inconceivably rapid spread of ice crystals across the windscreen and along power cables as everything that moments before served a purpose, that had been designed to support life and progress, crystallises into entropy almost instantaneously. The only pilot to survive the inevitable crash claws open the door, and we witness the last seconds of life in his face before the frost metastasises up his throat and over his features. It is not ice, or even fear, that freezes my interior in this moment – it is sudden and devastating disillusionment. The scales have fallen from my eyes, and I know that I cannot have Cam for much longer.

Autumn Term
Late September – mid-December

Kass Session 12

I watch Kass dart across the quad – almost running. The wind, rippling across the horse chestnuts in the car park, plucks leaves from their branches and lifts them high. From my window, I watch them dance across the sky, carried along air currents, before they drop to the quad, where they end up by the maths stair corner, which on breezy days hosts its own miniature tornado, swirling leaves, crisp packets and sweetie wrappers in its invisible vortex.

Kass enters quickly, sits down in my chair as usual. She seems less concerned now about being seen here, but she is still cautious. I've been looking forward to seeing her, hopeful that the progress she's made in the last month has continued. Something really does seem to have shifted, and I know I mustn't get ahead of myself but...

I smile at Kass, at the blue sky through the window behind her – an advantage of temporarily giving up my chair. Sunlight slants into the room, striking my *Hoya*. Its small, pointed leaves are doubled by the sun in black and grey shadows on the white wall under the shelf where it sits.

'It's good to see you, Kass.'

'Good to see you too.'

She does a double-take, says, 'Are you wearing

contour?'

'No.'

'Right, you just look... I just never noticed how great your cheekbones were before.'

I can see that by the end of the sentence she has realised I've lost weight. But she is not, thankfully, one of those women who feels the need to point it out, mistakenly believing they are either giving a compliment or imparting information of which the other woman is unaccountably unaware.

What else can she see? Is Kass eagle-eyed like my mother, who would comment if I had moved the parting in my hair by a centimetre? *Hair looks good, love!*

I may not be wearing contour, but would she notice the concealer I've rubbed over the blueish shadows which recently emerged from the inner corners of my eyes? Which, millimetre by millimetre are spreading faster, travelling more quickly across my skin than any of those other signifiers of aging which, though not particularly welcome, are less unexpected, like the frown lines on my forehead that don't disappear when I stop scowling, or the barely-there-but-only-gonna-get-worse chicken-skin texture the backs of my hands have taken on. The lines, the texture, these things are subtle – the shuffle and shift as my youth slowly side-steps around me, taking up its place behind me, the first whispered suggestions that I have irrevocably moved into new territory, that I am no longer young. The shadows are not like that. The shadows are something else, something fast and potent.

'Thanks,' I say, and leave it at that. This is not the time to be thinking about the shadows round my eyes, or why my bra is gaping and my jeans no longer fit.

Kass basks in silence the way other people do in sunshine. So that's generally how we start.

After a minute or so, she speaks.

'I wanted to tell you about bedtime – Lewis's bedtime.'

'Okay…'

Now she smiles, looks vaguely embarrassed.

'When it's time for lights out, after stories and stuff, Lewis lies on his back and I curl into him, so my face is against his peachy cheeks, and I just kind of inhale him… His warm neck, you know? He's got like this white-golden down on the sides of his cheeks that is just so… And then, every time, he throws his arm back like this,' she lifts her left arm and imitates hooking it around the head of someone next to her, '…and curls it around my head, finding my hair, then he kneads it like a kitten, you know the way they do? Like a *cub*. It's the sweetest thing…'

She puts her fingers to her lips, stares at the carpet.

'I don't move a muscle,' she continues, 'even if I'm dog-tired and have loads to do in the house before I can get to bed myself, I will stay there until he falls asleep and stops kneading. It's my favourite part of the day.'

She shakes her head, as if she can't get over how great it is.

'It's a tenderness that's bearable…'

'Not just bearable. I actually want it, I crave it. It's like nutrients going into me – it nourishes me, makes me feel like I'm a real person. There's nothing in it except goodness.'

I nod. Kass's long brown hair is perfectly GHD straight and slippery-looking, as it has been for the last four or five sessions: a good sign. I imagine a small hand running through it, twirling it around little fingers, scrunching to a marvellous tangle.

Often she describes this little boy, this unplanned miracle, as the thing that saved her. The thing that brings her joy. New mums are advised to sleep when their newborns are sleeping, but some do the dishes, or watch daytime TV, or hang the washing. Kass sat and watched Lewis sleep. The thought of anyone harming Lewis preoccupies her, gives her nightmares. She once came to her session with a red raised lump on her forehead where she had headbutted the wall next to her bed, dreaming it was some man, who may or may not have been her brother, come to take her child.

She looks like she's gathering her thoughts.

'I thought it might get easier the older he got…'

'But it doesn't?' I ask, not sure I know what she's referring to, but going with it.

'No. Well, maybe a little, but no, not really. I'm wondering if it might stop when he's fourteen.'

Ah, I get it now. For every parent who feels the stop-you-in-your-tracks rush of love for their child, seeing them emerge, smaller than you remember them, into the playground with their teacher and class at pick-up time, scanning the crowd for you, the relief on their faces when they find yours, or in those moments they show kindness to another child, or when you watch them laugh uncontrollably at some slapstick humour, or just sometimes when they turn and look at you with bright faces – that feeling is always counterpointed by the pain of their vulnerability, and how devastation lurks around every corner.

Or so they tell me. Often in the rawest and most visceral of terms. This is when my empathy is at its most painful.

The bittersweetness of loving a child lays us bare and exposed to the possibility of unimaginable pain. Kass feels all this, but for her there is another layer.

'Because fourteen is how old you were when it stopped?'

'Yes... Lewis is only six. Looks just like I did. Both got light brown hair.'

'It's good that he looks like you, but also hard...'

She gazes at the tissue box, doesn't speak for what feels like forever, then says, 'It's very good that he looks like me. To be fair I don't remember what his biological thingummy looked like, but I doubt he was anything to write home about. But maybe it would be better if Lewis didn't look like me, because then it wouldn't make me think so much of myself at that age. I've blocked out that kid-me for so long...'

I wait to see if she will say any more.

She doesn't. So I say, 'But could remembering that, and seeing this – this almost mini-you, help you to deal with the shame, and the times you think you could have done something? Help you to not just understand, but really internalise – to know in your bones – how defenceless, how innocent you were?'

Kass exhales sharply through her nostrils.

'Yeah maybe, if things worked how they do in the self-help books. If I could get over the feeling of horror I have when I look at my son.'

'It's not all the time, though. And it's not your fault.'

'You don't think anything's my fault,' she remarks.

'Because it's not.'

She gives a half-smile and shakes her head. She started this session, if not happy, with a good thing – describing a tenderness she can cope with – but now we are back to pain, and I'm wondering did I direct her away from the good too quickly?

'I've not been having a good week,' she says, and looks directly at me.

By this she means that living inside her body has, this week, been unbearable. I nod in acknowledgement that I have heard her, and to prompt her to continue. I will not take up her challenge. I will not judge her for whatever she has done this week in order to cope with intolerable feelings. And if she has done something terrible in order to deal with them, I will try to take it from her, try to neutralise it, attempt to compassion-the-fuck out of her shame.

I'm not sure this approach has ever worked. Sometimes I get so frustrated with her I could kill her. What did you do, Kass? Where did you cut this time? Did you slice along the edges of your pubic hair? Did you go further than that? Did it sting when you showered with the lights off?

You hate the dark because that's when it happened, but you hate your body more because your body is the object that he desired; if you hadn't had a vagina, he *might* not have wanted you and you might have been safe. You might have had a childhood. If you hadn't grown breasts, he might have grown bored of you, moved on to someone else more quickly.

You hate your body because often it would respond to the abuse, not only by freezing or dissociating, but by lubricating itself. I've explained that this is just another way in which the body can attempt to protect itself from harm, but you still struggle with the deep shame you feel because of it.

When you got older, you'd seek out men who would hurt you, make you feel something other than numb. You stopped that when you found out you were pregnant with your luminescent wonder. You thought the pregnancy might kill you – but you felt like you had some other woman's body for a while, and you gave birth to a miracle.

Even though you went back to rejecting your body, you loved it long enough for Lewis to be born. You don't even like men. You'd have a girlfriend if only you could imagine deserving love, tolerating tenderness. I know you're challenging me to ask you, Kass, but I challenge you to live your life well.

Eventually she says, 'Aren't you going to ask me if I cut?'

I give in. 'Well, did you?'

'No,' she says quietly. 'I put Lewis to bed and my neighbour came over and we drank tea.'

She laughs as I let my mouth drop open.

'No way...?' She has completely blindsided me. 'What, hot neighbour with the massive dog?'

Kass smiles, 'I'm like a mirror: people look at me every day, but they only really see me when I'm broken. Even then, it's easier for them to just give me the afternoon off so they don't have to see me any more. But hot neighbour...'

I know I'm grinning from ear to ear.

'You don't have to be broken for hot neighbour to see you...'

'Jane, sometimes your mirroring sounds like you're reading straight out of an *Introduction to Counselling* book. But yeah, no, she sees me. And you see me.'

General Hospital

I'm standing outside the automatic glass doors. I've not been here for years. I made sure of it. I have looked after myself rigorously. I eat healthily. I exercise. I don't smoke or drink and I don't do drugs – not since the odd joint in my teens. I keep everything clean, and I hold my breath whenever I pass a car exhaust pipe chugging out fumes. I do nothing which might risk injury. No contact sports, no cycling, no fairground rides, no travelling in a taxi without the seatbelt on. No risky sexual situations. So I won't have to come here.

But now it's time.

In through the nostrils for four, out through the mouth for six. Always longer on the exhale – that's key. Breathe into the diaphragm, not the chest. Oxygen in, adrenaline and cortisol out. That's the ticket – is what my father used to say when I did something correctly. *That's the ticket, Janey love.*

Inside has had a paint job. Utility green, my mother would have called it. It's nice. Better than the brown and cream it used to be. Why would you paint a hospital the colour of shit?

Two more visits. Surely that's all that's required. The MRI today, then the meeting with the consultant to discuss the results.

Breathe.

I haven't had a flashback for years. I will walk through these doors and across the floor to the stairs. I will not be triggered.

I hear that word said so often by people on their phones, chatting to their friends. Triggered, triggers, triggering. *Yeah, I was really triggered,* and *it was just so triggering.* When a kid tells me how, whenever he hears a certain song, he cannot move, cannot think, cannot speak, because it was the song that was on the radio at the time when that unspeakable thing happened to him, I say, *you know how everyone says they get triggered these days?* And he says *yeah.* And I say, *well what you are describing is what being triggered really means.* It is a world away from feeling pissed off or upset. It is not ordinary distress, however unpleasant. What it is, is being attacked by your own mind and body. An absence of air to breathe. The sudden prickling slick of sweat all over. Palpitations and, for some, a chest-clutching pain so severe that they are convinced they are having a heart attack. Sometimes it is being plunged back inside a memory so intense that in that moment you are actually back there; terrified and powerless again.

I will walk through those doors, and I will not be triggered.

Breathe.

I move towards the glass doors on the inhale, across the floor on the exhale, in time with my steps, in time with my steps, in time with my steps.

God help the person who gets in the way of me.

And up the stairs.

I remember climbing the stepladder up to Cam's attic bedroom that first time. First, the dark, dust-mote warmth of his parents' creaky-floored landing in summer, then emerging into the brightness of his bedroom under the eaves... That place was our world for a while, and falling in love was life spreading itself wide open before me.

I am okay.

As I know will be the case, in the waiting room are older people gazing up apathetically from their seats at the muted TV in the far corner of the room. I feel conspicuous. I'm not meant to be here. To differentiate myself further, and because I am nervous, I open my bag and take out the pen and notebook I use for client notes. I open a fresh page and write today's date in the top right-hand corner. On the first line I put the initials of the first kid I saw this morning, then try to remember what we talked about. Which is pointless, so I give up and close the book.

On *Bargain Hunt*, a short woman with bobbed grey hair is rooting about in an antiques shop in one of those picturesque English villages. She finds a vintage tobacco tin and a white chamber pot with pink carnations glazed onto it. The large green subtitles make it hard to see the items properly, but she looks chuffed to bits.

Two of the old people are called in front of me, but now it's my turn. A young nurse in blue scrubs shows me to a cubicle.

'This is for you,' she says, handing me a hospital gown and a key on what looks like a long red shoelace.

'Strip down to just your pants and tights and pop this on. Leave your clothes in there, as well as all your jewellery, and take the key with you to your scan. Your things will be quite safe.' She gives me a mask without metal to wear during the scan and leaves me to it.

Once inside, I make sure the door of the cubicle is locked. There are a stool, a mirror, and pegs on the back of the door. Surprisingly the mirror is more flattering than the ones in John Lewis changing rooms, or maybe it's the lighting in here, which is a little subterranean. I strip down to just my pants and tights as instructed and put on the hospital gown, which is white with a tiny blue geometric print. My face in the mirror, as I fix the ties at the back of my neck, is more my mother's than mine. As is increasingly so these days.

I hang my bra on one of the pegs and feel shame. The bra is greying, threadbare – my mother would never have worn a bra like this. Nor would she have worn the cheap polyester blouse that I fold and place on the stool along with my skirt and cardigan. But she earned more money than I do, and there was my father's income too. I remove her engagement ring and the gold hoops from my ears, put them in the zip pocket of my handbag.

Another nurse, a man in his sixties this time, with an Irish accent, leads me through to a room with windows all along one side looking onto the ambulance bay, where two heavily pregnant women in dressing gowns and slippers are smoking cigarettes and chatting. He gestures for me to sit down on a wipe-clean reclining chair and pulls up a stool to perch beside me.

'Okay, Jane, I'm going to pop the cannula in your arm now. Have you read the leaflet?'

'Yes.'

'Good, good. So no history of allergic reactions or blood clotting problems?'

'No, nothing like that.'

No history of anything much. Fit as a fiddle, me. But that doesn't mean anything, does it? I used to think that I'd be undone when I stopped paying attention, but lately I've had the feeling that all the looking after myself has been for nothing. Sometimes our bodies know what our minds do not.

'Great,' he says, adjusting his glasses.

I look to the side while he gets himself ready. 'Not like needles, no?'

'Not really.'

'You'll be grand. I've done this a million times.'

I look out the window to the twilight beyond. In through the nose...

'Just a wee sharp scratch…'

It's nothing like a sharp scratch. It is a blunt, painful intrusion which makes me gasp.

'There now, Jane. All done.'

'Thank you.'

'Now, you just wait here, and you'll be called in shortly. Okay?'

'Okay.'

'Good girl.'

A door at the far end of the room opens and a tall young man walks through, pulls his mask to the side for long enough to smile at me. 'Jane?'

'Yes.'

'If you'd like to come with me, please.'

He holds the door open for me. He's wearing a lighter blue version of the tunics that the nurses wear, but with him I'm much more aware, as he holds the door open for me, of the long limbs and smooth brown skin beneath the material. I'd like to snap my fingers, for the clothes to just drop off his body.

I walk under his arm feeling like an overgrown child in a nightie, or a mad little old lady, clutching my key on its shoelace.

The room is windowless. There is an examination table and a white machine which looks like a giant plastic doughnut. At one end of the room is an isolation booth with a glass wall, like the ones I've seen in movies about famous singers recording albums. I can see a woman behind the glass.

I stand awkwardly, key in hand.

'I'm the radiographer,' the man says.

He is *really* handsome, and I'm embarrassed.

'Why don't you put your key on that table over there, then come and lie down. My colleague is through there setting up…' he points to the woman behind the glass. 'First thing we have to do is pop in some contrast dye.'

Irish guy said he was 'popping' in the cannula. This had better not hurt like that did. Handsome bloke must be a mind reader because he says, 'No need to worry. It won't hurt and it doesn't take long. But you might experience a warm feeling around the thighs, a bit like you've wet yourself.'

Just to add to the glamour.

I do as he says, put the key on the table and lie myself down. The ceiling is made of squares.

'Right, pop your arms over your head… That's right, good. I'm just going to inject the dye now, so you should start to feel something…'

I do. It's quite a nice feeling: warmth spreading around my pelvis and thighs like he said it would.

'That okay?'

'Yes, it's fine.'

'Great. I'm going to join my colleague now, but you'll hear me over the intercom.'

Once he's behind the glass he gives me instructions. Keep still, breathe in…and breathe out. The doughnut moves smoothly up and down across my body. It is fine, it is nothing. It doesn't take long.

Then he's beside me once more. 'Right, that's you. You can sit up now. You did great.' Professional and kind.

I sit up and swing my feet down to the floor. He is too beautiful, too never-going-to-happen. I just want to be away from him.

Five weeks ago, my GP told me that the NHS does not have the resources to indulge intuition. That the symptoms I'm presenting with – tiredness and a bit of weight loss – aren't enough to warrant an X-ray. He said it was more likely to be something hormonal, maybe a bit of anxiety. And he was right, my symptoms aren't much, and only started creeping up on me a few months ago. But I know. Or at least heavily suspect. And I need confirmation so that I can make plans.

He changed his tune when I explained my history. When I explained why the blood tests he was offering were not enough – that I needed to look inside my body, and that I would go mad if he didn't help me. My local treatment centre carried out the X-ray a fortnight later, and the next day my GP called me to tell me that something had shown up on the scan – probably just a nipple shadow, but better safe than sorry.

Handsome bloke says that he can't tell me anything right now, but I will get my results soon. He and his colleague have just seen what is inside of me, and I know it's not a nipple shadow.

I retrieve my key, thank him and leave.

Back in the room with Irish guy, he is so gentle, asking me how it went and giving me water. He removes the cannula and puts a plaster where it has been.

'Now you just sit here for fifteen minutes or so and then I'll let you go... It'll soon be teatime. What you having tonight?' he asks.

'I don't know, I haven't really thought about it...'

'Just focusing on getting this out the way, I bet.'

'Yes. What are you having?'

'Me? Mince probably. There aren't a lot of options round my house...'

'Why not?'

'My wife only eats meat from the butcher and potatoes. No veg, no tomatoes.'

'What?'

'She doesn't like anything else.'

'What, no pasta, or soup, or salads or anything?'

'Nope, nothing. No fruit or veg. She says she once tried raspberries and her face turned bright blue...'

'What on earth...? How does she not get scurvy?'

'She's not daft. She takes her vitamins.'

'Right. And what about you? What do you like to eat?' I ask, as he opens and closes cabinet drawers, wipes down surfaces.

'Oh, I love all that Italian stuff, and curries,' he says. 'Don't get a chance to eat it much, though.'

'You should jack this in and go work in a restaurant...'

He laughs. 'Yeah, I probably should. But I like it here. And the canteen's actually not as bad as most people make out.'

I bet he's been here for most of his working life. Good to find one's place in the world. I think I found mine eventually. I am a keeper of secrets, witness to what happens behind closed doors. I spend my time sipping tea and listening to stories which are sometimes so implausible, so unlikely, so fantastical, that they would never be believed were I to put them down in print. It is my deep privilege, my great honour, to sit before the bright faces of teenagers hungry for connection, for compassion – for life. I've got the best job in the world. I mean, how lucky am I?

Irish guy doesn't ask why I'm crying about the canteen being really quite good. Just hands me a tissue. And when, like a toddler, I indecorously reach out to him with both hands, he kneels down by my chair, gathers me into his arms and lets me weep into his scrubs.

Kass Session 14

She brought it up. But it may as well have been me, because she is firing every possible argument against reaching out to her parents straight at my face.

I don't know how I thought this session – possibly one of our last together (not that she's aware of it) – would go, but I didn't envisage her raging at me for agreeing with her. Of course it's not really me she's raging at. I'm just reflecting back so she can have the argument with herself. So I can show her anything she's showing me but isn't aware of showing me, if you get what I mean.

The key points are that she has felt better for a while now. She's in a new relationship – her first in fact, and miraculously it's going well. She misses her parents madly and daydreams about them meeting her son.

'What about them? Do they never contact you?'

Kass twists a lock of shiny hair, her finger working its way down the ringlet it's created. Her hair has grown since first we met, and the longer length suits her.

'They tried for years. They blamed themselves, though they didn't know what for. I could never tell them what he did. I broke them, I know I did. I suppose people can only take so much rejection. Then when I moved here, I didn't tell anyone. They don't know about Lewis.'

What a fucking enormous mess. A family ripped apart by an evil none of them could have foreseen. Gorgeous, uproarious, utterly enchanting little Lewis, unknown to his grandparents.

'Do you think you could tell them now?'

'No! Getting in touch means *explaining*. That's why I can't get in touch. Well, one of the reasons, but it's a pretty big one. That and obviously *him*; he'd find out where I am.'

'You still think they wouldn't believe you over your brother? Even if it would make sense to them, I mean of everything that happened. Surely they'd have to see the truth, no?'

In order to emphasise her point she sits forward in her chair, crosses her jeaned legs at the ankles, unaware of how graceful her movements are.

'Jane, you have no idea how powerful he is. They would never believe me, and the accusation would wreck their world.'

'Their world's already wrecked – they lost their daughter! I just... Why are you so convinced they wouldn't believe you?'

'Jane, I know. I know it in my bones.'

'Yeah, but can you trust that feeling in your bones? Or might he have planted it there? How many times did he tell you no one would ever believe you? Don't you see? That was the way he kept control, by feeding you lies, by filling you with fear and hopelessness. It worked for a long time, but that doesn't mean to say it has to stay that way. You have power too, Kass. You deserve to live your life how you want to live it. You don't have to hide any more.'

Kass sighs and cradles her face in her hands. We sit in her safe silence.

Eventually she says, 'I love that you want that for

me, but he is a master manipulator. Sure, it might make sense to them, but he would fight it so hard. He would find a way to counter every last little doubt in their minds, and I would be left in the dirt. While there is breath in his body, I can never tell my parents.

And Lewis will never have grandparents.

Behind her, outside the window, a crow lands on the sill where I've put down birdseed. It sees me, and the manner in which it blinks its black eye reminds me of the shutter on a camera Cam once had.

I say, 'I hear you, Kass. Really, I hear you.'

And I hope that all is not how I fear it is, and that I will be able to have more sessions with you. I know that I should be preparing our ending, but it's not the right time. How can I abandon you now? When you need me.

Two Days Later

I've taken the week off work. I'm knackered, and the appointment with the Respiratory Consultant is tomorrow. I rarely take time off, but I know that it's what Jessie would insist I do, had I told her anything about any of this, which I've not.

But now this email from Kass, desperate to meet, saying she's got something to tell me that can't wait until our next session. I'm avoiding supervision because I cannot simply relay to Estelle what is said between Kass and me – I would also have to be honest about where my thoughts are going, and right now the idea of doing that leaves me ice-cold. I know this is precisely why supervision exists – to stop therapists going off-piste – but right now I just can't deal with it.

I'm walking towards the park on a morning as grey

and indistinct as the day we last met here, in a different season; that's Scotland for you. Though this time there are clusters of bright berries on the trees and the first fallen leaves scattered across the path. The faded scarlet ropes of the amaranth cling wretchedly to their dying foliage. Love-lies-bleeding indeed; I'm embarrassed for them. When your time's up it's better to just accept it, no? At least that's what I've spent the last twenty-six years trying to tell myself.

I should be worrying about the fact that we are meeting outwith the counselling room yet again, outwith our scheduled appointment, and at a time when my future as a therapist may or may not be cut short; everything just so precarious. But I'm not. I feel high – I've got butterflies at the thought of seeing Lewis again.

I used to dream of a girl who was mine. But somewhere along the way, over the course of this year, she morphed into a boy, a little like Logan, with the potential to be someone like Fraser, but now it's Lewis's blue eyes which stare out from my dreams. Lewis that I'm thinking about when my mind wanders from whatever I'm supposed to be doing. Worries about Lewis's future that sit immovable as lead weights in my stomach.

I arrive at the gate. There's Kass in the green puffer, but where is Lewis? I scan the playpark – he's nowhere to be seen. Kass, rather than wait for me to get to her, hurries over.

'Thank you for seeing me,' she says, taking hold of

my arm and looking over my shoulder. I do a double-take. She's wide-eyed with exhaustion and wired with adrenaline – something's really wrong.

'Where's Lewis?' I ask, ignoring the fact she's leading me by the elbow to the bench, which would be a bizarre enough thing to do even if it wasn't the first time that we've ever had any kind of physical contact.

'He's at school.'

Of course he is. She must have called in sick, like me. I'm so disappointed, I can't even muster the will to hide it, but she doesn't notice. She can barely wait to tell me whatever it is that's plaguing her thoughts.

Before we're even sitting down, she blurts out, 'Jane, he found me.'

I hear myself asking 'What?' but I heard her just fine and I know exactly who it is that she's referring to.

Try again. 'What happened?'

We sit on the bench, knees pressed together like best friends or sisters. Now I understand why she looks so wild.

'A text message. He says he knows where I am. Not just me, he says he knows about Lewis and wants to get to know him!'

'How could he possibly?'

'I told you – he has ways and means.'

There she goes again, alluding to her brother being somehow powerful, knowing people.

'Kass I don't get it: what is he – some kind of gangster? A mafia boss?'

'No,' she replies, shaking her head, but still not saying.

'Well then, what then? Why won't you tell me?'

She scrunches up her features in frustration, as if the answer is obvious. 'Because you'll be able to find him instantly, and then I'll lose all control. You'll call the police because you have a duty of care. It's safeguarding, basic child protection – we've all done the training at work. You'll have to report him – he's dangerous.'

I mean, there is now a definite risk of serious harm to both Kass and Lewis, but reporting her brother also comes with huge risks for them.

'Kass, I wouldn't do that to you! Not if you didn't want me to. But I really think that this changes everything – he's actually threatened you, for the first time in years. You and Lewis are in danger; we need to call the police.'

Did I just contradict myself? Maybe. But the danger was never so imminent before, and I've not had a minute to think.

'Don't you get it, Jane? There's no point. My word against his is all there is. There's no evidence!'

'But the text message…'

'Oh it was all nicey-nicey. No one reading it would realise the threat behind the words. He sounds like a loving brother suggesting he makes a Christmas visit. The police won't do a thing. No one will ever be able to do a thing. I'm this nothing, this single mum with no money, no contacts, and he's…he's…'

She gives up, rakes her hand through her hair.

An idea occurs, and I can't believe I've never thought of it before.

'Is he a copper?'

'No!'

'Or someone like that?' I ask.

'A lawyer?'

'No. Just trust me Jane – nothing touches him, he's bulletproof. He always was and he always will be.'

It's got to be hyperbole; no one is bulletproof.

She still won't tell me. Still doesn't believe that I won't be obliged to do the *right thing*.

'You said last time that as long as there was breath left in his body you couldn't tell your parents, because they would believe your omnipotent brother over you…' I don't add that it had seemed so terrible that she and Lewis would remain alone, that my thoughts have been spooling off into dark places worrying what might happen to them. 'But at least you hadn't seen him for years. The threat was always there but not imminent. The situation has changed now. You've got to go to the police!'

She shakes her head, says vehemently, 'Jane, you have to trust that I can't. He would deny it all, and the process would end me. I just want a chance to bring up my son without him anywhere near me.'

'Then what will you do?'

'We have to move, somewhere far away from here.'

'But that's not realistic. You said yourself – you have no money, no contacts, and if he's that well-resourced he will find you wherever you go.'

She simultaneously shrugs and flings out her hands in a tight, exaggerated gesture.

'Then you tell me. What am I going to do?'

For a moment she appears frozen within the terror which glosses her blue eyes, before burying her face in her hands.

She's desperate.

He found her, and he found out about Lewis. I ask to see the message. It's short, amiable – *Looking forward to getting to know my nephew. Might pop round at Christmas.*

I see Lewis's round face in my mind – as perfect and open as a camellia flower in full bloom.

She's described their Christmases to me before. How hard she works to give Lewis a day worth looking forward to, despite the shoestring budget, the painful absence of family, and the trauma like a cobra always ready to strike.

How hard their Christmases are, but they make do, she makes it right.

I place a hand on her shoulder, hear myself say, 'We'll think of something.'

We have to, because whether or not her brother comes good on his threat, if something, anything, should happen to Kass, Lewis will need somewhere to go. And it's feasible that well-meaning social services could place him with his uncle.

Thoughts are forming thick and fast. Years of feeling powerless, ineffectual, rolling together. Waking dreams colliding. All that anger that felt so useless, so corrosive and pointless – what if there was a point after all? What if it was all leading here?

We listen. That's the therapist's job. But what if

circumstances change and opportunities arise that previously only existed in the imaginings of our shadow-sides?

What then?

Respiratory Consultant's Office

I wonder if I've been in this room before. I don't think so. It's small for a consultant's office. Or maybe it isn't. It's small in comparison with the imaginary consultant's office in my head. Dr Miller, sitting behind his desk, is a big guy, in a rugby-playing kind of a way, not an overweight way, which adds to the feeling that the room is too little.

I could really do with some air, but the windows look like they don't open. Which reminds me of those fancy new black cabs whose windows won't open and feel like ovens in the summer.

I could really do with some air. I undo the top button of my shirt. *In through the nose and out through the mouth...*

The cancer charity woman sits on a chair at the

side of the room, out of the way but not really. She is straight-backed, feet together. Meerkat-ish. At any moment she might spring up and run a marathon. Does she get paid? Or is she a volunteer?

It must really be hot in here because she's in a T-shirt and the consultant's shirt sleeves are rolled up. His huge forearms, covered in curly black hair – meaty, unlike Hazel's thighs – rest on the desk like two ham hocks.

In through the nose… My mask sticks to my face. Dr Miller must be able to tell I'm having a hard time because he removes his mask and gestures to me to do the same, which I do gratefully. He glances at cancer charity woman who gives a slight shake of the head and a thumbs-up that says, *I won't, thanks, but you two go for it.*

His face is nothing but serious. A big serious coupon. Hope – an emotion I rarely allow myself to feel, makes an appearance unbidden. This is the last-chance saloon. That face may be about to break open into a big reassuring smile. But if that were the case, then cancer charity woman would not be poised and ready, would she?

'I'm sorry, I don't have good news…' he says, and hope flits off and away through the useless air vent.

He taps his keyboard, and an X-ray, presumably my CT scan, appears on the computer screen which he has already turned to face me.

'So, this mass here…on your lower lobe…is just over five centimetres…' He points to a white cloud sitting in the blackness of my left lung. It reminds me of those delicate balls of empty egg cases you sometimes find on the beach. *There were whelk babies in there once,* my dad said. But this thing isn't full of babies, nor is it empty.

'...And then this little spot here on your lymph nodes...'

'Are cancer,' I say, to save him from having to.

'Yes.'

'And the fact there are two in the one lung means it's stage two, yes?'

'Yes. But there is nothing in your bones or other organs...'

'Yet.'

'Yes. Thinking about your symptoms... It says in the notes from your GP that you've been feeling tired and have lost some weight. Both of which could have been down to any number of things. No cough, no shortness of breath or chest pain – I'm very surprised that you knew anything was wrong at all.'

Does it say that I'm a nutcase who was ready to scratch the GP's eyes out if he didn't agree to a scan?

'And it's very rare for someone of your age who has never smoked heavily, but of course it happens. Have you ever been exposed to asbestos, that you know of? Or lived in an area with high levels of nitrous oxide gases?'

I have no idea about that.

'I don't know, I don't think so... You see I've been waiting for it for a long time. It's hard to explain but I always knew that I'd *just know* when it was time...'

'But why?' he says, his face full of concern and confusion – fatherly, even though he can't be much older than me. 'As I said, it's very rare in someone so young…'

I close my eyes. Open them again.

'Both my parents died young of lung cancer… I know, I know, I was told that was extremely unusual too. A fluke, a freak – I was the teenager whose parents both died of the same disease within two years of each other. Mum first, then Dad.'

The serious face is so full of sympathy now, it's hard for me to bear. Is that what my face looks like when I'm listening to my clients' stories for the first time?

'This should have been on your notes… Were you offered genetic testing?'

'I was, yes. Because it wasn't just my parents – there is a history of multiple cancers on both sides of my family, though not lung cancer and mostly all over the age of sixty. My parents were hope-over-experience kind of people, but they should probably never have got together.'

'Did you have it? The genetic testing, I mean?'

'No. I didn't need it.'

I'm surprised when he doesn't ask me why not. Just looks at me with a kind of knowing intensity. Maybe he gets it.

Then the moment is gone, and he says, 'Well, we are very lucky that your intuition led you here today. I know you must be in shock, but I'm afraid we need to talk about treatment options ASAP, which means now.'

I'm not in shock. Or I am, but have been this way for years.

'I'm not here for treatment, I came to get confirmation

that it has started.'

'Jane, I'm not going to lie to you. The situation you find yourself in is not great, but at this stage the cancer is treatable, through a combination of surgery and chemotherapy. You have a decent chance of surviving five years and possibly much longer. But without treatment...'

That's what a man just like you said to my parents, and they had the surgery and all the therapies, but they still died within two years of each other.

'No thank you.'

The concern on this guy's face is heart-breaking. I wish he'd stop looking at me like that.

'Are you absolutely certain you don't want to even hear the options? At worst, treatment will buy you more time to do things you want to do – a bucket-list perhaps? But at best, you could still live a good long life... And of course, you can go away and think it through. It doesn't need to be decided right now while you're understandably in shock, but don't take *too* long. Caroline here can help you think about it...'

Now Caroline here speaks for the first time since she introduced herself when I first came in. 'Yes, dear. Here's my card. You can call me anytime and we can have a chat...'

She hands me her card, which I take. It's pink and white with sharp edges. Expensive paper. Not hospital issue.

'I don't want treatment. I saw what it did to my parents. I have always known this was coming, so I am ready for it. I chose not to have children for precisely this reason.'

Caroline here glances at Dr Miller, unsure what to do.

'Do you have anyone you can call?' she asks.

She's in her sixties but looks younger. Slim and neat in a white T-shirt and navy jogging bottoms, but smart ones, and spanking new white trainers. A woman who has never been short of the love of others.

'There is no one I want to call.'

'A friend? A parent or sibling perhaps?' Dr Miller asks.

I wait for him to realise his mistake, which he does quickly and apologises. He's a nice guy. With a photo on his desk of a woman who must be his wife, kissing the fat cheek of a baby with a twist of jet-black hair who looks just like him.

'My parents are dead, and I am an only child. My friends all have kids – they don't have the space to deal with this and I won't put them and their children, whom I love as much as if I was their real auntie, through what I had to go through.'

My parents knew those treatments wouldn't work; I realise that now. They did it for me, so I wouldn't feel like they'd just given up, so I wouldn't feel abandoned, and maybe some of the hope they peddled to me was as real to them as it seemed to me at the time, at least for a while. But it meant I spent years watching them die instead of months. If it hadn't been for me, maybe they could have found an easier way out – one without pain and that horrific whittling away of their minds and bodies. I won't do this to my friends, and I won't do it to myself. I have always known I won't, and now the time has come, I'm more determined than ever. I know it won't last, but right now I feel calm – calm and resolute, purposeful even.

I look at his big, kind face and take pity on him.

'It's okay,' I say. 'I'm used to being on my own. I will tell my friends eventually.'

This is a lie. My friends won't know a thing until I am dead and gone. There is only one item on my bucket-list, one wish that could never be fulfilled had I not received this news today. Phantasy will finally become reality, and, even without any treatment, I have time enough to do it.

I don't believe in karma – that we automatically reap what we sow. Life doesn't work like that for most people. Sometimes we must act. People can't recover from trauma unless the threat is removed. For once, I have the opportunity to go out there and actually do something to remove a threat. Illegality does not concern me – I don't have long left. Immorality is another matter, but I'm just going to have to trust my gut that what I'm going to do will provide a kind of retributive justice that has no other way of being realised.

I don't think it would surprise anyone to learn that I don't like goodbyes. If this is avoidance, sue me. My clients, Estelle, my supervision group, I will not see again. Kass and Lewis… I will remember how I felt the last time I saw them, and they will remember me how I was then.

But my friends.

Jessie's House

Years ago, I stopped going dancing with my friends on a Friday night, as one by one they started having babies. Now on Friday nights I will be at one of their houses, having the kind of rowdy, kiddy dinners where you never get to complete a sentence because of the constant interruptions. Which is where I am now, sipping bitter lemon from a champagne coupe and cradling Jessie's third and only red-headed child in my arms. A baby so unplanned, and for much of the pregnancy so unwanted, she is lucky that, unlike her siblings, she looks so like her mother. With the other two, Jessie always said she didn't know how it was possible to grow someone inside you for so long, only for them to come out with someone else's face on.

My decision not to have children of my own started

that day in the photographic studio with Cam. As certain as he was that he'd have kids, I knew with equal certainty that having them would not be part of my life. The knowledge did not feel new, or surprising – it was something I carried around unconsciously, it just hadn't come into awareness before then, presumably because of the pain it would bring when it did.

Cam is good with broken people, and he deserved more than I could offer. We'd had a good run. I loved him too much to take away his chance of children, to die early on him, leave him widowed. He tried again and again to get me to change my mind. Then, when he finally accepted that I wouldn't, he told me he would be happy for it to be just the two of us, that he could live with that.

But I couldn't live with any of it – I loved him way too much to let him make the sacrifice he was offering, let alone risk him having to watch me die as I had watched my parents. I wouldn't do that to him. He said there was a chance that I'd be fine, a good chance. That I had to live positively, hopefully. I said he was wrong, he said I couldn't know that. If he was here today, I could say I told you so; not that I would, because *sometimes it is more important to be kind than to be right – remember that my Janey-Jane.*

After giving up the love of my life, I gave up fashion too. It wasn't for me, not the person I had become, not me without Cam. I worked in the pub for a few years and finally went to see another counsellor – a woman this time. She listened. I mean, really listened, and she was interested but not intrigued or thirsty for information. Only once did she cry, and for a moment it felt like I had my mother back with me, because she got up from her chair and came over and held me in her arms.

I told her I wasn't going to have a family, a traditional life – that I wanted to find a way to live with myself, by myself. I remembered shit therapist, wondered how things might have been if he'd been any good at his job. Good therapist was the one who suggested I try counselling training. I thought I'd be the youngest in the class but there were two others younger than me, and even if there hadn't been, in time I realised that it is not age that makes a good therapist, but the capacity to love.

I will never forget that first time sitting in a circle in the counselling and psychotherapy department up at the university. The ridiculous opposite-of-pep talk we got from the head of department, about how there is no money in therapy, and very few jobs. How most counsellors are volunteers and still paying back the loans they took out to afford the training, years after qualifying. How, once you are qualified, another barrier to employment will be the fact you are not yet accredited, which will only be possible after countless hours of probably unpaid client work and then another year for the very expensive accreditation course. Weighty, gloomy caveats tempered by oddly grandiose hints of therapy being a vocation with a higher purpose.

Grief, if it ever really went away, returned in a tsunami of a second wave. I had to make room for it, to meet it again, as an altered person. As a teenager, 'broken' had become my identity. As an adult I no longer felt broken, perhaps because I'd made powerful, grown-up decisions about my life.

In those years of studying, I missed my parents and mourned the life I'd thought I'd have, with a ferocity that could turn me inside out, raw and exposed, in the space of an evening. In time I learned to contain these moments, to survive them and come back to the reality of my home without my parents in it.

I knew it was likely I would get cancer young, but I wasn't going to usher it in, so I gave up alcohol, started eating more healthily and kept everything very clean. I had my studies, my tutors, new friends from my course and of course my school pals, most of whom were coming home or not far from coming home.

We crowd into Jessie's flat, because she's the head of legal at some company whose name always escapes me but has something to with *solutions,* so her flat is the one with the most space. Tonight, round the table there is Neil and his husband Joe, Angie, and of course Jessie and her husband Mike. Leila and Ross are both working late shifts at the hospital, so their children are staying here. All the kids except the baby are in the living room watching a film so that we can get some peace. Light streams through the French doors that open out onto a garden glossy and dripping after a rain shower. Jessie is standing by the cooker, wearing green-rimmed reading glasses and frowning at her phone, curls blazing in the evening sunshine.

Jessie's husband Mike slams his empty beer bottle down on the table and gets up, saying, 'I can't stand it any more, Jess. If you need a recipe for spag bol you shouldn't be making it.'

Jessie scowls at him, grey-green eyes magnified through the glasses. 'I'm just reminding myself...'

'Sit down,' he says, and pulls the apron from over her head.

Her shirt rides up momentarily, exposing an expanse of spongy stomach forever disfigured by her pregnancies. The first baby left startling crimson stretch marks reaching like flames from her pubis towards her breasts, which stubbornly remained while her slim middle returned. The second caused a little thickening which she'd resolved to eradicate when she fell (unintentionally) pregnant again, but the third has robbed her entirely of her waist. She's shown me, grabbed handfuls of her own fat, wielded it in my direction, disgusted. *What the fuck am I supposed to do with this, Janey?*

'Thank fuck,' she says as she sits down and pours herself a glass of red wine from the open bottle on the table.

'Shh,' I say, covering the baby's ears.

'Oh, she doesn't mind, she's not even awake!' says Jessie, reaching out to stroke her daughter's cheek. 'She's a pet. No bother at all. I like her so much better than the other two.'

Mike, who is doing things with pots and pans, snorts,

and says, 'You might like them better if you got to know them…'

'Well, that's a low blow…' Jessie shrieks at Mike's back 'And anyway I was only joking – I have an extremely close bond with all my children, *despite* the fact I have to be out at work so much. Don't know why you're being such a prick all of a sudden.'

Mike makes snapping beaks with his hands to mimic Jessie talking. Neil rolls his eyes.

'Please stop swearing, Jess.'

'Oh Jane, she's only six months…'

'So? You two are awful. Always arguing and swearing in front of your kids – it's not good for them.'

'Agreed,' says Neil. 'And you should listen to Jane; she knows her stuff.'

'It's not me,' says Mike, from inside a cloud of onion sizzle. 'It's that ginger bastard…'

Jessie laughing, says, 'The kids are fine.'

Neil and Joe's toddler Amy, in a terrible salmon-pink puff of a dress, appears at the door, followed by Janey, Jessie and Mike's eldest, who must be about twelve by now.

'Here she is!' says Joe, getting up from his chair to scoop up his daughter and take her over to the window to look at the garden.

Janey, in head-to-toe black, hoodie up, goes to the fridge and looks inside.

Without turning from the cooker, Mike says, 'Get out of there. Tea will be ready soon.'

Janey makes a face, but flashes me, her namesake,

a toothy smile before leaving the room. Angie's son would usually be here on a night like this, but just this week he started work in a supermarket.

'I'll never get how you two can fight like that and then it's all just fine,' Neil says, fiddling with the button on his shirt sleeve, seeming to have forgotten the thousands of play fights that he himself has had with Jess.

'It's weird, is what it is,' adds Angie, pausing to lick the gum on her roll-up. 'But the weirdest thing about it is that of all the relationships, I get the feeling theirs is the one strong enough, the one most likely to last.'

'How's that?' asks Neil, 'What's so flimsy about me and Joe, or Ross and Leila?'

'Oh, don't be so sensitive,' Angie says, reaching into the top pocket of her shirt for her lighter.

'I don't know…' says Jessie, blinking as a shaft of sunlight falls directly into the middle of the table, hitting her in the eyes. 'Sometimes I think I'd do just about anything to be free of it all…kids, husband, job…'

Mike, emptying a can of tomatoes into a frying pan, sings *Freedom's just another word for nothing left to lose* in as raspy a voice as he can manage, then takes the dishcloth off his shoulder and wipes at the hob where tomato juice has sploshed.

Jessie hoots and shouts, 'Alexa! Play "Me And Bobby McGee" by Janis Joplin!'

'Please,' I say.

'Pleeeease,' says Jessie, rolling her eyes.

At forty-one, Jessie is as striking and as self-assured as she was at sixteen, and Mike – if we are to believe the matching hypothesis taught in A-level psychology classes up and down the land – is punching well above his weight. But Mike is very kind, and he makes her laugh. He's good at knowing what homework needs doing and when for, and whose feet have grown and need new socks. Mike is the Tooth Fairy and the Easter Bunny, and he is rarely in the family photos because he is the one taking them. The walls and surfaces in their home are covered in pictures of his three beautiful children and his glorious wife. In the wedding photo on the kitchen wall, Jessie, tall in red stilettos (which make her two inches taller than her husband) and a sleeveless sage-green silk dress, holds his upturned face in her hands. It's not one of the professional photographs; I took it. Got lucky and captured a fleeting intimate moment, there for a second, then gone again. They are drunk and a bit sweaty-looking, but it's a great photo.

The song begins and still the baby in my arms sleeps.

'When she's asleep she's *really* asleep isn't she?' I say. 'So like you, Jess. Though she doesn't snore.'

'God, the snoring,' says Angie, getting up to go outside for a smoke.

Neil laughs. 'Remember at the Solstice Festival, when we were all in that tent and she just wouldn't shut up? That was murder. How do you cope, Mike?'

Mike, filling a pan of water from the kitchen sink, says, 'Earplugs, but they don't work for the base rumble – it's like sleeping next to Sakurajima.'

'Oh, shut up,' says Jessie. 'Listen to Janis... Do you guys know that she recorded this just a couple of days before her death? So tragic. They released the album posthumously.'

Freedom's just another word for nothin' left to lose Nothin', and that's all that Bobby left me...

Quite.

I look down at the little sleeping face and kiss the tip of her nose.

'That's me,' I say to no one in particular.

'What's you?' asks Neil. I look from the baby to him. There is silver in his sideburns that wasn't there two weeks ago. Finally.

'Nothing left to lose...'

Neil frowns, 'What you on about? You okay?'

I smile brightly. I so want this to be just another ordinary night together, and I don't know why those words just came out my mouth. 'Yes, I'm fine. I was just thinking about something I'm going to try with a client. That's all.'

'Care to share?' Jessie asks.

I shake my head, 'No. Let's just say I have a plan, and it's a good one.'

'Good for you!' says Jessie, the wine really kicking in. 'Let's drink to Janey's plan...' She raises her glass and Neil follows suit.

Angie comes back in. 'Forgot this...' she says, picking up her lighter from the table. 'What are we drinking to?'

'To Janey and her brilliant plan,' says Neil.

Angie replies, 'I have no idea what you're on about, but *slàinte!* Here's to our Jane!'

'And to freedom!' says Jessie.

My Flat

After a long week of work and the lively evening at Jessie and Mike's, I'm dog-tired, but I know I won't sleep until I've done what I need to do, and the adrenaline my body is producing at the prospect is keeping me alert. My houseplants are bugging me. I know they're dry, but I just googled *is it okay to water houseplants at night* and came up with a resounding no. So they'll just have to wait until the morning. I've got a cup of tea, and my laptop is open in front of me.

I know what I want to do, but I have no way of knowing if it's even possible. I have no plan as such, because I need details to make one, and these are what I'm about to start searching for. I don't even know if he's alive. What if he is alive but he's a shell of a man? Maybe all Kass's talk of him being somehow powerful is just nonsense; what if he runs a sanctuary for abandoned pets, or… I can't think of anything else right now, but something wonderfully worthy (that doesn't involve working with women or children!) What then?

What if I hatch a plan and it backfires horribly? Where will I be then?

But at least I'll have tried.

Kass said her brother's first name only once, and not on purpose. She didn't disclose that it was he who abused her until our fourth session. I filed his name away in my mind, and when the session ended and she left the room, I tore off a corner from a page in my notebook and wrote the name there. I folded it up, put it in my pocket and, when I got home, put the folded note inside my copy of *Trauma and Recovery* by Judith Herman. Which is where I retrieve it from now.

He is six years older than Kass, and she had a birthday not long ago, so he must be thirty-eight. I don't have his surname, but hers is Erskine, and she has never married. I put the folded note on the desk beside the laptop and light a jar candle, place it on the windowsill. Then I flick the switch for the ceiling lamp so that the only light in my living room is the warm glow of the candle and the cold glare from the screen.

I don't know why I unfold the note, because I have never forgotten the name inside. There it is, among the creases, clean and clear.

I google Christopher Erskine.

The first entry is a Wikipedia page for an American baseball player. I hit the link and see that this Chris

Erskine is in his mid-twenties and looks nothing like Kass. Back to the search page. More entries for the baseball star. Then a company director who, when I hit images, looks at least seventy. Next is a LinkedIn page with no photo, and a Facebook page with no photo and no content, which suggests to me that this Christopher Erskine joined Facebook when it became a thing but barely used it. I click on Family and Relationships. Relationship Status is set to 'married'. I click on family members.

Bingo.

Samantha Erskine is all over Facebook. Image after image of Samantha with her beachy blonde hair, (I could tell her stories that would make that hair curl), never looking anything less than immaculate. Sporty Samantha in Nike runners and pastel gym gear, with perfect ponytail. Mum Samantha, arms draped round the shoulders of her two children, head slightly cocked and smiling prettily to camera (children, after all, are a great excuse for yet another selfie). Sexy, night-out-with-the-girls Samantha, in black halter-neck top, skinny jeans, heels and eyeliner, pouting to camera with her equally hot friend. And of course, date-night-at-a-trendy-restaurant-with-hubby Samantha, who is still sexy but with cutesy smile: and this is not a selfie. Hubby is taking this one.

Where is hubby?

I click on image after image, endless variations of Samantha, and suddenly there he is, and I know immediately that this is my Christopher Erskine.

Found you.

On the terrace of a swanky bar in some hot country, an apricot-coloured sunset fanning out across the darkening sky behind him. Tall knife-edged buildings, then a haze of scrub and sand. It's not Europe; I'm guessing Dubai.

Soft, mouse-coloured hair and light eyes. A masculine version of your sister's symmetrical features. Easy on the eye. You are the kind of man Carrie Bradshaw would refer to as *a tall drink of water.*

I scroll for more. There is a snap captioned *so proud of hubby,* where you, Christopher Erskine, stand in front of the Houses of Parliament wearing a dark suit. Some more images of you and the kids splashing in a pool on what is obviously a very expensive holiday.

Ah, Samantha's Instagram handle. I pick up my phone and search for her. She's there and her account is public. When they are older, will her kids thank her for posting zillions of photos of them on the internet, I wonder? It's mostly all the same photos as Facebook. Why does she bother?

Scroll.

Scroll.

Scroll.

What's this? Our Sam a few years back with a baby on her knee and a toddler clinging to her side, caption *so blessed the universe brought me this pair #adoptive mums.*

More scrolling and here is Samantha again, and again humble-bragging about her beautiful and, it would appear, adopted children. I click on who she's following, only to see she is part of a network of other adoptive parents and adoption organisations and support groups.

So, Chris, does this mean you're firing blanks then? Is that what saved your sister from pregnancy for all those years?

Now, what is it you do for a living…?

I hit the original tab for the LinkedIn page and see a jumble of jargon. It would appear that you are a director of operations in some deliberately abstruse-sounding government department which has something to do with the Ministry of Defence. Christopher Erskine from Scotland – Tory bitch.

Exactly what you do is unclear, but I can immediately see why Kass believes you are powerful. There is a covert, classified feeling to the information on your LinkedIn page, and your internet presence is limited. Even still, Chris, can you really earn the kind of money necessary to keep Samantha in Lululemon joggers and the extremely fancy holidays to which she's clearly accustomed? I know you don't come from money. If I can only find Samantha's maiden name…

Google.

Google.

Here it is. Samantha is a Beaumont-Calthorpe, whose family estate is somewhere called Horsham. Lucky Christopher! Tell me, I'm wondering, what was it that first attracted you to Miss Moneybags? And should you really have adopted children? Did you never consider that the fact you fire blanks might be the universe's way of telling *you* something?

Google.

Samantha used to be in marketing but now looks after the kids, is on the PTA etc.

More Google.

The Erskines live in Surrey, which Google informs me, takes one hour and three minutes to get to from London, where Christopher works.

You started abusing your sister when you were twelve – a child yourself, just entering puberty – and she was six. You stopped when she was sixteen and you were twenty, I bet because you left to move to London, and because she started to resist you. I know you left home at seventeen, went to university in Scotland, but continued to abuse Kass on visits home. When she reached fourteen you were hardly ever in the family home because you were starting this life in London, and it was no longer so easy to abuse your sister because she was a near fully grown teenage girl.

Your mother despaired at her own inability to work out why her six, seven, eight-year-old daughter would regularly wet the bed. Your father, who prided himself on being the only one in the family who passed his eleven-plus, just couldn't work out where your sister's inability to concentrate in class came from. He couldn't fathom why his son was such an academic star while his daughter…

Both parents struggled with why Kass would become wildly ambivalent at bedtime, either clinging to them like her life depended on it or rejecting them outright, becoming completely withdrawn, taking herself and her duvet to the farthest corner of the bed. Any good Child Protection training advises teachers that what might be seen as restlessness, refusal to sit still, may actually be the presence of a sexually transmitted disease or bruised and torn body parts. But mostly these things are missed – put down to bad behaviour.

Kass's teacher asked, in front of the whole class, if she had ants in her pants, and because Kass blushed beetroot red, finding no words available to her (as there never were, because she lived in a state of permanent toxic stress because her amygdala was constantly activated), her teacher kindly took her aside at the end of class to ask if anything was wrong. But of course you had her well-versed in what to say should this kind of intervention arise. *No miss, thank you miss, I'm fine.*

Young people who have been abused, who have previously been compliant and totally controlled by their abusers, will often start 'acting out' around the onset of puberty, behave 'badly' in high school and draw attention to themselves. You would've wanted to avoid this. Continuing to abuse her would have been riskier now than ever it was.

However, Christopher, you always remained a threat, so much so that Kass had to give up her family and start a new life entirely on her own, just to keep safe from you. And now you've found her, and – any fool can read between the lines of your message – plan to hurt her again. Why now? Why, when you got away with the monstrous things you did back then, would you now decide to risk everything you have, just to hurt her again?

You're a psychopath, aren't you, Chris? And a paedophile; perhaps not in the most traditional sense, though certainly that label still fits. You abused Kass because you had urges and she was right there in your home – she was convenient. I don't know why you are like this when by Kass's account the rest of your family are not, but it happens.

Google.

Google.

And boom, there is the email address for your assistant, Laura.

I never thought it would be this easy.

I spend the next half an hour creating a new email address and, in my brightly lit bathroom, taking selfies and trying all the different filters in my phone.

Back to the laptop.

Dear Mr Erskine,

My name is Melanie Klein, and I'm starting up my own men's grooming and wellness line, Clean and Klein. I'm looking for successful, handsome Londoners to interview about their own grooming routines and fitness regimes for my marketing campaign. And, who knows, it could go further than this – have you ever considered doing any modelling?

Kind regards,

Melanie

Short and sweet.

I'm banking on the fact Chris won't mind that Melanie has no internet presence, since he himself has so little. But no doubt Laura is savvier. Will she google Melanie, then delete the email when she realises Melanie is a nobody? Unlike her legendary eponym, a pioneer of child psychoanalysis who became convinced that young infants have an innate destructive drive to destroy everything that is good. Which seems somehow fitting when thinking about Christopher Erskine.

It's 3am. I close the laptop.

Then open it again.

I swore never to look for Cam, even when the internet made it easy. If I came across him randomly, then fine, but not *actively look*. But my circumstances have changed, and I am no longer scared of however I'm going to feel.

So many images.

I still remember the day we found each other again at the festival – what the light looked like.

He's alive, and he's middle-aged like me. He has grey in his hair and in a beard that I've never known; this boy-man who saw me at my worst and still fought and fought to keep me. Even now I can conjure his smell, and the heat from his skin just before my lips touched his sleeping shoulder blades. He was perfect back then, as flawless and hopeful as the first page of a new jotter on which I could have written the date, printed my name and claimed as mine.

A celebrated photojournalist working in war zones, just like he always wanted, he's won award after award, and has the leathery, weathered face that comes from doing what he does. But the easy confidence is missing; he's lost something far greater than me. I wouldn't believe the things you've seen, would I, Cam?

Home is Reykjavik, Iceland, with his tiny dark-haired wife and their little girl. The three, dressed head to toe in waterproof jackets and trousers, beam to camera. He holds his precious ones close to him, as he should. Despite all that he can't unsee, Cam is the cat that got the canary and I know now that I did the right thing. I made the right call; his child does not have my faulty genes, and when she reaches her teens, instead of watching her mother die, instead of that protracted horror show, she will get to see her mother grow old. She will take every triumph, every heartbreak, and pour it into her good-enough, alive-enough mother, and when she falls in love for the very first time, her father might tell of *his* first love, and how it was like magic, like the most wonderful gift. Warmth spreads through my muscles and into my heart, which feels like it might burst. How lucky I was to have had that love.

I dream I'm in a grand, breathtakingly beautiful city – Rome, maybe – under a pale blue opaline sky. Across a river is a huge round building with a domed roof shining golden in the bright, hazy light. I stare into the gold and notice its surface isn't smooth, as gold should be. Instead, there are the hollows and pits and bright spreading spangles of the moon – the roof is the moon! Flocks of birds, hundreds of them, fly over the city, over the moon, over me. Each bird has a peony in its mouth, and petals are dropping from the sky. I stretch out my hand to catch one, somehow knowing that now I have it, everything is going to be alright.

I wake earlier than intended because my back is hurting – a dull ache from halfway down my spine that gnaws its way up to my shoulder. The pain propels me out of bed and to the medicine box in the bathroom cabinet. I neck a couple of ibuprofen and drink cold water straight from the tap. The plants!

I get my watering can from under the kitchen sink and fill it from the tap. It is another lovely, early-autumn day and sunlight is filtering into my small living room through the leafy curtain of my hanging plants, making them glow. I touch the fleshy leaves of the trailing jade, round as pennies and warm. Plants thrive if looked after carefully, given the right conditions, even the tricky topicals like the *Psychotrias*, fully grown now and showing off the bright berries as I hoped they would.

Counselling young people is like nurturing plants – you have to work out what they need, then find a way to help them get it. Whether that's a new schoolbag or just a compassionate presence. All these kids – I know what they need, but I can't provide it. Hopefully time will. Until something comes along that is just too much, too big. All we can hope for is that the life we have lived was a good one. My friends will take my plants. I'll make sure that my solicitor emphasises that they must be well cared for, by anyone but Jess.

I know that, when I check my phone, there will be an email reply waiting for me. I don't know *how* I know – maybe cancer sharpens one's intuition. Less clear is what the email will say.

I remain at the window after the watering is done. Standing in my nightie, letting the sun warm through to my bones, trying to stretch away the pain in my back. When I can stand the suspense no longer, I make myself a cup of tea and take it back to bed. I pick up my mobile from the nightstand and press the button on the side.

It is Christopher himself who replies to Melanie. Suggesting a post-work drink to discuss my proposal. I smile as I read this – the photo that I popped next to my electronic signature (a winning combination of my newly emerged cheekbones courtesy of cancer and sparkling blue eyes courtesy of Photoshop) has done its job.

Is this madness? Or just a really great opportunity? Winnicott said *we are poor indeed if we are only sane.* That'll do.

London

Never having owned a full-length mirror, I was stopped in my tracks by my reflection the minute I entered the hotel room. The no-longer-unexplained weight loss is quite something; I have a short window of time where I will have the figure I've dreamed of. How utterly macabre, like admiring roses grown specifically for my own funeral.

I'm reminded of George and his magical thinking; that if he stared his body down for long enough, it might eventually change shape. What if you fill your mouth with the same word over and over again, will it lose its meaning, come to describe something else entirely? Sometimes, maybe, but not in this case. Cancer, the word which fills my mouth but which, since leaving my consultant's office, I've been unable to speak, means only one thing now.

Earlier today I went to La Perla on Sloane Street and spent the money for a new boiler on the slivers of pink silk and lace which now encase my breasts and pelvis. Then it was Alexander Wang for a stretchy, ruched black dress in spandex jersey, and a black crepe tuxedo jacket, courtesy of my share of roof repairs. The council tax and home insurance paid for a spree in Liberty's Fragrance Room and beauty hall. Now it's all out of the bags and on me, and I'm looking at my reflection again. My transformation from plain Jane, school counsellor, to Melanie Klein, wellness entrepreneur, is complete.

I hardly recognise the woman in the glass.

She's ready.

I sling my bag over my shoulder and pick up my copy of *Home is Where We Start From* by D.W. Winnicott, with its child's picture of a yellow house with a red roof, smoke bubbling from the chimney, blue scribble sky and smiling kids in the garden. I pat the cover and place it in the middle of the bed.

The Artesian bar at the Langham Hotel, where Christopher suggested we meet, is the most beautiful place I have ever been. The bar staff are also beautiful. The clientele not so much, though all are well dressed, or at least expensively dressed. The drinks menu describes the décor as *modern oriental,* which I think works. There are lots of Far Eastern touches like the glass-shelved backbar with its ornate woodwork inlaid in places with mother-of-pearl, alongside plush bar stools, opulent floor-length curtains and elegant leather sofas the colour and texture of ripe damsons. And almost everything appears to be gilt-edged, just like me.

I order an Aviation, a cocktail involving Crème de Violette that I saw in *Vogue* years ago. The young bartender says 'Old-school, nice!' in a kind way – approving, rather than patronising. Mind you, why would he feel he has to be kind? I am not some frumpy therapist here; I absolutely look the part. The drink tastes extraordinary, of fresh lime and parma violets, and is an ineffably chic shade of dove-grey with the barest trace of lilac.

Jessie would love this; no doubt she's been here before.

Jessie.

After everyone else had gone, I'd surprised her by asking for a cigarette for the first time in nearly two decades. She stopped moons ago too, but I know she keeps a supply of Vogue Menthol bought in French duty-free in a shoebox at the back of her wardrobe. Rather than questioning my sudden desire to smoke, she looked delighted. Mike was dealing with the kids, and it was the first time I'd had my best friend to myself all evening.

The unusual triangular garden, with high walls on two sides and Jessie's kitchen on the third, feels very private, even though inner-city and surrounded by neighbours. The space is relatively small, with a paving of little rectangular bricks in concentric circles which looks old and like what you'd get in some gorgeous ancient Italian villa, but is actually fairly new, having been bought by Jessie when she purchased the house six years ago. There are pots of blowsy annuals, a rowan tree bejewelled with berries, swathes of glossy ivy and stunning red Virginia creeper across the brickwork: I felt folded inside nature. My favourite place in all the world, with my favourite person.

Side by side on the garden bench, the late-blooming clematis throwing alabaster stars across one wall, fairy lights strung around the open French doors, I felt like we had sat in that exact position for a thousand twilights, a thousand midnights, particularly during the lockdowns, in sundresses and jumpers in the warmer months, or under thick blankets when the weather turned.

'What's up then?' she asked, biting slightly at her lip – an affectation she picked up watching the movie *Betty Blue* and never lost. She'd crammed her curls into a tortoiseshell clip just big enough for the job (her foray into wearing hairspray ended because I could never resist snapping the crispy spun-sugar curls) and, when she turned to look at me, her face lighting up with the glow of the cigarette from which she was taking a long drag, I felt like I was looking at the teenager she once was.

I knew in that moment that she knew. Nothing definite, nothing conclusive, but she knew…something. And if I gave her the spiel I'd rehearsed in my head a million times – the one where I said goodbye without saying goodbye, the one where I told her what she meant to me without telling her what she meant to me

– if I gave her that, then she'd most definitely twig, and all my plans would collapse around me.

So I didn't. I made up some nonsense about being pre-menstrual and just really fancying a fag. On another day she might not have swallowed it; she'd have put two and two together and concluded I must have the diagnosis I'd spent my life worrying about. On another day. But not that day, not that night, exhausted, sleep-deprived, maternally preoccupied with beautiful number three. That night I got to just be with my Jessie, and we smoked and gossiped and laughed under the stars until our eyelids grew so heavy that I knew it was time to leave.

In walks Christopher Erskine, unconscionable cunt *extraordinaire,* wearing an expensive suit jacket over a cashmere sweater so fine he need wear nothing beneath it. He immediately sees me, sitting at the bar, and comes over.

'Melanie?' he asks, smiling brightly. Kass's same pale blue eyes.

'Christopher!' I say, returning the smile. He leans in and kisses my cheek. He smells of leather and pine forests and warm things.

Suddenly I don't feel as confident. It was all a fantasy before. Now it's real, and not how I imagined. Am I really going to go through with this? Is my plan just crazy dying-person nonsense? Maybe I will see where the night takes me, then go back north where I belong.

Regardless, I'm here right now, or rather Melanie is,

and she needs to get her game on.

'What would you like to drink?' I ask, keeping my voice steady.

'You're Scottish! Why didn't you say in your email?' He looks delighted.

'Em, I didn't think it was relevant.'

He laughs and says, 'Of course it's relevant; we're both Scots abroad – we have to stick together. Where are you from originally?'

I get the impression he thinks I live in London. 'Ayr,' I lie.

He beams as if I'd just told him I grew up in the house next to his. 'I'm from Glasgow!'

Are you now? I'm not the only one who's lying.

'Well, there you go,' I say stupidly.

'That looks good,' he says, pointing to my drink. The bartender who has been discreetly hovering comes over. 'Hi, how are you?' says Christopher.

'I'm great. Now what can I get for you, sir?'

'Please may I have what she's having?'

Please may I have what she's having. What is he? Six? I'd imagined he'd be the type to click his fingers and have as little interaction as possible with serving staff.

Kass's brother takes off his jacket and hangs it on one of the hooks under the bar, then sits on the stool next to me. Samantha keeps him nice. There is no polyester in the Erskine household. His cashmere sweater, a close fit, skims over the defined musculature of his arms. He is recently clean-shaven, and his honey-coloured skin is in great condition. His light blue eyes immediately make me think of the blue-scribble sky on Donald's book cover. He is incredibly handsome and the perfect ambassador for Clean and Klein, if it were really a thing.

'So, Melanie, I was immensely flattered by your email. Very different from the types of email I usually receive.'

I smile. 'Well, I'm glad to hear that.'

'I'm just surprised you even knew about me,' he says, and I feel a prickle of anxiety.

You're a director of operations – not the Scarlet Pimpernel.

'You must be more famous that you know.'

'Ha! Yeah, maybe, but not necessarily in a good way.'

I hope he doesn't ask any more about how I've heard of him, but he just says, 'Anyway, enough about me,' even though he has said literally nothing about himself, at least nothing true, '…Tell me all about yourself, Melanie. Tell me everything.'

I tell him all about Melanie Klein, who did a degree in fashion and textiles, who worked as a buyer for a high-end internet retailer before deciding to start her own brand, and whose parents still live in their cottage by the sea. Me in a parallel life perhaps – it's not so hard to imagine; not so outlandish. He asks question after question, as if there is no more fascinating person in the world to him than me.

And now I know why Kass never told anyone. No one would have believed her. Her brother is completely, disarmingly charming.

Outside the windows the daylight is dying, but in

here we are cocooned in the glow from candles and well-placed lamps. I feel slightly woozy. Despite the adrenaline, and maybe because of the cocktail, and because tiredness is a symptom of my cancer, I suddenly yawn, and it is a massive thing like a cat's yawn. I feel unbelievably embarrassed.

'I'm so sorry! I didn't sleep well last night.'

He smiles. 'Don't be. I don't think the Langham has a no-yawning policy.' Then he leans in, conspiratorially and whispers, 'Though I have something in my pocket that might help wake you up a bit… If you're into that sort of thing?'

I know he's talking about drugs. 'Christopher, are you propositioning me?' I ask.

'No,' he says, '…but I will if you want me to…'

He doesn't say it smarmily. He says it honestly, the way you would want someone to say it to you if you wanted them to say it in the first place. Which I of course don't, but Melanie does, because it's part of her plan.

We regard each other, considering possibilities. Eventually I say, 'Yes, I'm into that sort of thing… By which I mean your first offer.'

He laughs and turns to order us another round of Aviations, while simultaneously dipping his hand in his pocket, then discreetly pressing it onto my lap under the bar. I glance around the room and, satisfied no one is watching, retrieve the little bag he has left there.

I take my handbag and follow the sign for the bathrooms. I don't have to turn around to know he's watching me leave the room.

Walking down the hall, exhaustion hits me as if its origin were outside of me – like a punch in the face, or a tidal wave. Stunned, I rock on my high heels. Then it's over and I continue on my way.

The bathroom is bigger than my entire flat, all cream and black marble and low lighting. A woman in a blue dress applies lipstick in front of the mirror. I head for the farthest cubicle, the interior of which is as spotless as the rest of the hotel. I feel like this pristine, unsullied place has been designed especially for me. I don't think I really understood before now that the world inside *Vogue* magazine is one where real people actually exist. If I'm going to do class-A drugs for the first time, it may as well be here.

I watched my friends, off their faces, on so many nights before the babies started coming. I suppose I could've snorted my way through my grief, but I've never been one to self-destruct. I was all about self-preservation, and I could never get over the knowledge that pills and powders might be cut with something that could kill me. But now I'm on my way out, so fuck it.

I open my handbag and take out the clear bag. Inside is a £20 note curling around itself in a loose spiral, and another, smaller bag a quarter full of white powder, which I presume is cocaine. Ket is all I hear about at work, but Christopher Erskine doesn't seem the type.

I close the toilet seat and open the bag. Carefully, I tap out a little mound onto the lid of the toilet cistern and smile at a memory from long ago, when I worked in a bar where we used to smear Vaseline over the cistern lids on Friday and Saturday nights then laugh at the yuppies as they emerged furious from the WCs. I close the bag and take out the curled note, roll it into a tight tube.

I've seen this done in a thousand edgy movies, not to mention watched my friends do it, so I press one nostril with my free hand and snort the coke with the other.

An unpleasant chemical taste, bitter and soapy with a ferric edge, floods my throat. Not that I care – I feel like Uma Thurman. I carefully put the powder and the note back inside the bag and push it down to the bottom of the zipped compartment in my handbag, which I hang on the peg on the back of the door. I hitch up my dress and while I pee, I google *how long does cocaine take to work?* on my phone. Damn, there is no reception in here.

Christopher is talking to the bartender as I take my place back on my stool and hang up my handbag.

He turns to me, asks, 'You good?'

I say, 'Oh, I'm great.' And I really am. The tiredness is completely gone. I feel incredibly clear-headed and full of energy. Around the room, flickering candle flames, which had seemed fuzzy before my trip to the loo, have sharpened, and the purples and golds of the room have intensified.

Under the bar I hand the bag back to Christopher who excuses himself to 'make a phone-call'. I take a sip from my Aviation which fizzes slightly in my mouth. Parma violets. My mother's favourite.

Coldingham Bay. I can smell the sea, even though the tide has taken it a million miles away from where we are sitting on a picnic rug on the beach. My mother is pulling apart the twist of cellophane to get to the parma violets, now handing me some of the tiny purple sweeties as she pops hers in her mouth. My father's voice – *I'll never understand why you love those things so much – they taste like soap!* My mother's laughter high and airy – *Jane, cover your ears, your dad is blaspheming...* Gesturing at me to hold my hands over my ears as she is doing, both of us looking mutinously at my father. I'm giggling, delighted. He shakes his head slowly and the sun flashes on his glasses. Then he smiles and leans in to plant kisses on our flowery mouths.

Christopher is back from the bathroom and taking a drink from his glass. I realise we haven't talked at all about the fake interview Melanie plans to conduct with him and I'm about to bring it up when he says, 'Ever crashed a wedding?'

'No.'

'Excellent!'

'Why? Have you?'

'Nope, but we're about to remedy that. One more thing off the bucket list.'

For a moment I think he knows somehow, then quickly chalk it up to coincidence.

'What do you mean?'

'There's a wedding party in the ballroom and we're going for a dance!' he says, grabbing my hands and pulling me off my stool.

'I can't!'

'Oh yes you can,' he says, letting go of me to fetch our jackets.

I don't know how to stop him. 'We haven't paid!'

'Oh yeah,' he says and produces two fifty-pound notes which he slaps on the bar.

Imagine what Kass would do with an unexpected hundred quid. How carefully she would consider how to spend it. She'd know that she should probably keep it for the electricity meter, but the knees in Lewis's joggers are nearly gone, and she can get a two-pack new for £12 from Tesco. They could get yumyums from Greggs, the flaky coating of water icing so good with a cup of tea, though she won't buy Tetley because it's too dear. Lewis can have his yumyum with milk. She could buy Loreal shampoo and conditioner instead of Lidl's cheapo versions, but she won't, because he really needs new school shoes and with this money she can buy him Nike, just this once, to be like the other kids.

Kass in Primark, Chris in Prada.

'That's too much.'

'Oh, *come on* Melanie, live a little!' he says, careless of his privilege, and I'm getting whisked out of the Artesian and into the grand hall, where his demeanour changes from excited, care-free teenager to urbane criminal of the George Clooney variety, as he holds out my tuxedo jacket for me to slip myself into. Exhilaration rushes through me as I watch him shrug on his own jacket. He takes my hand, and we nod at each other in silent complicity before striding off towards the ballroom.

*

Everything is shining. We've danced to song after song, taken trip after trip to the bathroom, passed a bottle of champagne between us as we jumped about to every type of music I can think of. Now my cheek is pressed against cashmere as Cindy Lauper belts out 'Time After Time', the wedding party a slow silken swirl around us.

When the song ends, we leave the Langham and hail a cab. In the lift of my hotel we're stumbling, laughing – now entwined, eyes locked. Maybe he isn't trying to kiss me because that would properly count as cheating on Samantha. Is that how men's minds work? But Christopher is not an ordinary man. Christopher is a man who raped his little sister over and over again, year after year. He put on a good show of conviviality and good manners at the bar but he has no real regard for others. This is not a man who has spent years regretting and attempting to rectify what he did. Oh no, Christopher feels entitled to do whatever the fuck Christopher feels like doing. He is dangerous, and I have to be careful.

In my fifth-floor room Christopher throws his jacket on the bed and the bag of coke on the coffee table, beside which he kneels.

'No offence, but I thought a woman like you might choose to stay somewhere more…more luxurious than this…'

He's used to better.

Swaying a little, I see disdain in the soft flare of his nostrils. He can't even begin to know what a woman like me might do.

He has no idea what a hard time I had finding this place. Two nights trawling through Tripadvisor reviews, searching for customer complaints about hotel rooms with hazardously low balconies. I eventually found one, fortuitously above water, but was dismayed to discover it isn't even that low! Still, Melanie is a woman who knows how to plan ahead, even with short notice.

'Yes, it's not exactly the Savoy is it!' I bleat. 'But they want to stock my products in all their hotels, which is rather a lucrative coup, don't you agree?'

He snorts one of the lines he's racked up on the coffee table. I watch the way his muscles move under the sweater and my mouth fills again with the sweetness of parma violets.

The evening we have had, the hotel room... This could all be a different story. He could be a different man, and I could not be dying. But he is not, and I most certainly am. Adrenaline screeches through my body.

No time is the right time.

No time like the present.

All anyone has is the here and now, nothing more.

Make these last moments of your life count, Jane.

He looks up at me, hands me the rolled note. Pupils so dilated as to leave only the slightest of sapphire outlines. 'Well, if that doesn't call for a celebration, I don't know what does – congratulations, Melanie!'

'Thank you very much, kind sir!' I say, taking the note from him and kneeling down. I snort and throw my head back as the powder hits, feel myself unfurling towards ultra-lucid pin-sharp clarity again. 'There's a bottle of fizz in the fridge. Let's have a drink on the balcony.'

I look out across the river at a completely different London to the one in my childhood imaginings. No Big Ben, Tower Bridge, or St Paul's Cathedral blurry with pigeons. Instead a jagged skyline of darkly glittering skyscrapers more reminiscent of 80s New York in the opening credits of *The Equalizer* than the setting for *Mary Poppins*.

Most of the windows in those towers still blaze with fluorescent light. Wasn't there a fuss about leaving lights on after working hours? It's bad for the planet. Not so long ago this crowded, lively city, like all the others, withdrew into itself, only the wind and the ambulances rushing through deserted streets. A herd of fallow deer appeared on the lawns of a housing estate, walking on their tiptoes as ballerinas do. Fallow deer graze on grass, heather, conifer, holly and bramble, but turn their noses up at ragwort, foxgloves and stinging nettles.

'Good to know,' says Christopher and chuckles softly. How much of what I was just thinking have I actually said out loud? Probably just the bit about deer, apropos of exactly nothing. Maybe he thinks me cute.

The oily, gleaming dock below our balcony is a long

way down, and the sky above us black and bright with stars. For once it doesn't make me feel like I'm trapped in a box into whose lid someone has punched holes. For once the stars aren't somewhere I'd rather be. I want to be right here with Christopher forever. I don't recall the last time I felt this happy or alive.

We watch it all twinkle before us.

But I see a photograph.

Oh Lewis, with your smile and your bucket – thriving, poppy-like, despite growing among the disturbed ground of your mother's mind. Because she fought and fought for you, even though, with that much trauma, the odds were against her, against you.

Lewis who scrambled down an octopus to meet me. Kass who joined us, and together we spent all that shitty grey perfect afternoon being the bright underwater creatures of her bioluminescent fantasies. We glowed; we really did. And I will make sure that they keep on glowing even after I'm long gone. And that they are safe.

I made sure it was me who walked out the glass doors and onto the balcony first. Me who dictated where we now stand.

The night is very still as Christopher clinks his glass against mine and says '*Slàinte mhath*. Congratulations again you clever, beautiful woman.'

We drink then put our glasses down.

I pull him to me, inhale his warm, clean, woody, smell, and whisper, 'I'm so glad I finally met you, Christopher Erskine.'

He leans in to kiss me and with my arms still around his neck I push forward with every last iota of strength in my body.

And the last thing I think as we crash through the railings is how proud my mother would be that I'm such a dab-hand with an angle grinder.

2034

Lewis jogs onto the pitch into the sunshine, wearing his captain's armband for the last time. School's out forever, and though he can't know it yet, his exam results in August will be so good that he will receive unconditional offers from all the art colleges he has applied to. Not that he cares in this moment – all that matters is the football, is captaining his team for one last time before the season ends for the summer.

No muddy park pitches for them today. This morning his team are in the small outdoor stadium attached to the local sports centre, but it may as well be Hampden. There is all to play for, as today's result will decide the winners of the league. Lewis might not be as tall as the others, but he is fast and agile and can play as well with his left foot as his right. His teammates and coaches he has known since he was tiny, trained with them, won and lost with them, for thirteen years now – as long as he can remember, and he's not sure, when it comes to it, that he will be able to leave them without crying.

He squints into the sun, shields the light from his eyes with his hand, and scans the people in the stands. He can't know that the conspiracy of girls, all long locks, bare midriffs and gallus laughter, propelled out of their beds and into the stadium this early on a Saturday morning, are here to catch a blue flash of his pale eyes, a glimmer of sun reflected gold on his mouse-coloured hair.

He's searching for his mother. Finds her, front row, his grandparents either side, chatting away. He still remembers when it was just her at the sidelines, the way she'd run out at the slightest sign of injury – so embarrassing. How he'd had to teach her to hang back, because it was never what she feared, no broken ankles or career-ending hamstring injury. Just knocks and bumps and bruises, and enough for him to know she was there watching, the other end of the invisible thread that runs between them.

Now his grandparents have been here for longer than they weren't. He knows their arrival in his life was something to do with his uncle's death, but he doesn't know exactly what. At the time, snatches of eavesdropped adult conversations over phones, then around kitchen tables, pointed towards some scandal, an uncle he never knew he had, dying in a hotel room with a strange woman not his wife. He never knew more than that and learned not to ask. Whatever it was, it changed everything.

The guy, his uncle, must have been a wanker, the opposite of Lewis's coaches who are all here today. These patient, cheerful, enthusiastic men, joiners and plumbers and taxi drivers – most of whom were other kids' dads or granddads, but still called him *son* and *pal*, still grinned and high-fived him when he did something good, said *better luck next time* and ruffled his hair when he messed up, the hundreds of pep-talks, the care and kindness, and expressions of belief in him, given on their knees so as to be at his eye level – these men have devoted their Wednesday evenings and Sunday mornings to him since he was five. They can't know what they mean to him. Can't know the need they meet in him. Lewis remembers how he felt the day his mum mentioned that, of course, they didn't get paid – how he'd loved them even more.

His grandparents had been hungry for him, like the monsters in *Where the Wild Things Are*. He'd let them eat him up, spoil him rotten. A room in their house, all kitted out for him. A PlayStation 5, the football strips of his favourite European teams, scooters, bikes and pretty much everything he wanted until his mum put her foot down. Said she wouldn't let him stay over with them while she was studying for her teaching assistant qualification, if every time she picked him up, he had yet another bag of new stuff.

She'd been kind of quiet for a while, watched him being adored by her parents, but set herself apart. Lewis couldn't even begin to articulate the confusion that caused in him. Then, in time, it changed. She started to laugh properly around them, not in that guarded way she had before. She'd stay for tea instead of whisking him away the second she got there. Lewis found his granddad hugging her in the back green, watched her shoulders heave in his arms while tears streamed down the old man's cheeks.

Recently he's noticed that his mum and his granny have started holding hands while they watch Lewis play, their bodies tense with excitement.

His team won't win today, but this will mean little later, when he's laughing with his family round the kitchen table, tangled in invisible thread.

Just another thing he can't know yet.

Acknowledgements

To Dan Hiscocks for believing in the book and making it all possible – I'm still not convinced that you are actually real. To Simon Edge, for being gracious in the face of my ineptitude at Microsoft Word and just generally brilliant. And to the rest of the team at Eye Books, particularly Nell Wood for her amazing and patient work on the cover, and to Clio Mitchell for typesetting.

To Mike Bryce, who'd have us believe he's 'just an ordinary lad from Duns', ha!, and hot tramp Janice Baines; both of them wild and wise in equal measure. And to the team at work – the last place I expected to find a home.

To lovely, clever, creative Gary Smith.

To Susan Smith for her dustbin mind and generous spirit.

To Leslie Hills for loving the original short story (and me), for encouragement and for meticulously editing one particular chapter that had me beat.

To Simon Stephenson and Lee Randall for their enthusiasm, and for taking the time to give me the detailed feedback which led to the changes that got me published.

To the exceptionally talented artist Craig Murray.

To courageous, huge-hearted Mark Taylor, and his lovely bibliomaniac daughter Sophia Taylor.

To Emma Patterson, who dreamt Jane's dream – I hope you don't mind that I stole it for this book!

To Satveer Landa, Ward Campbell, Pip Hills, Maggie Braid, Trina McKendrick, Kev Theaker, Val McDermid, Malcolm Chisholm, Mikey Crook, Susan Miller, Matthew Stephenson, Sarah Stephenson, Angela Jackson, Ian Rankin, Emma and Aaron Shaw, Cai Williams, Claire Laing, Dylan Blackstock and Pete Irvine – for encouragement and enthusiasm, for reading early drafts, for useful advice, helpful conversations, for all these things. To Katie and Omar Dellal for their help, encouragement and exquisite designs.

To linguist and wordsmith Stephanie Hills: Laura to my Lizzie, or the other way round, no matter.

To the kids, parents and particularly the coaches of Leith Athletic 2015, whose incredible, trauma-informed coaching inspired my final page.

To Keir McKendrick for his unwavering belief that *Words Fail Me* would find a publisher.

To Elise Walker, whose compassionate, intelligent take on some of the issues raised in this book leaves me awestruck.

To Ben McKendrick for showing me that this was the story I should be telling, and because '*that man takes care of all o' my pains and my ills*'. Thank you, love.

Also from Lightning

The Darlings

Angela Jackson

**The daring new novel from the award-winning author
of *The Emergence of Judy Taylor***

At fifteen, Mark Darling is the golden boy, captain of the
school football team, admired by all who know him. Then he
kills his best friend in a freak accident.

He spends the next decade drifting between the therapy
couch and dead-end pursuits until he marries Sadie. A mender
by nature, she tries her best to fix him, and has enough energy
to carry them both through the next few years.

One evening, Mark bumps into an old schoolfriend, Ruby.
She saw the accident first hand. He is pulled towards her by
a force stronger than logic: the universal need to reconcile
one's childhood wounds. This is his chance to, once again,
feel the enveloping warmth of unconditional love.

But can he leave behind the woman who rescued him from
the pit of despair, the wife he loves? His unborn child?

*Exactly the kind of humane, life-affirming, humorous read I
needed*
Catherine Simpson

Angela is a true writer and an extremely powerful voice
Bidisha

*Eccentric...compelling...subtle... A dark, humorous novel, led
by domestic scenes and keen observations, in which a troubled
man's crises have clear consequences*
Foreword Reviews

The Tick and the Tock of the Crocodile Clock

Kenny Boyle

Wendy just wants to be a poet. So how comes she's on the run after an art heist?

An aspiring writer from the Southside of Glasgow, Wendy is in a rut. Jobless and depressed after walking out of her call-centre job, she finds consolation in a surprise friendship with another disgruntled ex-colleague, wild-child painter Cat, who encourages her to live more dangerously.

It's just what Wendy needs and it's also brilliant for her creative juices. But a black cloud is about to overshadow this new-found liberation, as well as to put Wendy on the wrong side of the law.

Fresh, insightful and funny, as well as unflinchingly honest about the tougher side of life, Kenny Boyle's debut novel takes us deep into the psyche of a likeable misfit who treads a fine line between reality and fantasy – and just wants the world to see her true self.

May well be the best book I've read in years
Peter May

A quirky and honest portrayal of early twenties friendship. Disarmingly intimate… A sweet, sad and funny book
Scotland on Sunday

One of the nation's best writers
The Scotsman

A charming, funny and unique story that tackles tough issues with a gentleness and poignancy that really resonated with me
Clare Grogan

Ocean

Polly Clark

A powerful yacht, a warring family, the unforgiving deep...

Caught in a terrorist explosion on the London Underground, inner-city schoolteacher Helen is pregnant and lost until a stranger leads her to safety then vanishes. Obsessed with finding him, she begins to lose her grip on reality – and her family.

As their marriage fractures, her husband Frank proposes a daring plan: sell up and sail the Atlantic with their son Nicholas and troubled foster daughter Sindi on the *Innisfree*, the very boat where the couple first fell in love.

What begins as a daring bid for salvation turns into an epic journey. The ocean proves as wild and unpredictable as the heartbreak Helen is trying to outrun. Will the voyage meant to save them destroy them instead?

With a fiercely funny and maverick heroine at its helm, *Ocean* is a powerful exploration of the uncharted waters of the human heart. The award-winning author of *Larchfield* takes us on a gripping, beautifully written voyage into the depths of what it means to heal – and to live.

A ferociously intense portrait of a mind, marriage and family in extreme turbulence. Startling and dramatic, it made me very glad to be on terra firma
Amanda Craig

Clark has a wonderful eye for detail and a light comic touch
The Times

Ocean is out in June 2025

If you have enjoyed *Words Fail Me,* do please help us spread the word – by putting a review online; by posting something on social media; or in the old-fashioned way by simply telling your friends or family about it.

Book publishing is a very competitive business these days, in a saturated market, and small independent publishers such as ourselves are often crowded out by the big houses. Support from readers like you can make all the difference to a book's success.

Many thanks.
Dan Hiscocks
Publisher, Eye Books